Hegira
By
Jim Cronin

Cover Art:
MLCDesigns4U

Publisher's Note:

This is a work of fiction. All names, characters, places, and
events are the work of the author's imagination.

Any resemblance to real persons, places, or events is
coincidental.

Solstice Publishing - www.solsticepublishing.com

This book is dedicated to my family, all of you. Without you, I would never have become the person I am... For good or ill, I'll let you be the judge. But especially to my brand new granddaughter, Hanora Alice. May your future be as incredible as you have made our present.

Preface

"Come in, Latonia Base…come in Latonia Base. This is Starship Hegira, repeat, this is Hegira. Come in, Latonia."

Static crackled from the speaker. The lieutenant, bleeding and dying from the injuries he received during the mutiny trembled feebly as he gripped the microphone. Blood soaked his crest feathers; his talons broken and jagged from the hand-to-hand combat in the spaceship's passageways. He knew his wounds were fatal, but his duty was clear: to report back to base about the failure of the mission. His body tensed as the next wave of pain shot through him.

"Latonia Base, this is Hegira. Come in. Priority clearance Falcon, Delta. Come in Base. Damn you to strix!" the soldier shouted in desperation. "Somebody answer! Come in, Latonia!" The microphone dropped from his talons, clattering on the control panel before falling to the metal plated floor. The lieutenant slumped back into the chair, pressing a blood soaked rag to his shoulder. Staring out the view port he watched the star-filled blackness and wondered at the cruel turn fate had taken over the past few days.

A pounding on the hatch caused the lieutenant to reach for his sidearm. "Lieutenant Yardef! It's Vedak. Let me in, sir!"

The lieutenant pulled himself up in the chair and reached out with a fractured, bloodstained talon to press the door release circuit. With a sharp hiss, the door slid open and in hobbled Sergeant Vedak, one of his few remaining platoon members.

"It worked, sir," the soldier said, crashing into the second chair in the room.

Yardef surveyed his subordinate's injuries, noting several which would prove to be fatal. "You okay, Sarge? You don't look so good."

"Look who's talking," said the young soldier. He tugged at his uniform, checking his wounds.

"We got most of them sealed in the lower decks and opened the cargo hatches to space. They didn't stand a chance once we decompressed decks one through ten. They're all dead now. Just a few survivors are holed up one deck above us." Ripping a piece from his ruined shirt he wrapped the makeshift bandage around the laser shot in his arm.

"Good. Were you able to get the hatches closed again?"

The sergeant looked his superior in the eyes and shook his head. "Negative. All the controls are fried."

"I need you to go find the engineer. See if he can do anything."

"He's dead, sir. He bought it down in cargo bay C during the first assault."

The two sat in silence for several long minutes before either could speak. "That looks pretty bad, sir. Want me to look at it?" Vedak pointed at the lieutenant's shoulder, still bleeding heavily despite the thick bandage he pressed against it.

"Don't waste your time." The officer coughed and winced as the pain gripped him again. "At least I won't have to wait around to starve to death. Are those vials secured?"

"Yes, sir. We were able to pull them from cryogenics before those clerics overran us. I locked them up in the high security bay. No one can get to them now. What's so important about those two samples, sir? Out of the thousands of samples, why just those two?"

Lieutenant Yardef shrugged his shoulders, his face contorting at the new stab of pain. "Don't ask me, Sarge. All I know is the orders specified keeping those two samples out of fundamentalist hands at all cost. When the mutiny began, the Captain ordered me to make them our top priority. Way above my pay grade to ask why."

"I hope they're worth the lives they cost us," said the sergeant. "Any luck with communications?"

The older man shook his head in silence. "Nothing but static so far. I'll ..." He coughed again and dropped to the floor.

"Lieutenant!" Vedak jumped out of his chair and fell to his knees, lifting the lifeless body of the officer.

The sound of sporadic energy blasts tore his attention away from the dead lieutenant. He checked the monitor and stumbled to the intercom controls. "What's going on out there, soldier?" he demanded of the man he saw on the camera. The bright orange flash of a laser blast missed the soldier's head by inches.

"The fundie rebels, Sarge," called out the soldier as he fired several rounds down the corridor behind him. "They broke out of their makeshift fortress on deck twelve and forced us to regroup here. We got most of them, but it cost us. Only a few of us left now."

The sergeant quickly appraised the situation and made his decision. "Stand your ground, soldier. Nobody gets through you into this room. I've got to try to reach Latonia Base. Kill anything in a robe that's still breathing."

"Those fucking fundies are as good as dead, Sarge."

Another flash lit up the monitor and blood splattered the camera lens before he could acknowledge. As the sergeant stepped back into the ether wave room he heard the speakers come to life. "Hegira, this is Latonia Base. Do you read us, Hegira? Come in."

The sergeant lunged to the floor, grabbing the microphone in his shaking hand; the last remnants of his self-control dissolving rapidly. "Latonia Base, this is Hegira. I read you," he responded. "Praise The Eternal! You can hear me. Please help. They're killing each other. Only a few of us are left and badly wounded. Help us!"

Part One

Chapter One

Location: Deep Space, Catalan Sector

Alarms echoed throughout the ship.

"Alert code Delta...Alert code Delta," the ship-wide communications blared. "This is no drill...Repeat, this is no drill."

The *Helven* was the first of her kind. Built by the Skae Space Command to explore the farthest regions of space, she had traveled farther than any other vessel in the fleet. While designed for exploration, the *Helven* came equipped with the most advanced technology for both scientific and military encounters. The Skae had few rivals in exploration of the galaxy, but recently, the Gorvin had begun to challenge them in nearby sectors. After a year in Sector Beta 14, this was the Helven's first live action.

Captain Pok entered the bridge from his private briefing room. Senior commander of the fleet with twenty-seven years' experience, he was the natural choice for command of the Helven on such a mission. A jagged scar cut through the deep blue skin of his left temple, the result of action he saw during the Gorvin Wars. He scanned the banks of computer screens to read the ship's condition and to see if the sensors detected any threats.

"So what do we have?"

"Our communications buoys have picked up a ship distress signal. It appears to be from an alien vessel about three parsecs from our current position. The signal appears automated and we have not been able to raise anything in response. We are not close enough for sensors to pick up life signs or weapons status."

"Any sign of hostile activity?" Recent intel didn't mention any Gorvin activity out this far, but information about this sector was sketchy at best.

"No, sir," replied the first officer. "No enemy energy signatures within range of our sensors."

"Very well then, take us to the ship, Ensign Tagol. Keep weapons on alert status and sensors on full range. Cosmic string engine synchronization at point eight."

It took only a few moments for the flight crew to set their instruments to the assigned coordinates and flight pattern. The ship responded without sound or any apparent change in acceleration, but the control panels all indicated the approach of an appropriate cosmic string and alignment with their new trajectory toward the source of the distress signal. "How long till arrival, Ensign?"

"We should arrive at the coordinates in three days, Captain."

"Very well. Notify me if there are any changes or if sensors pick up anything unusual." Pok left the bridge after a glance and a nod to his second in command. He left for his quarters to catch up on the endless flow of reports and, hopefully, get at least a few hours of sleep before his duty watch arrived.

Seventy-five hours later, in the Captain's briefing room, the ensign of the watch reported on the latest updates regarding the alien vessel.

Captain Pok's brow furrowed as he raised his hand to interrupt the report. "Just this automated distress signal and no signs of life? What about weapons?"

"The ship contains only a minimum of weaponry and those are only standard lasers, no threat to our vessel. Their propulsion system is ionic thruster based. Power levels are barely registering. There are only faint life sign readings. Sensors show it to be a cargo vessel, probably fully automated and it seems to have had a mechanical malfunction of some sort."

"Any threat to a survey team?" asked the second in command.

"No, sir, no threat detected. Radiation levels are minimal. Sensors detect no evidence of active security measures on board. However, temperature and atmospheric conditions will require the use of environmental suits."

"Very well then. Dismissed, Ensign." The officer turned back to the Captain. Tagol saluted smartly and marched out of the briefing room.

"First contact with a new species is always a delicate business," said the Captain. "Let's do this one strictly by the book until we learn more."

On the main view screen a silvery space ship, shaped like a flattened ovoid approximately one hundred meters long, fifty meters wide and forty meters thick and bifurcated at the stern, showed numerous portholes indicating at least six decks. Three thrust manifolds protruded from aft, apparently inoperative, as the ship drifted aimlessly against the immensity of space. No lights or energy emissions of any sort were to be seen. Years of micro-meteorite impacts pitted the derelict ship's skin, as if some demented space demon had used it as a chew toy. There were a few small breeches in the hull originating from the ship's interior, but otherwise it seemed to be intact.

In the Captain's briefing room, the command crew sat around the oblong table.

"Those breeches came from some sort of small arms fire," said the chief weapons officer as he pointed at the holes in the vessel. "They could have been defending themselves from something."

The science officer examined the data on his screen. "Whatever happened occurred a long time ago. Sensor readings indicate the ship has been adrift for over twenty years."

Captain Pok leaned back in his chair, examining the faces of his officers. "Very well then. Have a survey team ready to board, but with caution and in full protective measures in place. If there was a crew, no telling what might have killed them, so we don't want any alien infections brought back here. Level ten decontamination upon return as well, just to be safe. And let's go in on full alert. If this was the result of hostile action we don't want to be caught with our drawers down."

Once they arrived, Pok dispatched several teams to check out the disabled vessel. "Explore Team One here, sir. We have entered the ship and are heading toward the bridge."

"Very good Team One, proceed with caution."

"Team Two here. The corridors are a bit short; we definitely need to be careful getting through these hatchways. Strange design, pointed archways on top, the bulkheads are slightly concave and the rooms are circular. Whoever they were, they didn't like straight lines or corners. No sign of any survivors. All we have here are the remains of the crew. There appears to have been some sort of battle among the crew. Bodies are scattered everywhere, some still frozen in their final struggle."

"Can you describe them, Ensign?" the Captain asked.

Tagol shined his light over the bodies floating in the room to his left. "Yes, sir, they are humanoid, but more avian in appearance. They are short, only around six feet tall. I can see colorful feather-like crests on the tops of their heads covering a portion of their skulls, shorter feathers covering the rest of their heads, except for their faces. They have four fingers on each hand with talons instead of fingernails. At least one of the fingers appears to be opposable. Their skin appears smooth, but there is a very faint texture of scales. Not visible unless the light hits them just right. No external ears are visible."

"Okay, Ensign, continue your search. Bag up a few of them for examination by medical. Stay in constant communication."

"Team Three here, we have found what appears to be the main bridge. More signs of a struggle here, too. Some of the crew had a small hand-held energy weapon. Others are armed with knives or metal pipes. This looks more like a mutiny than outside hostilities, Captain. We're commencing to download their data logs."

"Very good, Team Three. Return to base once you have the data collected. We will begin translation and analysis once you get back."

"Captain! Team Two here. We have found what scanners indicate to be a vast collection of DNA samples in one of the cargo bays. Thousands of them! Power is off so they've degraded significantly, but sensors show that two still seem to be viable. We will retrieve these and return."

***

Six hours later, Captain Pok called all department chiefs to a conference.

The young Ensign Tagol turned on his recording device and stood at attention behind the Captain as the officers filed into the briefing room. "All department seniors present and accounted for, Captain."

Pok surveyed the faces around the rectangular briefing table. "Let's get this over with quickly. I want to get on with our mission as soon as possible. Engineering…"

"Just as we suspected, sir," said the senior chief, reading his notes, scanning over the details. "The ship was a primitive design, ion impulse engines, no external weaponry, flowing electron operating systems throughout the vessel. Nothing worth salvaging, unless you want to stay an extra month to carve it up into scrap metal for reworking.

"Not likely," the Captain replied, shaking his head and signaling for the next officer to begin. "Security…"

"No threats, biological or weapons, sir. The ship lacked any external armament, the only sign of weapons were obsolete hand-held plasma beam in design. No survivors."

"Navigation, do we know where the ship came from?"

"We did locate the star system, Captain, but bad news there. The central star went supernova about twenty years ago. No chance of anything surviving anywhere in the system."

Captain Pok rocked back in his chair, and rubbed his chin. "Could this ship have been some sort of attempt to preserve some remnant of their world?"

"A distinct possibility, sir," replied the bioscience officer. "All those DNA samples and machinery were very likely some last ditch effort to find a new home for themselves. It looks like—"

"With that ship?" cut in the chief engineer, shaking his head, his hands raised with elbows on the table. "It never stood a chance of getting to another star system. Those engines weren't nearly enough for the task. If this was their best effort at saving themselves they must have been incredibly desperate."

"The data banks are still in pretty bad shape, Captain," said the communications chief. "We will know more once we finish reconstruction from the mirrored files."

Pok nodded, ending the topic for the moment and looked to the next officer for her report.

Moving from one to the next, each officer stated his or her findings, nothing unexpected or surprising, until…

"Bioscience, let's finish this up."

"We have a Red Dart indicator, sir," replied the chief after clearing her throat. All eyes turned to the chief, backs stiff, muscles tensed. Red Dart alerts were something mentioned only in the academy as part of their history courses. "While the specimens are ordinary carbon based life forms, similar to everything we have encountered so far, except for the avian features, the indicators popped up once we began to analyze their DNA. Whatever the computers saw to trigger the alarm is something way beyond my pay grade, Captain."

"Damn!" said Pok, slapping his hand on the table amidst a general groan from the officers assembled. "Alright everyone, this briefing is over. Red Dart protocols are in effect. Encrypt all reports at level omega and have them delivered to me within the hour. Get comfortable, everyone, we aren't going anywhere until High Command has a look at this."

***

At the appointed time, Captain Pok keyed in the series of codes to enable the Eyes Only Security Net and punched the communications connection. The image of High Commander Tobuk appeared on the screen, flanked by Admiral Contu, chief medical advisor to the Emperor.

"Captain Pok, your discovery of this alien DNA has created an immediate Red Dart Alpha priority revision of your mission." The high commander's imperious tone and stiff demeanor warned Pok to hold his tongue for now. "Until further notice you and your crew will consider yourself outside the regular command structure and under the sole command of Admiral Contu. No outside communications by any crewmember, including yourself, are permitted without clearance by the admiral himself."

Pok stiffened in his chair, his mind racing with a thousand questions, but duty and training restrained him... barely. "Understood, sir."

"Thank you, Commander," said Admiral Contu dismissing the man, silently waiting until he was alone. "Captain Pok," he said, eyes burning into the screen, his face held firm as if made of granite. "There has not been a Red Dart alert for over fifteen hundred years. Not since the loss of the Kolandi and the rise of the Gorvins. We've been searching for ways to eradicate the Kolandi infection and return them to their former strength alongside us in the Galactic Forces ever since. Without success as you know."

"Yes, sir," replied Pok. The Skae learned this horrific history lesson in their earliest school days, and tales of the Gorvin monsters permeated many of the stories parents told their children when they misbehaved. It was the darkest moment of their generally glorious past. The Gorvin effectively eliminated the Kolandi with a genetic plague and nearly conquered the galaxy. Only extreme daring and chance brought the war to a standoff, with occasional minor wars breaking out over the following centuries. Pok absently brought a finger to his facial scar as he remembered his own close call during the latest of these encounters.

"This new DNA you discovered contains sequences we believe will finally provide the solution we have searched for. In the next few days you will receive orders containing instructions on how to proceed, including details on what you are authorized to reveal to your crew and which of them, due to their specialized skills, will be cleared to proceed with the reanimation of the DNA."

"Excuse me, sir," said Pok, unable to restrain himself any longer. "Reanimate the DNA? Are you talking about cloning, sir?"

"That is only the beginning, Captain. Your orders will tell you as much as we dare allow, and will undoubtedly sound incredible, but we are desperate, Captain."

"Understood, sir," Pok said as he saluted the monitor.

"And, Captain," said the Admiral returning the salute. "Do not fail. The future of the galaxy may very well rest on the success of this mission."

***

A week later, Captain Pok stepped through the bridge entryway, assumed his place in the command chair and pressed the ship-wide communications switch.

"All sector chiefs report to the briefing room immediately, repeat, immediately. Captain out."

The assembled chiefs questioned each other as they sat around the table awaiting the Captain, who entered through his private passage only a minute later, going directly to his place at the head of the table.

"Alright, everyone, settle down. We are about to receive a priority Delta communication from High Command." He pressed a switch on the table and seconds later, a ghostly holographic image began to form.

Captain Pok hesitated briefly, his jaw dropping almost imperceptibly as he recognized the personage before them. Lifting two fingers of his left hand to his temple in salute, he stood to attention. "Your Highness, this is truly unexpected."

"Yes, Captain," replied the image of the supreme ruler of all Skae. "High Command analyzed the data you transmitted and relayed their conclusions to me personally." The officers remained speechless, only able to gape incredulously at each other and the hologram before them as it paused. "By now, Captain, you have received your orders from Admiral Contu. You are the finest crew ever assembled and we have the utmost faith in your ability to carry out these orders. We know all too well the extreme hardship our restrictions will cause, but they are necessary and the rewards of success are too great to risk. Good luck gentlemen. All of our hopes go with you."

The officers shared stunned looks across the table as the image vanished. Captain Pok keyed in the commands to bring up images on the main screen.

"This, gentlemen, is our new mission…"

***

A month later, deep in the bowels of the *Helven*, specialists in the sterile science labs wore the high-level protective wardrobe required by protocols when dealing with foreign materials. Computer banks blinked as they processed the information fed to them, and several screens displayed the information as it became available. Line after line of genetic code appeared on the main screen.

"Can you imagine, the entire crew gone…all fifty-eight killed off, and by each other's hand," said Zem, lab specialist level four.

"Yeah, deciphering their computer logs is taking some time to translate due to the high levels of corruption, but it appears to have been the result of some political struggle between crew members over their cargo," Bolt, chief of the labs, replied.

"Yep, nothing but completely degenerated vials of DNA and the equipment to reanimate them once they had reached their destination is what we figure."

Bolt continued to examine the specimens at his station, then glanced over his shoulder to see if anyone was close enough to overhear him. "Know anything about the other two vials? The ones the rumors are about?"

The conversation between the two technicians was brought to an immediate halt by the entrance of the principal science officer. "You two know the regulations regarding discussion of any matters dealing with the alien ship. All such information is limited to officers and those directly involved. We have enough rumors and matters of policy to deal with without you two adding to the list of difficulties. You know your duties, get back to work, and leave these other matters alone until the Captain sees fit to fill everyone in on what is happening."

"Yes, sir, but you would think that after a month of communication blackout and sections of the ship being placed on top level security clearance, somebody would tell us something, sir," said Bolt.

"Well, when you reach the rank of admiral and want to walk right up to the Captain and demand an answer, feel free to go right ahead, Specialist Bolt, but until then, I suggest you stick to your usual duties."

"Yes, sir, no harm or disrespect intended, sir. Just a lot of scientific curiosity, sir."

"Okay, okay, lighten up with the 'sirs', Bolt. You know what I mean. We are all just as anxious as you are to know what is going on. The Captain will inform us just as soon as he can straighten out all of the political crap. Got me?"

Chapter Two

Bolt mind wandered fitfully over the past two decades as he monitored his student's progress. He startled back to the present as his pupil interrupted once again with more questions.

"So this cosmic string is going to take us back in time so I can take control and avoid the situations which caused the destruction of the Brin ship...my ship?" asked Karm, running his talons through his long crest feathers.

"That is correct," replied his mentor Bolt. The Skae's nimble blue hands danced over the control panel to display more images. "Most cosmic strings allow us to travel quickly through the vast distances of space. However, we have learned there are some strings, which, if approached using extremely precise calculations, allow us to travel through time as well as space. Unfortunately, these time-traveling strings are not as precise as the others, and much more dangerous. We have located a string to send you back in time to your home planet, but we can only approximate, with a fair degree of certainty, when you will arrive. This particular string does seem to be far enough in the past to allow for reasonable error and still provide you with sufficient time to complete your mission, within the twelve percent margin of error. Your case is unique and has thus received approval, despite the inherent dangers."

"Won't my going back in time change things?"

Bolt nodded. "The planet will not survive long enough for most changes to the timeline to matter. In addition, that is why we have provided you with this biocomputer. It will provide you with precisely the information you need to prevent you from doing too much damage to the timeline. It took a bit of skillful plastic surgery and some minor changes to your anatomy to accommodate the device, but your appearance is still well within the norm for a Brin, according to the databanks retrieved from your ship. Listen to me, Karm," said Bolt as he looked into Karm's eyes. "You cannot allow the timeline to change beyond the parameters we have given you. There are some events, which, if altered even in the short term remaining, could have far-reaching effects for our plan. Events in time are like ripples in a pond. Your biocomputer should help keep you in the outer, less vital ripples, far from the central events, but beware, the data we collected from your ship was corrupted. There are many gaps in the records where we could only extrapolate probabilities for occurrence. There is still a danger if you change things too much."

Bolt had been the junior officer in charge of analyzing the DNA sequence data downloaded from the derelict ship after its discovery 21 years ago. After receiving a highly classified reply to his Red Dart Emergency communication, the Captain held an immediate briefing in his ready room for the command staff. The result of that meeting was a quarantining of three decks and Bolt's promotion to what became known as the Brin department. He was ordered to grow a clone from one of the surviving DNA samples so long as strict isolation and secrecy protocols were implemented. Bolt was restricted to the quarantined section of the ship for the duration of the project. He named the clone Karm, after a favorite character in a novel he read as a child. He was now the senior officer in charge of Karm's instruction and training.

Learning the Brin language was the toughest part of all, but if Karm was to save his people, he had to be taught how to communicate in proper Brin-speak. Fortunately, the Brin ship contained enough verbal data to manage the task reasonably well. To be fluent, Karm would simply have to be careful and learn the nuances of the language once he arrived.

"But can't you give me anything more?" asked Karm, pacing nervously, his talons fidgeting with the hem of his sleeve. "I feel as if I'm going in blind. I wish you would tell me everything you know."

Bolt raised his long, blue index finger and wagged it in Karm's direction. "You know we cannot do that. We have been over this many times, Karm."

"Yes, I know," Karm said as he sat back in his chair and recited his first lesson again. "Unless there is a direct and imminent threat of destruction to our vessel and its crew, all alien races must be allowed to progress without interference. In the event direct contact is unavoidable, contact must be minimal for the safety and protection of all concerned."

"But what happens if I die in some unforeseen accident?"

"We have contingencies in place. Besides, you won't have that much longer to worry about it. Soon enough you will be on your way back to your planet's past and your mission will begin. Want to test your holoprojection system and biocomputer connections again? Practicing with the holograms always seems to get your mind off things."

Karm held out his left hand, palm up, and thought about the projector. *Activate!* Instantly, a light glowed in his palm and a three dimensional projection appeared a few inches above his hand. As he thought again about information regarding Dyan'ta, its image appeared in fine detail. The entire Brin ship's database, along with vital knowledge possessed by the Skae regarding the destruction of the Brin's home planet had been downloaded into the biocomputer. This information, which was integrated into his body at formation, provided Karm with certain advantages. Even with the corruption gaps Karm could access enough data to ensure at least ninety two percent accuracy of historical events on Dyan'ta. At least this was Bolt's theory. After years of training, he had learned how to access almost every part of the databanks at will. Learning how to manipulate the biocomputer was never an easy task, requiring both concentration and focus, neither of which Karm possessed at first. Recalling his early days often became a source of merriment for Bolt and the others during mealtime, much to Karm's chagrin. The conversations usually started with: "Do you remember the first time he ever attempted to…?"

This was followed with a detailed description of how Karm nearly killed himself with a feedback loop, wiped out an entire circuit board, collapsed in spasms from an excessive overload, or simply received information regarding worms when he tried to study interdimensional worm holes. Karm always felt his muscles tense and his crest feathers prickle at these good-natured jabs as he tried to laugh along with his instructors, but he became determined to master the biocomputer and end the jests.

After years of practice Karm learned to manipulate the image with great precision so now, when called on, the device provided exactly the information requested in the detail required. Karm was able to see the oceans, land masses, and all the geography he might desire. He zoomed in to such a tiny scale, he could pick out individual Brin and identify them by the names he had invented, or their actual names if they were important enough to have their information on file in the ship's computers. He could even bring up printed data about any aspect of the planet, and the Brin civilization, he wanted, going back thousands of years.

"When will you trust me enough to allow me access to the entire database?" asked Karm.

"You know it is not a matter of trust, Karm," replied Bolt as he placed his long blue arm gently around Karm's shoulder. "Too much information might cause you to change events too soon and you know the data was corrupted so, in certain circumstances, it can provide only statistical probabilities of events, some with errors of up to thirty-four percent possibility. You will be provided access to the data you need when the time is right for you to have it, but there will be times when you will need to rely on your own instincts and intelligence." Bolt took Karm by the elbow and looked directly into his eyes. "Even the wisest might be sorely tempted to misuse that much information about the future. This is too important of a mission to risk failure due to greed or overconfidence."

Karm ran a frustrated hand through his top crest, clenching the feathers in a tight fist, and turned away. "I know…I know. I just get frustrated being cooped up in here for so long. I want to get started."

"Karm," Bolt said, softly raising his hand toward him.

Karm turned back to Bolt and reached up to touch Bolt's hand. A soft glow enveloped them both and Karm felt a sense of serenity flow through him, limited mind alteration links being one of the added advantages of his biocomputer. He relaxed and returned to his training.

Time passed slowly, but eventually they arrived at the cosmic string that would take Karm back in time. Passing through the long hallways, he began to reminisce.

Twenty years of training for this, and now it's finally here. The fate of so many rests in my hands. Am I ready for this? Karm lifted his head and squared his shoulders. *It's now or never. No more doubts, too much is at stake. Focus on the job and get it done.*

The two crew members accompanying him along the time curve were equally silent, but seemed more reflective. Karm did not want to intrude on his companions. He did not fully comprehend their sense of loss at leaving the ship, but he respected them and kept to himself.

They soon arrived at the hatchway leading to the small transport vessel. Reaching up to slap his hand on the bulkhead high above his head, Karm entered the ship and found his seat. The others entered as well, ducking slightly to avoid hitting their heads, and each settled into their places and prepared for departure.

"Docking clamps released…Engines at stand-by… All hatches secure. Ready for departure." They went through the familiar pre-launch checklist and prepared themselves for the journey ahead.

"Karm, hit the ignition switch."

Karm reached for the switch, but hesitated. A look of grave concern crossed his face.

"What's the matter?"

"Nothing, just a flashback to the Kreldig incident." Karm hit the switch and sat back, checking the security of his shoulder straps.

"I thought you were over that," said Bolt, his brows furrowing. "After all, everyone did survive…eventually."

In moments, the holding clamps released with a slight jolt, maneuvering thrusters gently steered the shuttle free. Its engines engaged and they set coordinates toward the string. Karm watched out his porthole as the *Helven* silently slipped away above him. Their sensors registered the position of the string and automatically aligned the ship for entry.

"String augmenter to full strength," Bolt said as he manipulated the dials on his console. "Curve directional controls set and aligned to target time dimensions."

"Entering cosmic string now," said Bolt as the ship lurched to one side. "Singularity compensators engaged. Hull stresses well within parameters."

Karm closed his eyes and white-knuckled the armrests of his seat. A faint odor of ozone filled the cabin.

The passage was jarring as the ship buffeted around, but uneventful until his companions began some unexpected activity.

"Countdown to biopod launch," announced Bolt.

"What's going on?" asked Karm, turning his head as best he could while under restraint, but they ignored him.

"Launch countdown confirmed for ten seconds," replied Zem. "Target branch in range and launch sequence is steady."

A slight shudder ran through the ship as the biopod launched. The shaking and noise ended abruptly as they completed their passage along the cosmic string and found themselves in the vicinity of Dyan'ta. Karm looked in amazement at the first planet he had ever seen without the aid of his holoprojector. *It looks so much less real than my projections somehow.*

Rousing himself from his fascination with the planet, he turned to Bolt. "I don't suppose you want to tell me what that biopod stuff is all about, do you?"

"Not now, Karm." Bolt glanced at Zem with a wink then returned his attention to the displays at his console. "Your biocomputer will let you know what to do about the pod when the proper time arrives. For now, trust us and your computer system to provide you with the appropriate information when you most require it."

Karm's neck feathers always ruffled a bit when Bolt said this. He preferred knowing more up front, but he trusted Bolt, accepted what his mentor told him, and focused on his mission. Always the mission. The ship's sensors confirmed they had arrived three years ahead of the mark, the moment in history calculated as the precise tipping point he had trained for. Bolt entered the coordinates to take them to their destination and they soon landed in a remote area of the planet.

Karm and Bolt left the tight confines of the ship together. They faced each other and Bolt smiled. "Even after all this time, you still struggle with personal connections."

The two companions stood together silently, breathing deeply, admiring the beauty of this world, enjoying the freedom after their long confinement aboard ship.

Karm dug his hands into his pockets and looked off into the distance. The tall buildings of a city rose in the distance, the setting sun reflecting flashes of orange off their windows. The blue tinged leaves of the nearby forest shimmered in the breeze, the branches rustled with the darting movements of brightly colored flying creatures Karm's biocomputer identified as Mutons, their leathery wings contrasting with the feathers covering the rest of their bodies. Small furry, six legged animals with dark eyes and long ears, identified as Dinters, swung from branch to branch using their prehensile tails. A herd of large, golden colored, six-legged animals with a single horn protruding from their heads grazed in the distance, unconcerned with the appearance of the visitors from above.

"It's difficult, but I'm getting better at it."

"Have you taken your medication, yet?"

Karm reached into his pocket and pulled out a large red pill. Swallowing it, he grimaced.

"First thing I need to do is find a way to improve the taste of these awful things."

Bolt smiled at his student and they stood a while longer looking across the scene stretching out before them. When the two could no longer delay the inevitable, they raised their hands and touched palms. The familiar tingle raced up their arms and the faint green glow surrounded their connected hands. Breaking the connection, Bolt turned toward the ship.

"What will you do now?" Karm asked his friend, knowing that cosmic string time travel followed a closed time curve and only worked in one direction.

"What we must."

Karm nodded and watched as Bolt left and climbed back up the ramp. As the ship rose into the sky, gradually diminishing into a barely visible speck, and then vanish beyond his sight. He looked down, picked up a few blades of grass at his feet and brought them to his nose. "Huh...I thought it would smell differently."

***

"Can you repeat that, stranger? Not quite sure I caught your meaning, what with your accent and all." The young man wearing the yellow smock held his pen over the notepad, confusion written all over his face.

Karm composed himself and attempted as genuine a smile as he tried again. His first attempt at communication with a living Brin proved to be more difficult than he had hoped.

"I request food...for consumption to eat...please... fruit with leaves of salad...and water liquid. Bring now here to me?" He pointed to a picture of what he hoped he was asking for on the menu cards.

"You want some fruit, a salad and some water?" repeated the serving man, also pointing to the items Karm indicated. "I swear, mister, no offense, but I haven't heard an accent like yours ever before. Where are you from?"

Swallowing hard and continuing to smile, the talons of his left hand clenched tight, Karm replied, "I from ocean...other side. Grepwon Island...town small."

The serving man, Karm's biocomputer now identified the profession as waiter, shook his head and ran the talons of one hand through his crest. "If you say so, mister. I'll be right back with your food." He hesitated, a frown growing on his brow. "You can pay for the food, can't you, mister?"

Karm reached into his pocket and pulled out several of the coins the Skae fabricated for him.

"Huh," he said taking one of the coins, turning it in his fingers, feeling its weight. "Must be another new one of them coins from the capital."

The young man turned and walked briskly toward the kitchen, glancing back over his shoulder at Karm as he pushed through the shiny metallic doors.

To avoid the embarrassment and frustration of similar encounters in the future, Karm devised his plan of visiting a busy section of town for several hours each day. He sat quietly on a bench or walked slowly through the crowds of Brin, listening to their conversations. The biocomputer recording each one for future reference. At night, alone in his small rented room with the yellowing wallpaper, thin brown rug and windows so dirty there was no need for curtains, he listened to the flow of the words, learning the syntax and nuances of the Brin language. He could not afford to stand out. His destiny required anonymity.

Chapter Three

"Feathers and Quills!" shouted Karm into the receiver, throwing his arms in the air, letting the stack of papers fly, his crest feathers turning crimson with rage. "How could this happen? How could I have lost everything so fast?"

In only five years, Karm found himself the master of a small fortune, the result of his biocomputer's suggestions for speculation in the money exchange market, judicious buying and selling of several land acquisitions, shares purchased in a number of small, but successful business ventures, and careful management of his growing estate. His greed also grew in proportion to his wealth to the point where he started ignoring the advice of his biocomputer and bankers, trusting instead his own ego driven wishes.

"Sir," replied the voice over the speaker, "we tried to warn you about investing in such marginal markets. Our data indicated, as we informed you last month, the strong possibility of collapse. Had you listened to us you would not be facing bankruptcy today. You will need to divest your holdings and—"

"Don't lecture me, sir." Karm drew out and emphasized the 'sir' mocking the banker's formality. "If I always listened to your timid advice I would never have accumulated enough to worry about losing in the first place! Just sell off whatever you need to and resolve this mess. I'll call later to make final arrangements and assess the damages. Save as much as you can." Karm hit the off switch with a shaking talon, rubbed his face and slumped heavily back in his chair. Breathing deeply to gather his emotions, he swiveled around, jumped to his feet and strode quickly out of the room, feeling the need for a drive into the countryside.

With the mag-lev's dome retracted, the air blew briskly through his crest, sending a chill down his spine. He loved driving, especially this time of year when he could set the controls to automatically follow the magnetic propulsion system buried beneath the roadbed and enjoy the new colors of the season. The crisp autumn air always helped clear his mind. Thick dark clouds gathered over the taller mountains in the distance, giving the ominous appearance of a building storm. He pulled off into the red dirt trailhead parking lot, one of his favorite places to escape and think, turned off the electromagnetic drive, and found the bench by the stream he always found soothing. There was something about the sound of water tumbling over the rocks and listening to the creek of the trunks as the wind gently blew through the yellow flowering Tark trees, their fragrant leaves smelling of fresh mint that calmed his mind, allowing him to think clearly. Downstream, a nearly silent Hodak waded into the flowing water, its single spiral horn sending out v-shaped ripples as the gentle creature bent its head for a drink.

"How could I have gotten so careless?" he muttered aloud to himself. His head hung low, resting in his hands, his elbows perched on his knees. Holding out his hand and thinking the activation command, he reviewed the biocomputer's analysis of his recent, and most disastrous, investments. "Negative ratings across the board. The machine was right all along. Bolt warned me about ignoring this thing." An hour later, Karm leaned over, picked up a grey flat rock and sent it skipping across the stream. "Never again," he growled at himself. He stood, straightening his shoulders and lifting his chin, having made the necessary decisions. Back in the city, he pulled into the first used mag-lev sales lot he found, haggled with the man in charge, and fed in the commands to transfer ownership. Turning up the collar of his overcoat to ward off the chill in the air, he walked home, determined to never fall prey to arrogance again. Wealth and authority over others were essential ingredients to accomplish his task. They were not his personal toys to play with as he wished. The mission is too important.

***

"I don't care what you think. You are an advisor, while I am the one spending the money here. You are paid, and rather well, I might add, regardless of whether my investments go bust or not. I expect you to carry out my instructions and not question them. If you cannot conduct business under these terms, let me know now so that I can stop wasting my time and go elsewhere." *I'm making this dinter-brain a fortune with my investments. It would take an army of accountants to unravel all of my dummy corporations, off-shore accounts and legal entities. I know the man's just doing his job, but the wrong question from a brainless broker could send up a red flag that sends an investigation my way. I can't allow sentiment to interfere with the mission. Maybe it is time to move on before he starts to wonder just where my information is coming from.*

Karm knew he could not afford to linger too long in any one location, yet he did enjoy being here in this small mountain town. People here were friendly. After the factory shut down most of the townspeople had moved on to the larger cities to find work, but enough remained to take advantage of the tourists. The town itself was like something out of a tourist bureau poster. The blue-leafed trees produced flowers of so many colors, they rivaled the rainbows. The highest peaks of distant mountains usually maintained at least some snow, no matter the season. A small stream flowing through town sparkled and held a number of great fishing spots within walking distance of his home here. Families of thick-furred Petzels using their tusks to root in the fields for their dinner made for great sport with youngsters learning to hunt. *Never expected I would get so addicted to standing in cold water trying to convince some fish to sacrifice itself for my enjoyment.*

Karm sat on his porch, enjoying the solitude and scenery before getting back to business. A pair of flightless Quol hunted in a nearby grove of trees. Their long legs and bulk made their graceful movements all the more beautiful. *Maybe just a couple more years? No. Not worth the risk. Fifteen years of following the plan I cannot get off track again. It is nice here, though. Maybe I'll get lucky again.*

Activate Accounts. And, holding out his hand, the soft glow of his palm presented a detailed and beautifully displayed holographic graph of the required information.

Total Assets §160,926,462.34. Good diversification in all the necessary areas as well. Construction, Pharmaceuticals, Engineering, R & D, all falling into place as planned.

Alright, everything seems in order and on schedule so far. Nothing like a bit of historical perspective to enhance one's portfolio. Activate Calendar: Appointments for the week.

With a satisfied nod, Karm surveyed the holographic calendar, noting the dates and times of upcoming meetings with executives of soon to be acquired additions to his growing empire, as well as the precious time he always set aside to indulge his beloved fly fishing habit.

All these years of pursuing the plan and, despite the set-backs I created, everything's on schedule. Still so much to do before everything is ready. Still a few hours of daylight left though. Deactivate.

The hologram vanished and the glow in his palm faded. Karm got up from the bench, crossed the porch, and grabbed his favorite fly rod and a box of flies. *That big fella is out there in those riffles and it's just about his dinner time.*

As he stood in the stream that evening watching the pool for rises, an idea struck him. *As the head of a financial empire, I am going to need someplace to bring potential clients and partners for meetings; someplace to impress them as they are wined and dined. This area offers some spectacular advantages for just such an enterprise. Lots of available land and a people starved for employment. I think this might work.* He cast his line one final time and watched as it floated downstream without taking a hit. He shrugged and reeled in the line absentmindedly as he considered his next move.

The following weeks were a blur of activity. Karm described his vision to a local architect whom he hired to create the blueprints and architectural drawings. Once everything was completed to his satisfaction he called together the local real estate broker, the banker, the mayor, and the town council. He explained his idea for the purchase of a large parcel of land and the development he envisioned.

"I want to build an estate home on several hundred acres back beyond those forested hills to the west," he told them. "This will be a type of resort home where I will be able to bring clients and entertain dignitaries in high style." He unveiled the series of artistic and architectural designs as he described the project. The drawings illustrated a large castle-like building surrounded by well-preserved natural settings. "Your town needs a strong financial base now that your factory is gone. And the quarry and masons could certainly use a boost to their business. This project will provide employment for everyone. I'll need hundreds of construction workers over the next decade. Once finished, there will be steady employment for many more. Staff will be needed to run the facility, cooks, maintenance and security personnel, grounds keepers, all hired locally."

The mayor looked over at the council members and stood to take the lead. "Now, just hold on a minute here, Karm. We like our nice quiet little town just the way it is. What you're talking about sounds like you want to turn our fine town into some sort of amusement park."

Karm shook his head in response. "Not at all, Mr. Mayor, quite the opposite I assure you. This will be a strictly private operation. The general public will not be allowed on the grounds. My plan is for the estate to be used for my private business affairs. The only people who come here will be at my invitation. Our town will not be changed in any way, except to be put on a much more permanent economic footing." He smiled at them and leaned in closer as if to bring them into his little conspiracy. "Of course exclusive contracts for all of my needs in the facility will be made only with your townspeople. No outside involvement. Imagine the boost to local business."

"Give us just a moment, Karm." The mayor and council members walked over to a corner of the room and whispered among themselves for a few minutes. When they returned, the mayor grabbed Karm's hand and shook it vigorously. "I think we have a deal."

"Wonderful! I'll have my people draw up some contracts right away." Karm picked up a glass of red valum, sniffed the fruity scent, and toasted his new partners.

The room buzzed with animated talk over the opportunities and potential this proposal had for the town. Council members drank and smiled as they considered their future. Then one of the council members called out to Karm over the noise. "What do you intend to call this project?"

He pointed to the central architectural drawing of the front façade of the castle and beamed, "I call it, The Citadel."

***

The noise was deafening. Heavy lifters roared in protest as they placed stone blocks into position in the walls of The Citadel. Excavators plowed up vast tracts of land for the landscaping. Construction supervisors shouting instructions to hundreds of workers who continued to pound, saw, drill and yell back in response all contributed to the organized chaos of the site. Karm sat in the manager's hut going over the blueprints with the architects.

"What is so difficult about this?" he asked the supervisor. "Your job is to see my wishes are carried out exactly as directed. Money is not your concern. No more alterations to any part of this design or the materials specified without my direct orders. Is that understood?"

The supervisor gathered up the diagrams and placed them back into their folders. "Yes, sir," he replied. "I wouldn't be doing my job if I didn't try to bring this job on time and under budget for you. Many of these specifications require materials and artisans that are nearly impossible to find. The locals are skilled, but would benefit from the guidance and training of a master guildsman. We're only six months into construction and delays are starting to build up."

Karm collected himself with a deep breath, then leaned forward, hands clasped on the table. His eyes fixed firmly on the supervisor. "There are reasons why these provisions are necessary. I am not worried about delays, just make sure the plans are followed exactly as required. I can provide you any extra help you need to find the specialists and rare materials."

At that moment the door to the small hut opened. Karm and the supervisor turned to see who was interrupting their meeting. A large man wearing a dark suit, carrying a valise entered the cramped quarters and closed the door behind him.

"I was told I would find Karm in here," he said, leveling his eyes at the two men inside.

"I'm Karm. Who let you in here and what do you mean by barging in here like this?"

"My name is Darkon." He held out a business disk to Karm. "I'm with the Securities and Exchange Division. We need to talk."

Karm's left palm itched and his eyes looked off as if distracted for a brief moment. "Excuse us for a bit," he said to the supervisor. "I'll be back tomorrow to discuss this further with you." He placed a hand on Darkon's shoulder and gave the government agent his most ingratiating smile. "It's such a nice day today, why don't we discuss this down by the river, away from all this noise. I have a nice pergola down there where we can order some lunch and talk in private."

Twenty minutes later they were seated in comfortable chairs listening to the sound of the flowing river. "So, what can I do for you, Darkon?"

Darkon opened his valise and brought out a thick folder, which he set on the table in front of him. "About three months ago we started receiving some very disturbing information about some of your operations, Karm. I was assigned to investigate the matter. I need to ask you some very serious questions about your finances."

Karm leaned back in his chair and took a sip of his tea. "What exactly is your concern, Darkon? I can assure you all of my finances are quite legitimate and above board. I've hired an army of lawyers and tax experts to make sure everything is double checked and completely legal."

"That is not precisely our concern," said Darkon as he opened the file and turned a few pages. "It is you yourself that is the real mystery here. You seem to be quite the financial genius, Karm. You always manage to invest in just the right companies at the exact moment of maximum value for your efforts. How do you manage that? Dozens of investments over the past ten years, all without fail. That is unprecedented and very suspect."

Karm's palm tingled again and he paused before replying, then smiled. "Come now, Darkon. I'm sure your investigation was very thorough and showed no illicit or illegal activity on any transactions. Surely it's no crime to be smarter than the other investors. What are you really after here?"

Darkon sat up straight and closed the folder. He looked Karm directly in the eye, studying him for a moment. "Very well, then. As I said, it is you that is the real mystery here. My investigation led me to look further into your background. Of course, all of the paperwork was in perfect order. Birth certificate, census and school records, all seemingly normal. Until I took it upon myself to take a more personal approach."

"And what did you turn up?" asked Karm, seemingly unconcerned and relaxed.

"I went to the university to talk with some of the professors in the economics department, which is your declared major according to the documents. I also visited your old neighborhoods listed in the census records, your old primary schools, even your parent's gravesite. It seems nobody has any personal recollection of you or your family. Nothing at all."

"It was a long time ago, Darkon. We were a very quiet family, nothing remarkable. I'm not surprised nobody remembers us."

"I am," said Darkon. "I've never experienced such a complete anonymity as yours. What are you hiding, Karm? Who are you?"

"Is there anything illegal, immoral, or unethical in anything you found?"

"No, nothing like that. In fact, I have already filed my report to my superiors clearing you of any suspicions.

My job was to try to discover anything illegal in your dealings. Your mysterious history is not illegal and therefore not their concern. As far as the Securities and Exchange Division is concerned, you are clean as a whistle. This was something I did on my own. I don't like unanswered questions."

"Come walk with me." Karm stood and headed down to the path next to the river. Darkon followed. A few minutes later, under the teal leaves of the trees overhanging the path and the gentle gurgling of the river in their ears, Karm placed his left hand on Darkon's shoulder. A faint blue glow surrounded the two men. "So what are your intentions now? Is it blackmail you're after?"

"Not at all," said Darkon. "as I said, I don't like unanswered questions. The more I dug, the less I found. Nobody is that well hidden, but you have managed it. I want to know how and why. I can offer you something valuable in return."

Karm removed his arm from Darkon's shoulder, turning to face him with narrowed eyes. "And what would that be? What can you possibly have that I would be interested in?"

Darkon stopped and turned to face Karm. "I'm not sure why, but I trust you, Karm. Anybody else who would go through all of this effort to hide their past would have done it for some nefarious purpose. You didn't. In my experience, you are a rarity, Karm. Despite my personal convictions to the contrary, I have been unable to uncover so much as a single shred of evidence of any wrongdoing. Oh, there were the normal bits of devious business acumen, perfectly reasonable for anyone in your position, but nothing to indicate subversive or other scandalous intent. And believe me, I have looked." He looked hard into Karm's eyes and held them for a moment. "You must have some powerful reasons for hiding yourself like this. If I discovered as much as I have about you, others may be able to as well. I can help you with the mistakes you made that roused my curiosity so much. Your trail was good, but not perfect. I can help you fix that…if you'll hire me as head of your security group."

"That is quite a bold statement, Darkon. Why should I trust you?"

Darkon held his ground. He opened his valise and took out the files inside, holding them out for Karm. "There are no copies of these, they are now yours. I came to you with this information when I could just as easily gone to the authorities. While your past is not illegal, it is very unusual. Something that would quickly get noticed by the monarch's security people." Darkon thought briefly before continuing, "I'll be honest. I first came here to get a sense of you in person. I wasn't sure what I wanted to do with what I discovered. I really don't like mysteries, but I do have a gut instinct about you now that we have talked. Maybe someday, if I prove my value to you, I will find the answers."

Karm smiled and reached out to shake talons with Darkon. "I won't promise you anything other than a job, Darkon. In fact, I can pretty well guarantee your questions will remain unanswered. I can, however, promise some very interesting times ahead. If you can live with that, we have a deal."

Darkon smiled in return and grasped Karm's talons in return. A faint blue nimbus again surrounded both men, then faded as quickly as it came.

"Do you like to fish, Mr. Darkon?" asked Karm, smiling as they headed off in the direction of the stream.

***

A tingling sensation in his left arm startled Karm awake. *Must have dozed off for a bit. What's going on now?* Shaking his head and running his fingers through his crest to help clear his mind, he looked down at his arm and saw the soft glow emanating from his palm. *Activate.* An image of Dyan'ta hovered above his outstretched hand and rotated to the northern hemisphere. Data filled his mind as if long suppressed memories suddenly awakened. Karm stared blankly as the images and details sorted themselves into understanding. Looking down at the image of Dyan'ta he saw that it zoomed to a particular location. A set of coordinates blazed in crimson. He took a deep breath, stood, and walked to his desk. Still rubbing his eyes, Karm pressed the video-intercom button for his secretary.

"Kirta, I need you to clear my schedule for the next four days."

"Yes, sir," she replied. "Is there a specific reason that I can provide?"

"No, use your best judgment on how to handle that, but don't get too creative."

"Yes, sir, right away. Shall I notify Krell to prepare your bags?"

He stopped his pacing and thought for a moment. "No, I'll handle that myself. Under no circumstances is anyone to contact me for anything. I don't care if The Eternal stops by for afternoon tea. No calls."

"Yes, sir. No calls." Kirta looked at Karm, studying him. "I do hope everything is alright, sir."

"Everything is fine. Thank you for your concern. Just tell Krell to have the levicoach ready. And call the airport. I want the jet ready in two hours."

"Alright, sir. Be well. See you in four days." She returned her attention to the papers on her desk.

"Thank you, Kirta." Karm went to his private quarters to pack.

Twenty-four hours later Karm found himself in the middle of the Latonian Desert, hundreds of miles from the nearest town. He sat by his campfire trying to eat the meal he had just burned. "What was he thinking?" Karm muttered aloud to himself, grimacing at the unpleasant taste of his attempt to cook. "Building and managing a financial empire I can deal with, but this?" He threw down his unfinished meat and stared at the night sky. *Bolt, my old friend, wherever you are now, I hope I'm making you proud. Our plans are going well. I just hope that I'm up for what's ahead.* He turned to look at the lopsided tent he had attempted to set up, checked the biocomputer for any signs of rebel activity in the vicinity, and decided it would be safer to sleep under the stars.

In the morning, he awoke to the familiar tingling in his left arm. The soft glow in his palm had taken on a greenish hue now. *Activate.* A two-hour countdown projected above his hand. *Good. Time for a bit of breakfast first. Let's see if I can avoid poisoning myself today.*

He dug through his pack and located a tin of eggs and some sort of breakfast meat. Setting it on some flat rocks surrounding the fire, he returned to the pack and found a bottle of fruit juice.

As the countdown neared zero, he stood at the edge of his camp looking up at the sky. He noticed a small light growing larger as it headed straight toward him. The bright object left a vapor trail in its wake as it streaked through the atmosphere. At an altitude of 100 meters, the object stopped and hovered for a moment. Karm's palm tingled in a rhythmic pattern. The floating object turned and headed in his direction. Two hundred yards from the camp, the object stopped and settled gently onto the ground.

Karm stared at the craft, then at his palm. With a shrug of his shoulders, he headed in the direction of the craft.

Karm recognized the biopod that Bolt had launched from their ship the day he arrived at Dyan'ta. It was no more than two meters long and only slightly scarred by the heat of passing through the atmosphere. There were no visible signs of a hatch. He reached out his left hand and placed it on the hull. A rectangular outline appeared. The hatch dropped down and slid to the side revealing the interior. He stood for a moment, examining the contents of the craft. His palm glowed in changing hues of orange, blue and red, reflecting the turmoil he felt within, but the glow soon settled into a pleasant shade of soft green.

Karm reached down, hands trembling slightly, and picked up the infant inside. He passed his left hand over the child and his glowing palm registered strong vital signs.

"Strixo, Maripa," he said in a voice he hoped was soothing, but came out a bit too shaky and high-pitched. "You don't seem to be any worse for wear after your journey."

Karm then reached inside, pressed a series of switches on the control panel and walked away. An energy field shimmered around the vessel. In a few seconds, the ship collapsed into dust. Karm looked back making sure no traces remained.

Back in camp, Karm sat stiffly with his new charge sleeping peacefully in his lap. *Activate: Infant Care: Female.* The data required to care for this child, and additional data concerning the most probable course for her future, raced through his mind.

"Well, young lady," Karm said. "Welcome to Dyan'ta. My name is Karm. Not sure I'm up to this particular challenge, but you are apparently a vital cog to this mission's success. I'll figure it out somehow."

Chapter Four

The stream flowed fast and cold. The air was crisp, the sky slightly overcast and the trees displayed their brilliant orange and red of the season. It was quiet as the sun rose above the horizon. Karm gazed fixedly as he studied a deep pool on the opposite bank. *I know he's hiding in there somewhere. Just need the right incentive to get him to rise.* He turned over a few rocks, identified the insect larvae hiding there, and made his choice. *Yes, just the thing. Now all I need is to land it gently and see if he's hungry.* Karm cast his line out and watched the indicator closely for a strike.

"Sir, important call for you," called out Karm's driver.

"Jetu, Matto, and Jopa!" cursed Karm. "Not now! Tell them I'm in a meeting."

"Sorry, sir, it's Bandu Pharmaceuticals. You said to notify you right away if a call came in about it."

Kak! Forgot about the time zone difference. "Tell the early bird bastards I'm wrapping up another meeting." As he reeled in his line, Karm saw a set of concentric circles form in the center of the pool. "Would have gotten you this time. Don't go anywhere, I'll be back!" he yelled.

Karm climbed up the stream bank, handed his gear to the driver, and slammed himself into his limousine.

Karm's assistant sat inside the levicoach examining some papers. "The Bandu group wants to alter the contract again, sir," he said as Karm grabbed a breakfast bar and juice from the limo's refrigerator.

"What good does it do to own a private river, if I can't ever enjoy it? I've worked for 20 years, I have more money than The Eternal, and I can't convince anyone to let me catch that quetzal down there!" He grumbled, bit off a chunk of the bar and guzzled half the bottle of juice.

The limousine drove through the security gate of Karm's mountain retreat. The iron arch above the gate spelled out The Citadel. The mansion sat in the center of a 300-acre forested estate. A thousand years ago this structure served as the summer castle of the Eastern continent's ruling family. Karm commissioned it to be moved and restored to its original glory by an army of resident artisans. Stonemasons from the local quarry expertly reconstructed those portions proving impossible to transport. The walls were hand carved stone three stories tall, curving magnificently and seamlessly into the floors and ceiling and displayed large stained glass windows. Rounded turrets stood at each corner, complete with conical roofs and flags. The archway into the main courtyard held a functioning drawbridge rising after the limo drove toward the main entrance. There were even a dozen or so gargoyles haunting the parapet.

Karm and his assistant exited the mag-lev and briskly headed into The Citadel. Karm's personal valet took his jacket as soon as he entered the foyer. The stoic manservant then cleared his throat and pointed to the antechamber before his employer took another step in his muddy boots. As he sat and changed into a comfortable pair of house shoes, another servant brought Karm a tray of food and morning cocktails. He grabbed a roll and a glass of juice, talons fitting precisely into the holes in the handle measured by expert craftsmen for him alone, then motioned for her to follow him to his second floor office.

The interior was even more of a museum than the outside. Imported marble floors reflected the light of the large crystal chandeliers hanging from the ceiling. Original paintings from several of the great masters hung prominently on every wall. Outrageously expensive antique furniture, hand-woven rugs, and rare collections adorned every room.

"Thank you, Brill," Karm said as the girl set her tray on the table by the fireplace.

"Will you need anything else, sir?"

"Not for now, thank you. I'll ring you if I need something."

"Very well then, sir. Have a good day." Brill left the room, gently closing the door behind her.

Karm sat behind his desk, glanced through the papers left for him there, and hit the intercom button on his phone. "Kirta, get Bandu on the line."

"I dialed them as you arrived, sir. Video conference is set up on line one."

Karm punched the top button. The view screen on the wall lit up to display five men surrounding a conference table. They looked up from their conversations as the call connected.

"What is it you want, gentlemen?"

The elderly man seated in the chair at the far end of the table spoke. "Yes, Karm. We wanted to discuss several of the provisions in the contract. Our board is not completely satisfied with some of them and we want to negotiate better terms." Their heads all nodded in agreement.

"And what gives you the idea that I am inclined to offer anything more than we have already discussed? With the death of the monarch and the uncertainties regarding his son's qualifications, you should be pleased I am offering this much."

The men turned to look at the one who sat at the end of the table. He shot a quick glance at them before focusing on Karm's image. "Some of the board believes the buyout you are offering is below market value and —"

"Have you had any better offers?"

The appointed speaker shuffled in his seat, then pointed at Karm's image in an attempt to take charge of the conversation. "That is completely beside the point…"

"I repeat, sir, have you had any better offers?" Karm sipped at the drink in his hand.

"No, sir, not yet," the man replied, dropping his hands to the table. A general confusion of discussions erupted among the other men, each trying to be heard above the others. Karm sipped his drink and waited until they quieted. "And you won't. I have controlling interest in all of the other companies that could possibly be in a position to do so and I have vetoed any efforts in that direction. You have no bargaining strength here, and I have no desire to pay you any more than the §43 billion I have set out already."

"Sir, that is hardly what this company is worth," the others all murmured in agreement.

"Your company's value is no more or less than what I say it is. Or would you rather let it go into corporate collapse where I can simply offer to take it off of the government's hands for taxes owed? You have no options left, gentlemen. My lawyers will bring you the papers to sign in the morning." Karm hung up, sat back, closed his eyes and rubbed his temples. He got up, walked across to the large world map on the wall and placed a red pin on the coast of the major continent. *Three more acquisitions and everything will be ready. Probably within the next three years.* Karm sat at the small table, kicked off his shoes, picked up a sandwich and turned on the ballgame. Nothing happened. He tried another button, then another. He flopped back into the sofa, sighed, tossed the remote aside and held out his palm. *Catalog* and the holographic image appeared above his glowing hand showing the latest in handcrafted fishing equipment.

***

Maripa's tenth birthday celebration was everything a young girl could want. All of her classmates attended. Her uncle spared no expense decorating the lavish mansion in the hills in her favorite colors. Music from a live band filled the air. Even life-size paper geldrigs (her favorite mythological creatures), complete with the long flowing, rainbow colored manes, six legs, hooves sparkling as they ran, hanging from strings as if they were guardian sentinels sent from The Eternal, a stable of Tals for riding, and plenty of servants with unending trays of food and drink for all. Why, then, did Karm find her drying tears from her face, alone in the library?

"What is the matter, child? Why aren't you out there with your friends enjoying your party?" He stood at a distance, hands clasped behind his back, eyes wandering from bookshelf to desktop, only briefly settling on his niece.

Wiping her nose on her sleeve, Maripa looked up at Karm, fighting back more tears. "Those are not my friends," she began. "I don't have any real friends, those are just my classmates. Why couldn't we just go somewhere, just you and me, instead? You never make any time just for me. That is what I really wanted."

Karm stiffened at her question, his shoulders fell slightly, but otherwise remained as he was. "I thought you would enjoy all of this. I consulted with the finest party managers in town. They assured me you would…"

"Why didn't you ask me? You never ask me what I want. Darkon would have known exactly what I wanted. He always knows." She stood her ground, refusing to look away or show any further weakness in front of him.

Karm strode to his desk and sat in the heavy padded chair. He leaned forward, supporting his chin with one hand, examining the young girl. "You are right, my dear. I should have discussed this with you. You are not a youngling any more, something I have a difficult time realizing."

Maripa smiled at this and approached the desk, but remained across the massive wooden fixture, not daring to come closer, fearing the appearance of weakness in his eyes. She stood facing Karm, unable to say what she so desperately longed for.

"If spending time together is what you would enjoy, then we shall do so," Karm said, leaning back in his chair, smiling broadly, his hands now folding behind his head. "How about next weekend?"

Maripa's heart leaped in her chest, her crest feathers flushed a brilliant combination of blue and green, but she resisted the impulse to rush into his arms, knowing the crushing result of any attempt at such familiarity. "I would like that, uncle," she replied with a smile. "Very much."

"It's settled then," he slapped the desk with his palm and brought two talons to his chest, tapping it three times to signal the promise. "Run along now and try to enjoy the rest of your party. We will discuss this later in the week. I have some business to deal with now, but I will see you for the blessing cheer later. We can discuss your acceptance as a cadet into The Academy, too. I'm very proud of you for that, you know."

"Thank you, uncle," Maripa said as she turned to leave. "Please don't forget again."

"Don't worry, my dear. We have a date next weekend."

As she opened the door, she saw Darkon approaching with the local newspaper in hand.

"Strixo, Squirt," he said, ruffling her top crest with his hand.

"I hate that name, you know." She strained a lopsided grin at the man.

The big man flashed a huge smile at her. "I know, Squirt. Join me for a game of tuttles later?"

Maripa nodded non-committedly as Darkon continued into the elliptical office, tossing the paper onto Karm's desk. The headline read:

MONARCH PRO-TEM DIES IN TRAGIC BOATING ACCIDENT. BRACH TO ASSUME THRONE.

Watching from the doorway, Maripa saw Karm reach for the phone and knew that once again, all plans were off. She silently closed the door behind her and headed off to her room.

Chapter Five

Brach, second son of Tallett, the ruling monarch of Dyan'ta, and First Chancellor to the Supreme Council, sat among the many family members and functionaries at his father's deathbed. He was tall for a Brin, slightly over six feet, and broad chested, with a thick and colorful head feathering. The crest feathers, long and well preened at all times, served to optimize a display of confidence and strength. To an outsider, the somber scene gave every appearance of a family grieving the passing of a beloved elder. The royal bedchambers were dark, lit only dimly by a few candles. Heavy velvet curtains blocked the many tall windows. A dozen heavy chairs surrounded the large canopied bed, each occupied by family members of various levels. Martek, the eldest son and heir to the throne sat slumped, his head bowed, shoulders shaking as he wept silently, ignoring the constant flow of dignitaries maneuvering for position once the dynasty changed hands. The queen mother stood behind Martek, one hand firmly on his shoulder, trying desperately to will some backbone into her hopeless son. Sitting opposite these two, Lerit, two years younger than Brach, remained impassive, eyes darting everywhere as he maintained the appropriate mask of sorrow and reflection. Everyone dressed in the violet hues of mourning. If anyone spoke, it was brief and hushed so as not to disturb the carefully maintained pose of others in the tableau. A half dozen servants lined the walls of the room awaiting the merest signal calling for their immediate attention. Everyone listened carefully to the erratically rasping breath of the pale, skeletal figure lying in the bed.

Unable to tolerate the charade any longer, Brach rose silently from his chair and approached his mother. Laying a hand gently on her shoulder he leaned in to whisper in her ear coverts. "I will return soon, mother, There are some important matters of state that cannot wait." He gave her a tender peck on top of her grey, sparsely feathered head, and turned to weave his way through the gathering.

"Wine! Now!" yelled Brach, bursting through the heavy doors of his personal chambers. Servants scrambled while his aides jumped to attention. The young royal grabbed the glass offered and slammed the contents down his throat in one sudden jerk. "If I have to sit one more second with those hypocrites I'm going to explode!" He held out the glass for the servant to refill. "They can't wait for that old bird to die so they can start fawning over my idiot brother and gain his favors. And if I don't play the game better than all of them then I'll be their first target." Brach downed the second glass just as quickly as the first and set it on the small table next to the chair he slumped into.

"Your Highness," Brach's senior aide, the Colonel, remained at attention, or at least always looked as though he was at attention as he spoke. "You are well protected and have no need to fear any plots against you. Our informant network will provide ample warning if anyone tries to subvert your position."

Brach stared at the Colonel. The man always dressed in his red and gold Royal Guard uniform, complete with the vast array of medals, ribbons and decorations he had earned throughout his long service to the monarch. The three silver tridents that signified his rank, prominently displayed on his cap and epaulets, reflected brilliantly the sunlight streaming through the tall windows. *How long have I known this man? I can't remember ever not knowing him.* The Colonel had always been an impressive figure, marked for rapid advancement by the heads of state even while he was still a student in the academy so long ago. Brach thought it odd that the Colonel was the only person who nobody ever seemed to address by name, only by his rank. Not even his father, the monarch, called him anything other than Colonel. *I may not know his name, but he is the only person whose loyalty to me is beyond reproach, at least so far. I would hate to have to eliminate such a valuable asset.*

Waving his talons dismissively, Brach brushed away the Colonel's statement. "Yes, yes, don't pay me any mind, Colonel. I'm just irritated right now." He stopped himself before continuing as he noticed the servants still in attendance. "All of you are dismissed now," Brach said. "I will ring if I need anything. Secure the door behind you and see that we are not disturbed."

"Why won't that old bird just get it over with and die already?" Brach said once the doors were closed. "He's been at it for over a week now. I never imagined anyone, even him, could hang on so long."

"Be patient, Your Highness. It cannot be much longer. Even your father must succumb eventually."

Brach pushed himself up from the chair and stomped across the circular room to refill his glass with more wine. "And to name Martek as his successor. That's the real feather twister." Brach swallowed the wine in another quick gulp. "Martek wouldn't know which talon to scratch his crest with if I wasn't there to remind him every day."

The Colonel stiffened, his face even more stone-like than normal. "It is customary for the eldest son to be successor to the throne."

Brach threw his empty glass against the wall, shattered shards danced as they scattered across the floor. "Well that custom is going to doom the kingdom! Those sycophant toadies will have him signing over all of the authority and power of the monarchy within a year. All Martek really cares about are his boats. He'll agree to anything if it will allow him to go race his sailing yacht. Something has to be done."

The Colonel shifted his stance slightly as he thought. "Tradition dictates six months of mourning before a successor can assume the throne, Your Highness. The senate cannot conduct anything more than the most basic of services until then. There is time. In the meantime, there are pressing matters needing your approval."

Two hours later, Brach sat at his desk reading the stack of official documents he had allowed to pile up while sitting by his father's bedside. The doors to his chambers creaked quietly as they opened. "I told you not to disturb me," he said without stopping his efforts.

"I am sorry, brother," said Lerit, waving a careless dismissal to the Colonel. "I must not have heard you amid all of the wailing down the hall."

"What do you want, Lerit?" Brach asked, rubbing his eyes with the palms of his hands. "I don't have time for visiting, or did you want to pour out your heart about dear old father?"

Lerit snorted, slipped his talons through the ornate holes in one of the goblets on the table, poured himself a drink and fell into the chair across the desk from Brach. "We have business to discuss, dear brother."

"We have nothing to—"

"Yes, we do. Neither of us believes for one second Martek is capable of being monarch."

"He will make a decent showing if I guide him; help him negotiate the flocks of sycophants bound to surround him."

Lerit took another long sip from his goblet, raised his eyes toward the high, arched ceiling, and sighed. "I hope you are right. Nevertheless, you know Martek as well as I do. He is weak and will inevitably fall prey to those who tell him what he wants to hear. We need to be prepared for this future, and I need you to know I have no aspirations for the throne and am no threat to you."

Brach set his pen aside, placed both hands on the table, drumming his talons rhythmically, narrowing his eyes as he studied his younger brother. "Explain yourself."

Lerit stood and leaned on Brach's desk, lowering his voice conspiratorially. "I sincerely hope your efforts to control Martek succeed, but I hold out little hope. I believe his incompetence will force you to remove him from the throne, preferably, but not necessarily preserving his life. When that happens, I plan to renounce all claims to the succession and take up the robes of a cleric."

Shaking his head, Brach chuckled in disbelief, and ran his talons through his crest. "Now why would you want to do such a fool thing? You are no more a cleric than I am. You would never…"

Lerit held up a hand, pointing a talon at his brother. "When you succeed poor Martek as our monarch, I would be next in line. You would never be free of my potential to usurp you unless I was legally bound to the church rather than the palace. We both know you are the one with the talent, ambition, and desire to rule. Neither of us will need to keep looking over our shoulders. I may not be a born cleric, but better that life than none at all. Besides, have you ever considered how completely pervasive and eternal the church is? Many ruling families have come and gone under the watchful eye of the church. I believe any thoughts of authority I may conceive will be amply fulfilled within their ranks."

"Would you be willing to state this intention in writing with the Grand Elder as witness?"

"With the understanding my joining the ranks of the bishops, my preferred rank to start with, would be delayed so long as Martek is monarch. After all, he will need both of us to guide him in this difficult role he is assuming."

Brach eyed his sibling up and down, searching for any trace of guile or deception. "I can find no fault with your plan," he replied after leaning back in his chair, arms folded across his chest. "We can have the papers drawn up in a day or two." He reached forward again, picked up his pen and returned to the stack of papers in front of him. Lerit smiled, raised his goblet in salute and strolled back to the table with the crystal decanters to refill his glass.

A knock on the heavy wooden doors broke the silence. The hinges creaked as the doors swung slowly open, light from the antechamber spilling into the room. "I am sorry, brothers, but father has died." Brach froze in mid signature and looked up to see Martek, eyes red and swollen, standing in the doorway. "Mother has asked me to come bring you both back to pay your respects." Martek used his sleeve to wipe his nose and dry his eyes.

Our future monarch. Brach hung his head and made his choice. *This, I cannot allow.* Crossing the room to join his elder brother, Brach embraced the now sobbing young man. "Be strong, brother," said Brach in his most reassuring manner. "You are our monarch now. You must be strong for the rest of us."

"I cannot replace Father," Martek continued to sob. "I don't know how to be monarch. Will you help me, brother?"

Brach took his brother by the shoulders and looked him in the eyes. "You know you can always count on me." Brach straightened his brother's collar, his talons deftly re-knotting the cravat. "I will be right by your side for as long as you need me." *Or at least as long as I let you live.* "Now go use my wash basin to rinse yourself off and we will go pay our respects to Father together."

***

Two months later, life was starting to return to normal in the palace. The royal funeral had been the grand affair people continued to talk about during the many state dinners. Brach resumed his duties as First Chancellor to the Supreme Council, but now with the added responsibility of guiding Martek through the intricacies of ruling as the new monarch. Martek tried hard to be a good monarch, but had the uncanny ability to surround himself with the worst possible sort of advisors. All of them were conniving in one way or another to undermine the monarchy in favor of their own interests. Despite Brach's best efforts, Martek continued to appoint individuals who appealed to his sensibilities and who whispered false praises in his ear whenever Brach was not around to intercede.

"But why shouldn't the mining guilders be exempt from the land use fee?" Martek's face twisted in confused concentration during one of his rare private moments with Brach. The two had managed to sneak away from the palace for a ride in the countryside. Their powerful Tals effortlessly galloped over the hilly terrain. Blooming wildflowers filled the air with invigorating aromas. The ever present royal guards maintained a discrete distance behind. "It is such a small fee, only three duckets per acre, and it will allow them enough of a profit margin to upgrade their equipment to make mining more efficient."

Brach fought to control his anger as he shook his head in dismay. Reigning in his Tal, he turned in his saddle to face his elder brother. "You still aren't seeing the long term effects," he explained. "The mining guilders pay that fee on tens of millions of acres across all of Dyan'ta. That would make a very significant reduction in the royal budget."

"Yes, but—"

"Wait, there's more. Those millions of duckets, even if they did go into upgrading equipment instead of lining the pockets of the head guilders, would eliminate the need for thousands of miners."

Martek squirmed, feigning interest in a flock of smats flying overhead. "Of course they will go towards equipment. Don't you think I asked about that already?"

"I'm sure you did. Did you get their promises written into the contracts and legislation?"

"Not yet, but they assure me it will all be there in the end."

"And you trust them? Are you still that naïve, brother?" Brach reigned in beside his brother, grabbed one arm and fixed him with a stern gaze. "What do you think will happen to all those miners who lose their jobs? They will join the ranks of so many others on government welfare, costing the royal treasury millions more every month. Even with government assistance, many will lose their homes, reducing our income even further without the income from those taxes. Can you see where this eventually leads? Do you want to reignite the terrorist movement out there after father fought so long to defeat them?"

Martek looked defeated as he faced his brother and slumped in his saddle. "I am trying, Brach, I really am trying to understand all of this. It's just so difficult to see everything the way you do."

"I know you are, Martek." Brach rubbed his temple with the knuckles of one hand, trying to drive out the frustration he felt building there. "You just need to remember that everyone is out for their own interests and you are in charge of protecting ours. You cannot afford to believe anything they tell you."

"But they're my friends. How can I —"

"No! They are NOT your friends!" Brach shouted, pounding his fist on his leg, startling his Tal. "The monarch has no friends. Those people only want to influence you so they will gain an advantage over their competitors, probably even over you and the rest of the government. They don't care about you, or anything else for that matter, except what will improve their own interests."

The two rode on in silence for a while. "I'll try harder, Brach. I won't let them fool me again," Martek said in a barely audible whisper.

"You must. You can't afford to do any less. I cannot watch over you all twenty six hours every day."

"I am so glad you are here to help me through all of this, brother. I don't know what I would do without you."

Brach nudged his Tal closer to Martek and reached out, taking his sibling's four-fingered hand in his. "You can always rely on me, brother," he said gently. "Why don't you head back home now. I have some pressing business to discuss with the Colonel that can't wait."

"Thank you, brother," said Martek, tears welling up in his eyes. He pulled on the reigns to head back the way they had come.

***

"I have tried, Colonel," Brach said as the two men slowly walked their mounts under the overhanging branches of a forested trail. "I have done everything I can to try to teach Martek how to be the monarch. He is simply not up to the task. If I had not been forcing him to bring me every piece of proposed legislation before he signed it we would be bankrupt and at the mercy of every guild on the planet as soon as the mourning period was over."

The Colonel stood at attention, talons clasped firmly behind his back. "There is no time to lose then. You must give approval to our plans to eliminate him before he does something you cannot prevent."

"I am afraid you are right, Colonel. I cannot allow Martek to be crowned monarch. How long will it take to set everything in motion once I give final approval?"

"The Darthon Cup Regatta is next week, Your Highness. It will be difficult to arrange in only ten days, but we can be ready by then."

"Alright. Just make certain nobody can possibly believe it is anything but a tragic accident."

"Of course, Highness. It will be as we discussed." The Colonel nodded and the two conspirators remounted increased their pace to a canter, and returned to the castle in time for the dinner hour.

***

The sky was a crisp and clear teal with a strong wind out of the west—perfect conditions for the premier regatta of the season. Martek's crew efficiently raced from one set of ropes to another, maintaining perfect tension on the sails and positioning themselves expertly for the next tack. It was in mid tack, as they cut through the eye of the wind and salt spray that the main halyard snapped. Martek gaped helplessly as the mainsail collapsed heavily around him. A sudden gust caught the loose fabric, tearing it from the boom as well. Now flying free in the wind, the sail wrapped itself around Martek and two other crew members, dragging them overboard. The water soaked fabric of the sail held the not yet coronated monarch under the waves for fifteen minutes. By the time rescue boats arrived, it was too late. Martek had drowned, unable to extricate himself from the tangle of sail and ropes.

Brach, now the new monarch-to-be, was grief stricken. He gave orders for his closest advisor, the Colonel, to lead an investigation into the tragic accident that took the life of his beloved brother. Once more, the nation was plunged into mourning at the passing of another leader. Once again, the state funeral was a grand event with all of the pomp and circumstance due such a young and promising monarch. And, after the appropriate six months of mourning, Brach assumed the throne. The day following the coronation, official statements from the palace announced not only the promotion of The Colonel to Volery General, but also the election of Lerit, youngest of the ruling house, to the bishopric of Elnon, the central authority of the clergy. Millions of faithful Brin viewed Lerit's consecration across the continent. The Grand Elder himself presided over the ceremony, accepting the newly ordained bishop's renunciation of all worldly claims, including those to the royal throne.

***

Before Brach even had an opportunity to settle comfortably on the throne, Dr. Malek, the aging curator of astronomy at the royal observatory, asked for an audience. The grandly curving and elevated bench of the science academy's governing board ascended high above the gallery. The dais normally accommodated a dozen members of the Science Academy. Only Dalvet, the president of the board, Clavarn, the chairman of the review committee and, due to the special invitation, Brach, His Highness the monarch, were in attendance. The thick maroon carpeting, padded chairs surrounding the room and heavy tapestries hanging on the walls of this oval-shaped chamber quieted the nearly empty room, giving it a tomb-like quality. Of course, the royal guards posted at every entrance also ensured the absence of prying ears and eyes. The glass-covered oculus provided only a dim light to the room. Holographic projections of the documents hung in the air before the only occupants today.

"These figures have been verified?" asked Dalvet. "There is no mistake?"

"None," Malek replied, sorting through the virtual images until he found the charts he was looking for. "As you can see in the supporting documents everything has been carefully examined by two outside sources, completely independent of each other. Our conclusions are accurate and reliable. Our sun is going supernova. I sincerely wish I could say otherwise."

A dreadful silence filled the room as everyone present absorbed this statement.

"I have spoken with both of the corroborating scientists, your Highness," said Clavarn, nervously clearing his throat. "There can be no doubt as to the correctness of the data, or the accuracy of the conclusions."

Brach cleared his throat and leaned forward as he folded his hands on the table in front of him. "So what you are saying is that our world is about to die, but you have no clear idea as to when?"

"Yes, Your Majesty," said Malek.

"And there is nothing anyone can do about it?"

"That is correct, Your Majesty."

Brach turned to the others at the bench beside him. "So what are your recommendations, gentlemen?"

After a brief silence, Dalvet responded. "After careful consideration of the possible consequences, Your Majesty, we believe it would be in everyone's best interest to reveal the truth of the matter to the world. News like this will inevitably leak out sooner or later. If we control the press releases we can manage the situation more effectively."

The monarch stared into his hands as he replied, "And just how trustworthy is your plan for building a fleet of spaceships to rescue the population of the planet? Sounds like feather fluff to me."

"Of course the technology does not exist at this time, Your Majesty," said Clavarn. "However, the knowledge that we most likely have a thousand years, give or take a few hundred, to develop the fleet will keep panic at bay. We Of course, lethal radiation levels will wipe out all life on the planet several hundred years before the actual eruption, but we can reassure everyone that they are completely safe here on Dyan'ta for many generations to come, and we are hard at work developing the plan to rescue those who are alive at some distant time in the future."

"But you said it may explode tomorrow. Why bother with all of this at all?"

The life of an average star spans roughly ten billion years. A few thousand years may seem like forever to us, but it is merely the blink of an eye to a star. In all probability we still have time to —"

Brach shoved the report away, scattering the loose papers on the floor. "I am not comfortable with that date," "It seems to me we lose all sense of urgency with something so far into the future. The people will need something a bit more concrete to wrap their brains around. What if we told them one hundred years instead?"

Dalvert and Clavarn glanced at each other for a moment and nodded their agreement. "That would be acceptable, Your Majesty," said Dalvert. "Still a couple of generations to come, but easier to grasp while still providing time to develop the technology. Yes, that should serve nicely. And it may even be accurate."

"Do you really believe we can find a way to get us all off Dyan'ta before the sun explodes?"

"I believe so, Your Majesty, but it will require a tremendous financial and political commitment from the government unprecedented in our history. Any wavering or political maneuvering would be a disastrous blow to public support."

"Good then. We are agreed." Brach rose and shook hands with the two scientists. His four-digit grip, well-practiced during his political career, was firm, but brief. His talons were heavy and sharp, always meticulously manicured. The translucent scales on the back of his hands and arms were slightly pearlescent in the dim light of the room. He looked directly at Malek. "Thank you, Dr. Malek. You handled this well so far. My office will call you soon to arrange the dates and times for you to make your public announcements. This is, after all, your discovery, but we must wait for the right moment. Once the people are mollified with the prosperity of the new work programs we are going to develop, only then will they be ready to handle the knowledge of what is to come. Even then there will be trouble, but not the total loss of control we would face otherwise. We might even arrange to give you the Prelim Award for your role in helping save our race from extinction."

Malek stood to leave. "Thank you, Your Majesty." He pushed his chair back under the table, gathered his papers, and walked up the sloping aisle toward the large double doors.

Once the doors shut behind Malek, Brach motioned for the two heads of the Science Academy to come closer. "Do you actually believe any of this will work?" he asked them in a hushed, conspiratorial voice. "I mean, is there honestly any hope of developing the technology to build spaceships large enough, and fast enough, to take so many Brin to another planet?"

Neither man responded for a minute, each hoping the other would speak. "In science, we never say anything is impossible, Your Majesty," said Dalvert nervously grasping his talons behind his back, his eyes shifting nervously to his colleague. "But in all honesty, I cannot see how it will be possible. Our current state of technology and the best minds in the field of rocket propulsion are far from any ability to accomplish something of this magnitude. With enough time and resources though, anything is possible."

"That then is our problem. How much time do we really have?"

"That is up to The Eternal, Your Majesty," said Clavarn. "We cannot say exactly when, although we do know with absolute certainty it will happen."

"Well then, my friends, let us hope future generations of Brin have the opportunity to solve this problem, and that they are more capable than we are." Brach walked around the bench, down the stairs and up the aisle. His guards snapped to attention as the giant doors opened and followed him back to the palace.

***

The monarch smiled as he inspected the newly dedicated mine. Crowds of miners cheered him as he passed by, demonstrating their appreciation of his efforts to increase employment throughout the realm. "What a difference from my father's constant battles with those insurgent uprisings centered here all those years ago. Prosperity finally accomplished what military might never could," said Brach as he waved to the gathered crowds. The immense hauling vehicles, processing and refining facilities, accommodations for the miners and their families, his gaze took in every detail, his ears rejoiced in the cheers of the workers as he passed by in the royal mag-lev limousine. "Only four years into the plan, and we are ready to start the controlled release of news about the supernova. Are the scientists and press prepared to handle this, General?"

"Yes, Your Majesty. I have seen to the briefings personally. Everyone is well aware of the consequences for any dissention or breaking ranks. There will be no trouble we are not ready to deal with."

"Very good. We cannot afford to overlook anything if this is going to succeed."

***

"Police departments throughout the continent tell us of sporadic looting and there are unconfirmed stories of minor rioting in some cities." Karm sat silently in his study watching the news reports on his monitors. "While some have resorted to violence in the aftermath of yesterday's news about our dying sun, churches everywhere show signs of unprecedented attendance during services." Scenes of violence interspersed with those of churches filled to capacity flashed on the screen as the reporter read his script. Interviews of individuals on the street ranged from those angrily accusing the government of vast conspiracies to others pleading for calm and a return to normalcy. Karm touched his talon to the remote, turning off the monitors.

"And so it begins." He poured himself a glass of orange colored Gorbett Ale and downed it in one swift shot. Karm grimaced as the too sweet draught flowed down his throat and wished the hour was late enough for a stronger bitter ale. It wasn't the first time he regretted instructing his staff to make sure he adhered to the social conventions, but his status required him to play this role so he would play the game. He held out his palm and called for it to activate. A brief perusal of the data reassured him everything was in place and on schedule. Setting his glass on the desk, Karm took in a deep breath, exhaled forcefully to release any lingering tensions, and reached for his communicator pad. "Time to get to work."

***

"I'm sorry, Lerit, but I cannot agree to your transfer out of the treasury." Corab, Elder of the church's treasury, peered over the top of his spectacles at the young bishop seated before him. "You are too valuable to me here. Your expertise has been invaluable in reorganizing our accounts."

Lerit kept his head bowed respectfully, his talons folded on the table. "If I may speak on my own behalf, Elder Corab. My education excelled in languages and I believe I can be of even greater value in the library translating ancient texts. It is as if The Eternal has led me to this goal my entire life. I feel his calling."

The Elder smiled and leaned forward as if to bestow some pearl of grandfatherly wisdom. "Patience Lerit. You are still young. There is plenty of time to learn the Eternal's plans for you. For now, you are to remain here with us."

"But Elder Corab, if I may…"

"My decision is final, Lerit." He hesitated, eyes searching the ceiling as he considered how to proceed. "I had not wished to discuss this with you until I had all of the facts, but there have been suspicious rumors regarding you and some apparent efforts to influence a number of the other bishops and clergy. Mind you these are unconfirmed, and, frankly, I consider them nothing more than jealousy over your rapid rise among us, but I must clear your name before your future can be discussed."

Lerit tensed, but quickly brought himself under control. "I am ashamed that my name has been brought under suspicion, Elder." Lerit bowed his head, covering his face with his hands. "I pray you will see there is nothing to these rumors. I am in your service. You have my blessings, Bishop Lerit. Go in the grace of The Eternal. I am sure my investigation will be brief and you may yet have your wish to work in the library."

"Thank you elder," Lerit said as he bowed and left the old cleric's chamber. Back in his own sparse room he slammed a fist into the stone wall. "No, Elder Corab, you will not get in my way. I will make you the sacrifice here. Your name will go down in shame once I am through with you.

CHAPTER SIX

"Mother! Where are you?" screamed Maripa. She strained to see through the mist. "I can't see you!"

"I'm here, darling," called her mother's voice, "I'm right here."

"Mother, I'm lost, help me!"

"I'm here, Maripa, sweetheart. I'm here."

Her mother's voice grew fainter as the mist thickened. Maripa could barely see her hand stretched out in front of her now. She ran after the fading voice into the mist.

Maripa bolted upright in her bed. Her heart raced and she gasped for breath in the darkness. "Mother! Don't leave me!"

"Ripa!" shouted Tessen as she leapt up from her bed across the room and turned on the lights. "What's wrong? Wake up!" She grabbed Maripa by the shoulders and shook her gently.

Maripa's eyes began to focus. "Tessen? What are you doing? What happened?"

What do you mean 'What happened?' You scared the mutes out of me, girl! You just started screaming. Something about your mother. That must have been one strix of a nightmare. I thought you were an orphan or something."

"It was nothing," said Maripa as she wiped her forehead with her nightgown sleeve. "Just a stupid dream. Go back to sleep."

"Oh no, not now. Something like that just doesn't come out of nowhere. Especially for someone like you. You aren't afraid of anything, honey. And you never talk about your family." Tessen pulled her feet up under her on the bed and turned Maripa to face her. "We've been friends and roommates here at the academy for two years now. I've been your sparring partner and your cadet unit second for over a year. We're graduating tomorrow. Talk to me." She reached under the mattress and removed a metallic flask. After pouring two small cups she handed one to Maripa. "Here, take a swig of this. It'll help."

"Thanks." Maripa took the glass and shot back the drink in one swift motion.

Maripa's shaking gradually subsided and her breathing became more regular. "There's nothing to tell. I used to have them all the time as a kid. It has been years though. Just turn off the light and go back to bed."

Tessen took Maripa's hands in hers and looked her straight in the eyes. "I said talk to me."

Maripa paused for a moment and then decided. "What the strix. You might as well know." She looked up at the ceiling shut her eyes as she spoke. "Did I ever tell you how my parents died?"

"Something about a levicoach wreck, I think."

"That's right. I was just an infant when it happened. They were both killed, but somehow I survived the accident. I don't remember them or the accident at all. I've been with my uncle ever since."

"Is he the rich uncle you go stay with during breaks?"

"Yeah, my father's brother. He was the only family I had left so he took me in and raised me the best he could. He wasn't really prepared to be a parent though. He was too busy with all of his financial dealings. He set me up with an army of nannies so he could leave town to take care of business."

Tessen flicked her lower lip with one talon in disgust. "What a quetzal!"

"Not really. I mean, I used to think so, but now I'm not so sure. I barely remember him when I lived with him as a child. He was always off to some part of the globe on business trips for weeks at a time. The nannies were great, and he always spent time with me when he got back, but he always had to leave again just as I was getting comfortable with him." Maripa leaned back against the wall and tucked her knees up under her chin. "Once I was old enough, he sent me off to boarding school. Straden Military Academy was the best so this is where I have been ever since."

"Like I said. A real quetzal. He didn't have time to waste on you so he just shipped you off while he got rich." Tessen spit into the trash can at the foot of the bed.

"Maybe," Maripa said, frowning as she stared at wall. "But he was so nice to me when I came home on breaks. He always seemed interested to hear about my school work and training. He often suggested courses that he thought I might be good at. It was Karm who got me interested in business administration as a career. He was even very supportive when I started showing some promise in combat skills."

"You are good at all of it, too. Not only are you at the top of your class, but you can whoop up on anyone twice your size. And your records on the shooting range may stand until the next century. Who would have thought such a tiny thing like you could be so bad ass?" Tessen refilled their cups and reached out, tipping her drink in salute.

Maripa smiled bit and shot a sideways glance at her roommate. "It is really fun sometimes. Darkon, his security chief, was always there for me. He's the one who taught me to play tuttle." She smiled briefly at the memories of Darkon and all of his small kindnesses toward her, even now. "And I love the look on Uncle Karm's face when I bring home a new trophy to put in my display case. He's always taken care of me so I do want him to be proud of me."

"Has he ever come to visit you here? I never see him at cadet reviews or when you receive an award. What's up with him?"

"He's just so busy all the time. It's like he's on some sort of mission. The corporation always comes first. He always made sure that I got the best of everything."

Tessen snorted and rolled her eyes at Maripa. "The best of everything except himself! That must have been a very lonely childhood for you. All by yourself up there at that castle of his with only the servants and nannies around. Did you ever have any friends to play with?"

"Oh, yes. There were always children around the place. The servants would bring their children to play with me most of the time. I had lots of friends."

"Friends? Sounds more like companions for hire." Tessen mimed spitting on the floor.

Maripa lowered her head. Her voice softened to a whisper. "I always thought they were friends, at least until I got older and heard one of them being scolded by her mother for playing too rough with me. I'll never forget the look of anger on the girl's face when she yelled back at her mother saying she never wanted to come here in the first place and ask why she couldn't stay home and play with her real friends."

"Ouch! That sucks."

"It was right after that when Karm sent me to boarding school. Misery loves company so I did make a few friends there. At least with some of the other girls who were in the same boat as me. Absentee parents and all." Maripa shook herself trying to regain her composure. "Don't get me wrong, Tessen, times weren't all rough like that. There were plenty of great times as well. Karm never forgot my birthdays, and most holidays he carved out at least one day to spend completely with me doing whatever I wanted. We had some great adventures together."

Tessen managed a dismal smile while shaking her head. "Still sounds like a rough way to grow up. I used to envy you when we first met, but now…I wouldn't trade my life for yours at all."

Maripa shook her head. "It made me strong. I learned how to cope with it all and take life as it came. I devoted myself to my studies and learned to defend myself. But that's all in the past now. Did you know he wants me to work for him after graduation? Some sort of personal assistant from the way he talks about it."

"Are you going to take the job?"

Maripa let her eyes and thoughts rise toward the high ceiling as she pondered a moment. "I think so. It sounds exciting. He travels all over Dyan'ta on business and I would accompany him. It might finally give us a chance to get to know each other. And I could start to repay him for everything he's done for me."

"I'm sure you would be great at it. Strix, you're great at everything you try. Is there anything you can't do?" Tessen laughed and punched Maripa on the arm.

Maripa threw off the covers and stomped over to the bathroom sink. She splashed cold water on her face, trying to regain her composure. "Kak! One little bad dream and I start blubbering like some freshman away from home for the first time. I've never told anyone that mutes before."

"Don't worry, your secret is safe with me, Ripa," Tessen said as she slid off the bed.

"It better be, Lieutenant. Or I'll have your ass in the ring in two shakes of a flea's tits."

"Now, that's the Cadet Captain Maripa that I know and love. Here, have one more for the road." Tessen poured another drink from her flask. They tapped glasses and downed their drinks in another single gulp. "Now go back to sleep. We don't want our class valedictorian to fall asleep in the middle of her commencement address."

***

Bishop Lerit, assistant to Zelph, Elder of church records, entered the Grand Elder's office carrying an ancient scroll and a packet of papers. "Holy Pater, I have momentous news." He genuflected before approaching the pale and wrinkled leader of the church.

Squinting through thick lenses, the Grand Elder smiled in recognition. "Ah, Lerit, my trusted friend, what has you so worked up today?"

"I believe I have found something in the holy scrolls of incredible import." He spread the papers in front of the Grand Elder. "Something that could possibly change the entire future of our beloved church."

"Lerit, my son," The elderly man, frail and bald, patted Lerit on the hand. "Always so full of zeal. Ever since you uncovered the unfortunate Corab's betrayals, your services to this office have been invaluable. I do miss the days of my youth. I, too, saw great import in nearly everything. Let me take a look at your latest discovery."

His head shaking slightly, the Elder adjusted his glasses and leaned forward, pulling the papers to within inches of his failing eyes. As he read the pages, the Elder's hands began to tremble violently. His smile faded into an open-mouthed gape, and he dropped the packet back onto the table, grasping unsteadily at his glasses, dropping them on top of the table as he rubbed his eyes. "Have you verified these translations? How could something of this magnitude have escaped us for so long?"

With a look of sincere shock on his face, Lerit rose and stepped quickly to a cabinet along one wall of the office and withdrew a vial of yellow, oily liquid. "Pater," he said with a nervous tremor in his voice, "let me get you your medicine. Then we can discuss my findings."

"Thank The Eternal for you, my boy," the trembling old cleric said as he swallowed the bitter tasting dosage. "If your translations are correct then we must waste no time in informing the High Council of Elders. There must be verification of this and plans drawn up to bring this new revelation to the people."

Lerit waited a moment as the Elder read through the information again, noticing the tremors subsiding. "Is the medicine helping, Grand Elder?"

The infirmed head of the church dropped the papers, some falling to the floor. His eyes lost their focus and his words slurred as he looked up toward Lerit. "Yes my son. I feel better now. Thank you. What were you about to say?"

Lerit relaxed visibly as he returned to his chair. "I was saying we should not rush into anything just yet, Grand Elder. What with the unrest everywhere now due to the news of our impending doom, is it really the wisest course to upset the people even further? Maybe you should let me handle this quietly."

Staring blankly ahead, face contorted in great effort the Grand Elder slumped, waved his hand and let his chin fall to his chest. "Yes, yes, Lerit. Of course, you are right, as always. So wise for your young years. I place this matter in your hands."

Chapter Seven

Banners proclaiming the grand elevation flew across every major thoroughfare. Although the public was not participating in the event itself, there were parades, concerts, public speeches, sporting events and pyrotechnic displays enough to satiate everyone. Booths serving foods of all descriptions, roast Quol in Tequel sauce, Petzel eggs cooked inside their brown and orange speckled sstrixs, sweet boiled pudding, along with cart after cart of fresh vegetables and homemade treats for sale. The mixing of aromas in the air watered mouths from one end of the grounds to the other. Colorful costumed characters on stilts portrayed the many heroes from the Book of The Eternal, tossing coins, food packages, and toys to the children. Lerit, the Bishop of Elnon, ranking bishop of the order, was celebrating the tenth anniversary of his installation. Having passed the initiation period, his installation as an Elder, and the traditional vote of the Elders to select their leader, as was proper whenever a new Elder joined the ranks, was a grand celebration. The election, a mere formality reaffirming the current Grand Elder's office, held little interest for anyone, but traditions must be upheld, no matter the added length to an already overly full schedule. Dignitaries, high officials, government and business leaders from all corners of Dyan'ta attended the gala.

The brothers stood together behind the screen of tall gold and silver curtains serving as a backdrop for the main stage. In the Grand Courtyard before the stage, a troop of elite dancers performed the ancient dance of the joining. A row of drums beat a steady rhythm, copied by the stamping feet of the dancers as pairs, male and female, circled each other. For several beats, the dancers hunched forward, shoulders rolled; arms extended and curled in front, heads bowed. They hooted and made guttural sounds in counterpoint to the drums. Suddenly, they jumped high, raised their faces to the sky, reaching high and wide, emitting a haunting, yet piercing shriek. At this moment, the audience joined in the cacophony, waving their arms in the air. This pattern repeated, with minor variations, for several minutes, until the pairs embraced each other, and began a new, more balletic portion of the dance.

"Well, brother," said Lerit to his oldest surviving sibling, "are you satisfied I have upheld my end of our agreement?"

Brach adjusted the ornate silver and gold robe of office on his brother's shoulders and slapped him on the back. "I never doubted you, Lerit. Our collaboration has succeeded beyond my wildest dreams. I am very proud of you. Are you ready to assume your new role?"

"I have been preparing for this day as long as I can remember. It will be a day nobody will ever forget." Lerit smiled at Brach, turned, and took his place behind the senior Elders as they formed the V-shaped procession, led by the Grand Elder, into the grand hall of the cathedral. Brach smiled and bowed his head in respect as the Grand Elder passed by, but the high priest only stared ahead, eyes glazed, his steps shaky, as if he was in a trance. Brach tilted his head, his crest ruffled and flushed; a sense of unease rose in his mind as he followed the procession and took his place on the royal throne to the left of the dais.

Three hours of speeches in the increasingly uncomfortable hall finally ended and the moment of election arrived. One by one, the elders rose from their wooden high backed chairs, vaguely reminiscent of a throne, took a small stone from a clay vessel, moved behind a translucent screen, made the mark of their selection, and deposited the stone into a gold, jewel encrusted vessel with the words: "This is my choice. May The Eternal grant him wisdom."

When all of the votes were cast, the Grand Elder rose, walked behind the screen and counted the votes. As he counted each stone, the Grand Elder dropped it into a grinder where it was pulverized. At the conclusion, he returned to the center of the dais, removed his sash of office and hung it on the central chair. Turning to the audience, his face and arms raised in beatific rapture, he announced the name of the elected.

"By the guiding hand of The Eternal and all the Prophets, all honor and praise go to Lerit, Elder of Elnon, on his elevation as our Grand Elder."

The gathered crowd sat silently for a moment before erupting into a clamor of shouting and disorder. Brach maintained his control by the slimmest of margins. Turning to the General, seated slightly behind and to his left, he commanded, "Find out what my idiot brother thinks he is doing! No novice has ever assumed the office of Grand Elder. I can't even recall the last time a new Grand Elder was elected before the death of his predecessor. Has he lost his mind?"

Amid the uproar and confusion, Lerit seated himself on the central chair while the former Grand Elder fitted the sash of office on his shoulders. Lerit rose and held his arms high, signaling for order and attention. "Today marks the opening of a new era. The Eternal himself foretold my election to this esteemed position to me. My prayers and studies have revealed to me many wrongdoings and shortcomings of this order. I have spent the past few years teaching these revelations to my fellow brothers and The Eternal has opened their eyes to the truth."

The crowd murmured, heads turning left and right to verify they were hearing everything correctly. Lerit paused for the commotion to subside before continuing.

"Henceforth, by the authority now invested in me by The Eternal and his clergy here in this realm, I am abolishing the old covenants. A new order, one known as

The Faith, will follow in its place. Our new mission, as revealed to me by The Eternal, will be to guide us away from the deceptions of our misplaced trust in government and science and into a life of purity and peace, led by His teachings. As a sign to all of our commitment to a new order, I take the name, and title of Pareth, Prior of Dregor, the noblest of our prophets. May his example be a shining light for us all."

He turned, arms wide, encompassing the gathered Elders behind him and continued, an orange glow appearing to enfold the holy men assembled on the stage, taking the form of a great flaming bird as it grew in size and intensity. The form then broke into smaller individual flames, one for each of the brothers on stage, appearing to absorb into their bodies. "In accordance with the dictates of The Eternal, as revealed to me, the Elders are no more. Instead, they are henceforth to be known as The Brothers of The Convocation, and I, as their chosen leader, will be known as the Prior. May the blessings of The Eternal be on you all." The assembly of Brothers approached their new leader, removed the ornate robe of the former office, and wrapped him instead with a plain, homespun cloth.

Pareth bowed, signaled to the brothers, turned and led the procession offstage. Brach rushed after them, his face no longer able to contain the rage in his mind. The assembled dignitaries, confused and dismayed, shoved their way to the exits. Hundreds of those gathered in the hushed crowd burst into awed proclamations of faith, arms raised up to the sky, tears streaming down their faces.

***

Brach slammed his fist into the wall of his carriage, upsetting the balance of the candlesticks mounted there, which toppled to the floor in response. "He refuses to see me!" He roared. "Me! His monarch! Not to mention his only surviving brother!" Grabbing the nearest object at hand, a crystal goblet awarded him by the merchants in honor of his newest tax relief measures, he hurled it across the carriage, shattering it into a thousand pieces against the wall next to the General's head.

The General sat, impassive as ever, waiting for Brach's temper to run its course. The clatter of the Tal's hooves, and the rumble of the carriage wheels on the cobblestones as they sped through the city drowned the monarch's continuing rants from outside ears. In due time, he poured his sovereign another drink, this time in a pewter goblet, and placed it in the holder next to him. "Your Majesty," he began cautiously, "While it is disturbing, and worth serious investigation, your brother's elevation to leadership of this new religion of his does not appear to be any immediate threat to your position. He did, after all, publicly renounce any claims to the throne."

"You know my brother," Brach said, downing the goblet in one swift gulp, falling heavily against the back of his padded seat. "He is intelligent and devious. How else do you explain his being able to hide this plot of his from me, and everyone else?" Brach ripped off his formal coat, tossing it aside and raked the wall again, his talons leaving deep gouges in the ornate woodwork as he continued to shout. "I don't fear his taking over the throne, but he is certainly in a position to wield sufficient power to influence, if not control a great many events."

"Unfortunately, there is very little you can do about it now, except to consolidate your base and limit the damage the new Prior can do."

"I had one brother killed, why not another? He surely has made some powerful enemies we could lay the blame on."

Shaking his head, the General leaned forward, placing himself directly in front of Brach, forcing him to listen. "That would be most unwise, Your Majesty. There are far more subtle ways of controlling the situation. The risks are far too great. And you certainly do not want to turn him into a martyr for their new cause."

Brach glared at his advisor, his body shaking in anger. "I don't just want him killed, I want him flayed alive and then his head stuck on a pike on the castle parapets."

The General remained impervious to Brach's rage.

"Perhaps you are right," said Brach, his shoulders slumping as he exhaled loudly. "We will need to set up an immediate surveillance team, infiltrate this new Brothers of The Convocation, and keep a close eye on my dear brother from now on. I don't want any more surprises. And find out how he pulled off that theatrical stunt with the lights!"

"I will see it done immediately, Your Majesty."

The royal carriage pulled into the palace courtyard, stopping in front of the massive doorway. Brach stormed out of the carriage before any of the footmen had a chance to assist him. Flailing his arms and shouting to nobody in particular, mostly in a variations of creative and most un-royal curses, Brach bulled his way to his private chambers.

***

A week later, the General walked into the monarch's office and waited to be recognized.

"Did you get what I wanted, General?" asked the monarch, still focused on the papers he was examining.

"Your suspicions were correct, Your Majesty. Almost all of the Elders, except the former Grand Elder, the doddering old fool, was connected to some sort of impropriety, some even criminal in nature, but your brother intervened on their behalf and their names were cleared. While there is no hard evidence, he appears to be directly connected to their elevation to the hierarchy. Your brother appears to have been very busy these past ten years."

Brach flipped through the papers, stopping occasionally to focus on some point of interest. "How are your efforts to infiltrate The Brotherhood proceeding?

"Not as well as expected, Your Majesty. They are extremely cautious and suspicious of anyone outside their organization. It will take some time to work our associates into their confidence."

"Very well. Keep at it. I need to know what Lerit… excuse me, Prior Pareth, is up to.

Chapter 8

"You worry too much, Maripa," Karm said. "This is just a dinner supporting my friend Noldar for a seat in Parliament."

Karm stood in front of the world map in his office, contemplating the dozens of various colored pins on every continent. Each color represented a different category of holding under his control. Reds indicated pharmaceutical companies; aerospace engineering firms were green. Yellow showed manufacturing plants. Blue pins for computer facilities. Other colors showed the locations of the many companies, universities, banks and other organizations he maintained interest in as either a board member or major stockholder. He pulled out one additional pin. A gold one. This he placed in the middle of the Latonian Desert.

Maripa tapped her foot rapidly, fists clenching at her side. "Yes, sir, but you have been attending a lot of these functions lately. You are becoming a celebrity. Are you sure all of the publicity is wise?" She sat at her small desk and began sorting through several files accumulating there.

"Nothing to concern yourself with. Just take care of these files and have my levicoach ready in an hour." Karm looked at Maripa, appraising her from head-to-toe. "Pick out something suitable to wear yourself. I think it is time you started accompanying me at these functions. You never know when I might need your special talents."

"As you wish, sir," said Maripa. She stood, organized the folders into neat stacks, with perhaps a bit too much force, and walked toward the door. "It is part of my job though to let you know when I believe there is a security risk. I haven't spent all these years training just to let you take unnecessary risks."

He sighed and turned to look at her. "I appreciate that, Maripa, but this is just a fundraiser. How much of a security risk can it be?"

"Not just this dinner, sir. It's all of the events you have been attending in the past few months. The more recognized you become, the bigger the target you make."

"Nothing I can't handle. I've been doing this for a long time, now. I know what I'm doing. Now, go get ready and meet me in an hour." He placed his hand on her shoulder. "Trust me."

"Yes, sir," she said, shutting the door behind her as she left.

The fundraiser was a lavish §10,000 a plate affair; all of the leading party representatives, corporate heads and celebrities received invitations. The men wore their dark tuxedos while the women dazzled the onlookers with their shimmering gowns in an incredible variety of colors. Internationally renowned chefs who flew in the week before prepared the food and the symphony orchestra hired for the evening performed from their alcove. Security personnel kept the news media, paparazzi, and protesters at a distance, but the flashes popped everywhere as each vehicle arrived.

Karm stepped out of his levicoach and extended a hand to Maripa. He was dressed in his finest tuxedo. She wore an iridescent jade gown she had specially made for ease of movement. She refused to wear heels despite Karm's protests.

"Heels will only get in the way if I have to act quickly," she told him. He decided not to press the matter any further.

He presented his arm to Maripa and they paraded down the walkway.

"Over here!"

"Look this way!"

"Who is your companion, Karm?"

Karm waved at the photographers and reporters as they called to him, but continued to walk toward the door. Maripa scanned the crowd for potential threats. Servants took their cloaks as they entered the foyer. Karm grabbed a drink from one of the trays circulating the room and walked toward a small group he recognized. Maripa followed at a respectful distance. She observed the crowd warily as they entered the gathering.

"Good evening, Prime Minister," Karm said as he approached the leading member of Parliament and shook his hand. "Looks like the money is pouring in for Noldar. What do you think of his chances?"

"With you on his side, how can he fail?" said the official, continuing to grasp Karm's hand. "Thanks to you we can pay for twice the campaign ads as any of his opponents. The polls show Noldar in a comfortable lead."

"Wonderful. And how is the little matter of the Anti-Cloning legislation coming? I hope there have been no difficulties."

"None at all. We've managed to tie up the bill in committee so deep it has no chance of surfacing for a vote." The Prime Minister leaned in closer to Karm and surveyed the room. "We have managed to counter every tactic mounted by the clergy and their people, so far. However, they are gaining in strength in some districts, particularly Elnon. We may not be able to contain them much longer."

"We need to keep clone research alive, Dolmak. I don't need to remind you of the consequences of failure here."

"Yes, we are in agreement there, Karm, but the monarch is not as solid as he was a couple of years ago. He may be starting to sympathize with the church and their ideology. I think he believes they have grown too powerful already, or perhaps he simply feels more secure with his own brother as the bishop. He may be courting them for support."

"That is concerning. Keep me informed if anything develops there." Karm raised his glass of champagne and tilted it toward the Prime Minister before taking a sip.

"Of course. Now, if you will excuse me, I have other matters to attend to." The Prime Minister walked off and found another group of dignitaries to engage.

There were many other officials with whom Karm met and discussed a wide assortment of issues. The dignitaries frequently pressed him into posing with them for photos by the official event photographers. Maripa, somehow, always managed to be at least partially hidden in each photo.

The tower clock struck midnight as Karm led Maripa out to their waiting levicoach. Karm scratched absentmindedly at his palm. *What is up with this thing? I thought it would give me some trouble warnings during the party, not afterwards.* While they waited for traffic to pass at the end of the private driveway, a series of blinding flashes erupted from outside to their left. Karm's palm suddenly glowed with a scarlet red, feeding his mind with immediate danger alerts.

"Maripa!" Karm shouted as he raised his hand to shield his eyes from the flashes. Before he could turn, he heard the coach door open. Maripa sprang into action.

The photographer retreated a few steps before Maripa seized his camera. "No, stay back! You can't do that!"

Maripa twisted the camera and easily relieved the man of his equipment. She dropped the camera on the ground, picked up a large rock, and smashed it.

"No pictures," she told the man. Reaching into her pocket, she pulled out §300 and tossed it on the ground. "For the damages." She turned, got back in the mag-lev, and closed the door. The driver accelerated onto the road, leaving the photographer behind.

"Did you get all that?" the paparazzo called to the bushes behind him.

A second man stood up from his concealment. "Yeah, got it. Who was that?"

"That is what we are getting paid to find out. Let's go." The two men walked to the levicoach they had hidden on a side road.

Karm returned to his office. "Kirta, please get me the Chancellor at the university now. No video this time." He grabbed a goblet and poured himself a drink, downing it in one quick shot. He reached into the top left desk drawer and pulled out a small silver box. From inside he removed a large violet capsule and swallowed it. He poured another drink and sat at his desk. *No more distractions. From here on, I stick to the plan. Keep focused on the priorities. Play time is over.*

"The Chancellor is on line two," said Kirta over the intercom.

Karm hit the second button and turned on the speaker phone. "Good morning, Chancellor."

"Karm, delighted to hear from you. I wasn't expecting your call until later though; what can I do for you?"

"I have been looking over the list of candidates for that associate Professor of genetics position you are trying to fill. I think I have a candidate for you."

"Wonderful, who did you have in mind?"

"A brilliant young man with some very novel ideas. He just got his appointment, recently married, very eager to get started."

"Sounds like someone we would be interested in. What is his name?"

"Dr. Jontar Rocker."

The Chancellor hesitated before speaking. "Oh, that one. We eliminated him from consideration. The background check revealed some information leading us to believe he did not fit in with our philosophy."

"Nonsense, Chancellor. I think he would be a perfect addition to the faculty."

"There are many other fine candidates, Karm. Surely we can find someone better suited to our needs."

"You don't understand, Chancellor. Jontar Rocker is my choice for the position. You will hire Dr. Rocker and convince the other board members of the wisdom in this decision. Or do I need to rethink my support for the new engineering building?"

There was a longer hesitation this time. "No, sir, that will not be necessary. I am sure Dr. Rocker will work out just fine."

"Thank you, Chancellor. I am glad you agree. We'll talk again soon."

Karm disconnected the line and sat back in his chair. He held out his hand. *Activate: Rocker.* His palm glowed and the image of Jontar Rocker, along with a detailed biography appeared, hovering above his hand. He grabbed his goblet and downed the drink in one shot as he read the dossier. *Dr. Rocker, this should be a very interesting meeting.*

Part Two

CHAPTER NINE

Campus police charged around the corner wearing full protective gear and with shock rods raised, ready for a confrontation. Rocker raced through the growing crowd toward the protection of the police. "Holy mutes!" he cried as he ducked, a rock grazing his head. Now protecting his skull with his tattered case as he dodged more missiles, he shoved through the angry crowd, their placards waving in the air: *The Eternal Hates Clones! You Can't Clone A Soul! Clones Are Brin Too! We Are All Brin!* Both factions exploded violently around him, their shouts seething with irrational hatred. A glass bottle exploded on the sidewalk after narrowly missing his head. *Mutes! That was too close. I've gotta get the* strix *out of here, and fast.* As he closed in on the barricades, an officer the size of a small house raised his shock rod and took aim at Rocker's noggin. Rocker held up his faculty ID badge with his talons and waved it as he ran closer. "I'm Professor Rocker, Head of Genetics!" he shouted.

The constable hesitated, and then lowered his weapon, but only slightly. Rocker noted that he still held it at the ready. "Good thing you ran into me instead of one of the rookies out here, Professor." Rocker slowed to catch his breath, bent over, leaning heavily on his knees. The officer frowned, holding the electrically charged baton tightly in his opposable talons. "You might have gotten your head bashed in if I hadn't recognized that faculty badge. Now get going before all strix breaks loose. This is going to get bad." The officer pointed the weapon in the direction of the nearest building behind him and shoved Rocker out of his way.

Rocker made it to the safety of his building just as the mob smashed through the barricades, trampling the officers in their path just before they attacked each other with signs and fists. The police let loose with repel-gas canisters and bystanders scrambled for safety. The scene before Rocker as he stared out at the chaos from behind the protective glass of the vestibule blurred slightly as his inner eyelids closed instinctively against the noxious fumes drifting toward the building.

"You okay, Jontar?" Rocker looked up to see one of the secretaries from the pool approaching.

"Yeah, I got caught in the middle of that mess out there. Nothing too serious."

"It's disgraceful," she replied. "Even when faced with our planet's destruction, we still fight amongst ourselves."

His head was starting to ache where the rock had hit him. He felt among his feathers and discovered a large bump beginning to form, but no blood. He winced as he pressed against the lump. "I would have thought everyone would be more afraid of the end of the world than clones. Honestly, we are only barely able to grow a few replacement organs, we're nowhere near being capable of accomplishing what they are accusing us of. I guess extinction is just too big to deal with right now." Rocker watched the chaotic scene a bit longer, then squared his shoulders and headed toward his classroom, waving goodbye to the woman as she turned to continue her duties.

Rocker nodded to the half-empty circular lecture hall and dropped his bag on the lectern. "Alright then, any questions from yesterday's lesson?"

"Professor?" Called out a student as she stood to address the class. She was tall, dressed in the colorful fashions of the well-to-do. Her impeccably preened red and yellow head feathers perfectly matched her painted talons. "I just don't get all this stuff about clones. I mean, they're just a bunch of animals the Progressives want to turn into a class of slaves, right? At least that is what my boyfriend says." She ran her talons through her crest, eyes rolling upward, as if searching her mind for further details before continuing. "Even some of the readings you have assigned us, and many of the recent news broadcasts seem to support this belief, but it doesn't feel right to me."

"And let the games begin," muttered Rocker softly as hands flew up. "Go ahead, Lokem," he said, pointing to a student in the third row.

"Your position appears to be grounded in research and verifiable data," stated the young man, "but I am not sure that your conclusions are a direct result of that data. Can you clarify your position?"

The girl squirmed at the lectern and scrunched her face as she searched through her papers. "I am just saying, if we ever do discover how to make clones, it seems like they will be our slaves and not free individuals."

"Your statements are not supported by scientific data," called out another student from the back of the room. "What you are saying is more personal opinion than evidence."

So far, so good, thought Rocker. The students were keeping the discussion to the ground rules, and after a few more questions, he almost started to relax. Then the inevitable happened.

"But doesn't The Faith tell us that a cloned individual, because it is manufactured by us and not created by The Eternal and therefore is without a soul, cannot be a true Brin?" the girl continued. Her comment opened the floodgates and the rules of discussion were as forgotten as yesterday's lecture. Students shouted out accusations and recriminations at will.

"You cannot be serious!" Hands flailing and voices raised, Rocker's students argued their perspective on the basic nature of clones. "How can you possibly believe clones are not true Brin?"

"Have you ever met one? Of course not, they don't exist, at least not yet," argued some students.

"So we just sit back and wait for these atrocities to exist? Not me." a second orated.

"Well, who appointed you the final judge of who is True Brin and who is not?" called out another student. "The Eternal loves all Brin, cloned or not."

Professor Rocker decided enough was enough and raked his talons across the chalk board to get their attention. Everyone suddenly cringed and covered their auricular as the spine wrenching screech filled the room. He then turned to the board and wrote in huge bold letters:

FOLLOW THE EVIDENCE!

FACTS NOT FEELINGS!

"Does everyone remember our discussion regarding the most basic rules of science?" he asked the class. "If you cannot maintain this sort of mental discipline, then may I suggest you change your major to Comparative Religions, or Philosophy?" Rocker replaced the chalk in its tray and turned to face the class. "This subject is not for everyone. I, too, struggle to keep my own personal beliefs out of my research. However, it is precisely this sort of discipline science requires. Especially now that our world is threatened and we search for ways to save ourselves." Rocker lowered his eyes and took a deep breath. "If we're lucky."

A student in the first row raised his hand. "Well, yes sir, what you say is true, but can you give us your perspective on this matter?" Rocker looked up and saw his top student, who also happened to be the son of the university's Chancellor, asked the question. The same Chancellor who was looking for any excuse to fire Rocker.

A few months ago, Rocker openly ridiculed his boss for introducing a proposal to include "Life, as designed by the Eternal" to the science curriculum. Rocker forced a smile and said, "Now, what good would it do you if I were to tell you my personal beliefs? I wouldn't be very good at this job if I influenced my students with my own personal biases, whatever they may be." Rocker winked at the class. His crest feathers ruffled and flashed just a bit of red.

"Feather Fluff!" the young man called out. He stood and waved his arms to emphasize his frustration. "That's a cop-out! Why don't you tell us what you think?"

Students turned, mouths open and eyes wide, first at the student, then at the Professor, holding their breath.

Rocker held himself in check and said, "Remember, a genetics classroom is for science, and is not the place for politics or philosophy. If you must debate philosophical matters then stick to the realities of technological advancement." Rocker studied the room for a moment before continuing. "What is the real fear of scientists with any new discovery or advancement?"

A shout from the back of the room answered. "Being ignored or dismissed as lunacy by our peers."

"No. While that does happen I am referring to something much more sinister." The lecture hall became silent except for the nervous shuffling of papers. Everyone tried to become invisible out of fear they would be called on to respond. "What I am talking about is the appropriation and misuse of our theories by the government or the military for their own destructive purposes. Think back through our history. How many times has the government taken scientific theories, originally intended for the benefit and advancement of society, then distorted and weaponized them?"

"Mag-lev technology," came a quiet voice from the audience. "It was first developed to improve transportation by making it safer for everyone. The military found a way to make their plasma weapons out of it."

"Precisely! Instead of worrying about whether clones have souls or not, imagine what the military could do if they chose to take over cloning technology to design the perfect soldier. Stick to the science, people. There are enough nightmares out there without inventing new ones to lose sleep over." Your first research paper is due in two days. I have extended my office hours today and tomorrow for any of you who need extra help. Class dismissed."

Dr. Rocker gathered his valise and mug and headed out the door. He turned left at the next hallway instead of heading to his office to stop off in the lab first He noticed the yellow "Experiment In Progress" light flashing above the doorway as he entered the room.

The lab, brightly lit by the solar panels in the ceiling, illuminated several rows of long tables filled the room. Shelves of ceramic containers and equipment lined the almost imperceptibly concave walls. Experiments conducted by the graduate students were in various stages of progress on each of the tables. *Now, this is where I belong.* Rocker smiled as he inhaled the scent of chemical reactions permeating the lab.

"Good morning, Professor," said Gardet, one of his lab assistants this semester. "Crebot asked me to remind you to talk to him when you arrived."

"Good morning, Gardet. That's why I'm here. How's the new technique working out?"

"Much better than what I was doing before. Thanks for the articles. They really helped." She beamed at him, pointed toward the intricate set of glassware gently percolating on the table, and handed him her notebook. "You can see the new data is very promising. Of course, the results are only preliminary, but I am hopeful."

Rocker perused the data tables and scribbled notes. "Yes…yes, I agree. Much more encouraging than before.

Your alterations to the design show a great deal of promise. You made sure to account for the new density variants?"

"Of course, Professor. You can see it right here." She turned a few pages of her notes and pointed to a set of calculations. "I should be ready for live tests on the eukaryotic cells in a few days, if everything turns out well."

Dr. Rocker leaned over, examining the set-up. He nodded his approval and patted her on the back. "Yes, looks much better. I have to run now, but I'll check in with you later. Keep up the good work, Gardet."

"Thank you, professor." Her voice was soft as it quavered. She wiped a hand over her eyes.

"Is anything wrong, Gardet?" asked Rocker, noticing the redness in her eyes and the slight trembling of her hands.

"It's nothing, professor, really. I'm just tired and overreacting to all the news about the supernova lately and all the terrible things happing." She hesitated, wiping her eyes again and grabbed for a tissue to blow her nose. "Don't mind me, I'm fine. That mob outside today just sort of got to me is all."

Rocker placed a hand gently on her shoulder and sat on the stool next to her. "Not all the news is bad, Gardet. Most individuals are taking it all in stride and just trying to get on with their lives. Many are even going out of their way to be better, kinder. The reporters just seem to get better ratings when they sensationalize the horrible things."

"I know, professor, I know. And I'm fine…really. It all just sort of ganged up on me for some reason. I know we will find a way to survive, after all, a hundred years is a long time to figure it all out."

"Those idiots out there haven't shaken your faith in our research have they?"

"Feathers no!" She replied, sitting up straighter and turning to face him. "Those crazies haven't got a clue about what they are saying so I usually don't pay them any mind at all. I don't know what got into me today. Just one of those things I guess. Thanks for talking to me about it though. It helped, but I better get back to work now."

Rocker stood up to leave, patting her on the shoulder as she picked up another tissue and blew out her sinuses again. "Good girl."

He turned and headed to the back of the room where Crebot, his most senior graduate assistant maintained his domain. The young man was huddled over his notebooks, writing furiously as he muttered to himself.

"Good morning, Crebot. How's your cervical vertebra cloning process going?"

Crebot startled and slammed shut his notebook. He jumped to his feet and spun to face the Professor. "I have some new ideas on that, Professor. I think I have a better approach."

Dr. Rocker shook his head. "Alright, slow down, let's not jump to conclusions. Show me what you have."

Crebot's eyes gleamed as he spoke. "As you know, one of the most common orthopedic injuries is to the cervical vertebrae. Sixteen small bones supporting our skulls is just not a practical arrangement."

Dr. Rocker nodded. "That's why I have you working on cloning replacement vertebrae."

"But why simply replace such an inefficient system? Why not improve it? This is what I am proposing." He opened his notebook to the calculations and diagrams of his latest theory.

Rocker twisted his mouth to one side and shook his head as he examined the notebook. "This looks like you want to reduce the number of vertebrae from sixteen to seven,"

Not noticing the negative reaction, Crebot continued his excited elucidation. "Exactly! Mammals have a much more efficient vertebral column. The cervical bones are thicker and less vulnerable. Instead of simply repairing the problem, why not fix it permanently? We have the ability to change our species. Why shouldn't we strive to improve ourselves?"

Dr. Rocker flipped through the pages of formulae and illustrations. His frown deepened as he read the young man's writings. "I admire your enthusiasm, Crebot," he said as he closed the manual, "but I have to tell you that, while this is an excellent exercise in the theoretical possibilities of genetics, I cannot allow you to proceed in this area. Stick to the original problem of cloning replacement vertebrae. We are not The Eternal. It's not our place to redesign our anatomy. We have no idea what the repercussions might be, or how such things might be misused."

Crebot's face and crest reddened and he fought to control his voice as he responded to the criticism. "Engineers improve their designs all the time. The world rewards them for developing new concepts that improve the efficiency and performance of our technology. We, on the other hand, are suppressed and vilified for any attempt to improve ourselves."

Dr. Rocker maintained his composure and tried to assume a more reassuring tone as he replied. "We've been over this before, Crebot. There are people out there suffering from spinal cord injuries. Your work here can provide them with real hope for a cure, if you don't allow yourself to get sidetracked. Do you want them to continue their struggles and live on in pain while you pursue some grand ideal of your own? They need relief now. Focus on the immediate concern before you go off on some flight of fancy. And, as we have already discussed, you know that society is just not ready for such extreme applications of our theories. Are you ready to accept the responsibility if some secret government program appropriates your work to create an invincible army of artificially created soldiers? You've got to learn more restraint. Your passions do you credit, but you let yourself get carried away by them too often. Wasn't it just last month that you wanted to reroute the arterial pathways instead of simply cloning the replacement blood vessels? And last year you proposed a strategy for developing retractable talons."

Crebot refused to back down. "Science is the pursuit of truth. We should not be constrained by the small minds of outsiders who cannot comprehend what we are doing."

Rocker shook his head again. "Science has nothing to do with truth, Crebot. It is simply the discovery and analysis of facts and evidence. Truth is an abstract concept. We deal in the concrete."

"What good is the evidence if it doesn't lead us to the truth, Professor?"

"Stick to the process. Let others worry about truth. I have to get back to my office now, but think about what we've discussed. Stop by my office later if you need to talk further. You have the makings of a great geneticist. Just learn to control your passions."

"Yes, sir," Crebot replied. He started to say something else, but stopped and returned to his notebooks.

Dr. Rocker stood watching for a moment, then left the lab, and walked toward his office. *That boy is brilliant, but he's becoming too concerned over truth.*

Dr. Rocker strode through the hallways of the building lost in concern over Crebot until he rounded the corner that held his office. The usual gaggle of students was already lining up outside his door with questions, concerns and a few brilliant insights that every geneticist in history had apparently missed.

"Give me ten minutes to get myself organized before you send in the first one," Rocker told his secretary. He went into his office and shut the door behind him.

Rocker sloughed into his uncomfortable chair behind his desk, deposited the notes in a random pile, took a long drink from his mug, and buried his head in his hands. Looking up between his talons, his eyes wandered among the framed certificates hanging on the wall and his most recent trophy from the Individual Rings Championship last semester, and settled on a photo of a younger self in his new Special Forces uniform surrounded by some friends from his unit. He held up the mug and took another drink in salute to the long lost comrades. He unconsciously felt for the gold ring hanging on its silver chain under his shirt and lingered there for only a moment.

Running his talons through his crest feathers and giving his head a shake, he got his mind back onto the matters at hand and he readied himself for the inevitable onslaught of students.

"Okay, Marique," he buzzed over the intercom on his desk, "you can let them in now."

"Yes, sir," came the slightly fuzzy, electronic reply.

All the usual complaints filled the next two hours, requests for deadline extensions and cries for help with understanding the latest set of lecture notes. Thankfully, the last of the supplicants concluded the afternoon's session with plenty of time left for a quick set of Rings before heading home. Rocker gathered his bags and turned out the lights as he left.

"Oh, Professor," called his secretary as he reached her desk. "This just came for you." She handed him a note. The official seal of the Chancellor was stamped on the front.

Rocker opened the note and read its contents:

"Your presence is required in my office no later than

eight o'clock tomorrow morning. Urgent matters concerning your most recent lecture will need to be discussed."

He refolded the note and placed it in his pocket. *Now what in Dyan'ta does that molting old buzzard want now? Hasn't anyone preened his tail enough today?*

"Okay, tell him I'll be there first thing in the morning." Rocker knew this could not be good. The Chancellor never wanted to talk to anybody who was not donating large sums of cash, or presenting him with some honorific. The mere mention of the Chancellor aroused vivid and unpleasant memories of the old man. Rocker shuddered as he recalled the summons he received only a month before. "Politicians should never be in charge of education," he muttered to himself.

Shaking his head to ward off the memories, Rocker rejoined the present. *Guess I better get going. No sense prolonging the inevitable.* Rocker grabbed his mug and downed the last of the tea. His gaze returned to the old photo. *I've survived worse than this. If Alpha Unit didn't kill me this certainly won't.* Rocker started to walk out of the office, but stopped and called back to his secretary. "Marique, after you contact the Chancellor could you please call Professor Barl and let him know I'm on my way to our Rings match. I'll just be a couple of minutes late. I want to stop by the cafeteria on my way."

"Will do, sir," he heard her reply just as the door closed behind him.

Chapter Ten

The room smelled of disinfectant, sterile and cold. The machines quietly beeped and displayed her vital signs in numbers and graphs that were meaningless to the uninitiated. Jontar Rocker sat silently holding his wife's hand as she lay comatose and dying in the hospital bed. Her body pale and gaunt from the ravages of bronchocilliary diskinesia, a rare genetic disorder. The late onset of her symptoms made the disease particularly virulent. A nurse, wearing the powder blue uniform of the night shift quietly entered the room and checked the monitors, recording a few notes on her pad. Her crest was long and flowing with a streak of green amid the yellow feathers.

"We don't normally see this sort of thing in adults. Children can usually survive, even with the disabilities. Tragic, but at least they live." She took a damp cloth from the basin and wiped her patient's forehead and arms to relieve some of the fever.

"No adult has ever survived this disease though," said Rocker. "At least nobody else will have to go through this." He lowered his head as tears welled up in his eyes.

"May I get you anything, Professor?" She asked, laying a gentle hand on his shoulder.

"I'm okay thank you," he replied hoarsely.

"Alright, then. You be sure to ring if you need anything." The young woman patted his shoulder and lingered at the door only a moment, holding back her own tears.

Professor Rocker wiped the tears falling down his cheeks with a single talon of his left hand. "I am so sorry, Betha. I should have worked harder. If only I had been smarter. It's just too late now. I should have seen the answer sooner. Our cure would only increase your suffering now. I am so sorry." His shoulders shook with the deep fits of sobbing overtaking him again.

Struggling to regain his composure, Dr. Rocker recalled all of his fondest memories of the years he and Betha had spent together before her illness stole her away. "Remember the weekend up at the cabin we rented for our second anniversary? How hard we tried to make a baby then? You were so disappointed when you didn't get pregnant." He entwined his four talons with hers and squeezed tightly. "We did keep trying though. It just wasn't in the stars for us I guess. You were so beautiful. Why didn't I try harder? If only the kaking university had parted with some more of their precious grant money to allow me some better equipment and more assistants."

As Rocker continued to speak and reminisce better times with his unconscious wife her breathing became shallow and rasping. The monitors sent a warning signal to the nurse's station down the hallway, summoning the head nurse within seconds.

"Are you sure you won't change your mind and allow us to take any further measures, Professor?" she asked after a brief check of the displays.

"I'm sure. We discussed this and she was adamant about not sustaining her life artificially when there was no longer any hope. Is this it?" Tears streamed down his face as the realization hit him.

The nurse struggled to maintain her own emotions as she turned to stand by her patient's husband, gently laying a hand on his arm. "I'm afraid so, Professor. It's only a matter of moments now. She is a strong woman though."

Rocker leaned in close and kissed his wife, then spoke quietly to her. "It's okay to go now, my love. You need to let go. I will always love and miss you, but your time here is over now. Go…be at peace." He kissed her again and sat back in his chair, still holding her hand.

Another minute passed and Betha's face seemed to relax. Her chest rose and fell one final time, and then she was gone.

Dr. Rocker awoke screaming. The nightmare had returned. He sat up, heart pounding and sweat soaking his sheets. "Holy strix!" He gasped, reaching for the light switch. "Been a long time since I had that one. What time is it?" Glancing toward the clock he saw the numbers read four twenty seven in the morning. His heart and breathing slowly returned to normal as he sat. "Feathers! Thought I was finally getting over her death. Guess I still have a few ghosts to deal with." He rubbed his eyes and stood, walking to the bathroom to splash some water on his face. "No sense trying to go back to sleep now. Might as well get up and face the day. Maybe I can get in a little practice before seeing the old bird this morning."

***

"Good morning, Professor," the Chancellor's secretary greeted Rocker as he entered the office. Gert was a fixture in the Chancellor's office. She was one of those indispensable personnel who each of the previous three Chancellors depended on to keep the office running seamlessly. Her crest was starting to grey now, but her eyes were bright and she had the reputation of knowing where all the bodies were buried.

"Strixo, Gert. Do I need to ask what His Lordship's mood is today?"

She gave him a sly smile and her eyes sparkled with mischief. "I would have thought he made that clear already. You did bring your spare ass with you, didn't you?"

"My spare ass?" Rocker cocked his head and hesitated as he began to sit.

"Yeah, you know, to replace the one he is going to chew off." Her eyes twinkled as she looked at Rocker.

"So just a normal inquisition then, okay," replied Rocker as he relaxed and continued to sit in the wobbly chair reserved for supplicants to the office.

"How do you put up with His Eminence? You could work for any department you wanted to with a fraction of the hassles you get here."

Gert tilted her head and smiled, "Now, Professor, you know these Chancellors couldn't tie their own shoes without me to help them. I am the sole force keeping this place functioning."

Just then a light flashed on the secretary's desk and she ushered him into the Chancellor's private office.

The office Rocker entered was plush, in the manner of most high officials. Large leather chairs populated several locations about the room. An ornate and highly polished wooden desk with an even grander throne of a chair behind it left no doubt as to who was in charge. Photos lined the wall of the Chancellor posing and shaking hands with all manner of government, religious and other immediately recognizable aristocrats testifying to the immense importance of the occupant of this office. A large embossed certificate announcing the Chancellor's nomination to the rank of High Director of The Faith hung prominently behind the desk.

The Chancellor stood looking out of the large window along one wall. The morning sun glowed deep orange as it rose above the horizon, its light casting a vibrant glow to the room. Tall and broad in the chest he wore brilliant silver and gold rings on each of the four fingers on his large, strong hands. His eyes were a penetrating deep brown. Even his top crest was artfully greyed just enough to give the impression of the wisdom of age, but still with eternal reserves of vitality. His suit, meticulously tailored in the fashion of a wealthy power broker. A large diamond graced the center of his university logo tie clasp. He stood, gazing out the window for a moment longer, forcing Rocker to remain standing.

"Good morning, Professor," he said, waving a hand to indicate a chair and permission to sit.

Sitting down at his desk, the Chancellor picked up his cigar and a small glass of translucent crimson liqueur. "Nothing like a fine Drasnian wine and an imported Pakish cigar, is there, Professor?" he said as he swirled the liquid in his glass and blew a cloud of smoke into the air above his head.

Rocker tensed, his hands clutched the arms of the chair and his crest reddened slightly. Then, fighting down the reaction he leaned back into the chair. "I'm a tea man myself, Chancellor, but with times the way they are, even that is getting out of financial reach now."

"Professor," said the Chancellor, ignoring Rocker's remark. "Are you aware of what keeps this university alive?"

Rocker locked eyes with the Chancellor. "The students and our research are our primary functions here, sir."

"No, Professor, in fact, they are not. It is money and the good will of those providing it is our primary responsibility. If I know about the inexcusable riot in your classroom today then rest assured others on the board know about it too, and so will a great many of our benefactors. I can guarantee you many of them will not like what they are hearing about you." He took a sip of his drink and another puff on the cigar to let his message sink in. Would you care to explain what happened yesterday?"

"To what are you referring, sir?"

"Don't be coy with me, Professor. I am not in the mood for games." The Chancellor looked as if he had eaten a dozen lemons right off the tree. "You know very well about the near riot you started among your students. Your new line of research is under a great deal of scrutiny and far from a second committee review. The probability of extending your grant in this area is highly doubtful at best. You have made some very impressive breakthroughs in your field, but your increasingly radical work and increasingly questionable teaching methods are bringing a great deal of negative scrutiny on yourself and this university. I am already under pressure to revoke your tenure. It won't take much to..."

The door to his office opened and in walked two very lethal-looking men in identical dark suits. They stood to either side of the doorway, admitting a small woman dressed impeccably in the latest designer fashions, but cut for functionality, not style. Her green eyes bore the look of a predator; her feathers and crest were preened short.

Rocker instinctively reached for the sidearm he had not worn for nearly ten years.

"What...who...what is the meaning of this?" sputtered the completely flummoxed Chancellor. He reached for the phone on his desk.

"Sit down, sir," commanded the young woman as she walked toward the Chancellor's desk. "This is official government business and we are in need of Professor Rocker." She effortlessly removed the phone from his grip and replaced it on the cradle.

"Who do you think you are, barging in here like this? I'm —"

The woman cut off the Chancellor's response. "Who we are is not important and is none of your concern. The only thing you need to know is that we need your office and you need to leave now, Chancellor."

"I will not stand for this, young lady. You need to leave before I call security."

"Answer your phone, Chancellor," she commanded.

"What do you mean, answer my..." The phone on the Chancellor's desk rang. He stared at it, then back at the implacable woman and her escorts. The Chancellor slumped back in his chair and answered the phone. "This is the Chancellor; who is this?" His eyes widened and his attempts to respond to the speaker at the other end instantly silenced. "Yes, sir, I understand," was all he could manage before hanging up. With an angry glare at the professor, and giving the woman a wide berth, he left his office. One of the escorts, stepping to the other side, closed the door behind him.

Rocker remained in his chair as the woman moved behind the large desk, placed a thick folder on its surface and sat in the Chancellor's chair. "Strixo, Professor. Nice to finally meet you."

Rocker nodded, taking inventory of possible weapons at his disposal.

"Well, first of all, we are not exactly from the government, Professor," she continued. "More precisely, we represent a private organization that is working independently on a project attempting to find a solution to the situation our world is facing, and we need your help."

Rocker kept his voice level and strong when he replied, "I'm an associate Professor at a level two university. What makes you think I can help you?"

The woman opened the folder she had placed on the desk and sorted through the papers it held. "Professor Jontar Rocker, only son of Gret and Martak Rocker?"

"Yes."

"Recipient of the Regent's award at age fifteen, graduated High School at age sixteen?"

"Yes."

"After your father's death in a levicoach wreck the night after your graduation there were several arrests for minor offenses, and then a felony charge that forced you into the military?"

Rocker tensed and glanced over his shoulder at the man who still stood at the door. "From where are you getting all of this information? Those are sealed juvenile records. Even the university could not gain access to those files when they hired me."

The woman glanced up at him, then back down and turned to the next page in the folder.

"Several field promotions for valor, Alpha Corp. Commander then promoted to Captain at the Galantar Marine training facilities. Married eight years ago, current status: widower."

The word "widower" stung, causing Rocker to jump out of his chair. The guard behind him reached out to grab his shoulder, but Rocker reacted. Grabbing the big man's wrist and twisting violently, he kicked the man in his knee, and brought his own elbow down to break the man's arm. There was a loud crack as the guard shouted out in pain, his arm bent at an unnatural angle. Before he could do any further damage, he heard a distinctive buzzing and felt the cold barrel of the second guard's energy pistol at his temple. He froze for a moment, picked up the chair and sat down again.

"Leave her out of this. You have no right..." The words strangled in his throat.

"Thank you, Professor," said the woman as if nothing had happened. "Let's proceed now." She turned to the next page of the dossier.

Rocker watched as the second guard removed the injured man from the office.

"Shortly after marrying you retired from military service and earned a degree in genetic engineering. You then gained employment in this university upon graduation. Currently involved in research developing new strategies to use chemical means to find a more stable process for the Somatic Cell Nuclear Transfer, more commonly known by its acronym, SCNT. Your research is being stonewalled due to political pressures trying to prevent publication of your theories."

"Now, just stop right there. How do you know all of this and why are you so interested in my life? What gives you the right to invade my privacy like this?"

The woman looked up with a puzzled expression. "Isn't it obvious? We have been following your career for some time now, Professor. Your work has the potential to solve some of the problems that have recently stalled our own progress. We are trying to save our society, Professor. And we're running out of time. The current political situation is threatening our future and we need your help."

Returning her attention to the report in front of her, she continued. "We are also aware that you have publicly expressed concerns over the potential ramifications of your work, however, you have no strong political convictions. Science is your true religion. We need you on our team. At this university your work is considered radical, even subversive. It's only a matter of time before the board of directors decides to let you go. Our facilities at GenCore are state of the art. We hire only the brightest and most innovative thinkers. We encourage our people to take their ideas as far as they can. GenCore will not pressure you or interfere with your research. You have become one of the leading authorities in cloning technology. With our team you will be surrounded by the personnel, equipment, and ideology that recognize and appreciate your genius."

Rocker's crest rose slightly, his eyes narrowed. "So why haven't I ever heard of GenCore? If it's everything you claim it to be, surely I would have heard something."

"GenCore is a new division of a much larger conglomerate of corporations. We see real potential in your work, Professor, and think there is a future in cloning technology. Our director believes your theories hold the most promise for a lucrative investment."

The professor scratched at his auricles and leaned forward in his chair. This proposition was just too good to be true. "Let me get this straight. You want to hire me so that I can continue my research on cloning technology without restrictions? What's the catch here? Are you looking to enhance your profits with some new military contracts or looking to cash in on the new advancements we're making in cloned organs?"

Nothing of the sort, Professor," she said, closing the file and leaned forward, folding her hands on the desk. "We assiduously avoid anything to do with the military, and our interests go far beyond the cloning of a few organs. You will have full publishing rights to anything you develop and you will lead a team of the finest geneticists on the planet. Think of it, Professor, an entire facility devoted to seeing your theories realized. Of course we would retain any patents on the technology resulting from your work, for which you will be generously compensated," said the woman as she smiled, sliding a contract across the table for him, "and did we mention full benefits at triple your current salary?"

Professor Rocker's letter of resignation was on the Chancellor's desk within the hour.

Chapter Eleven

Brach was unsettled. He was not used to being unsettled, which troubled him even more. He had been hearing rumors of some unidentified organization that was apparently manipulating recent legislation in a manner he did not appreciate. As monarch, he was supposed to control the passage or rejection of any act of Parliament that he desired. Current events were proving this assumption to be in error. He pressed the button on his desk.

The door opened and his chamberlain silently entered the private quarters. "Yes, Your Majesty?"

"Has the General arrived yet?"

"Only minutes ago, Sire. I was on my way to announce him when you rang."

"Admit him at once, then."

"Yes, Sire." The chamberlain retreated two precise steps, turned, and left the room.

The General entered the royal chambers, and the doors automatically closed and locked behind him with a solid thump. His formal gold and red uniform shone brilliantly in the sunlight streaming through the tall windows. Dozens of ribbons and medals decorated the sash across his chest. His trousers, crisply pressed, displayed a gold stripe down the side. His black boots, impeccably polished, resounded sharply as he marched across the stone floor.

Tapestries depicting fierce battle scenes hung from gently curved stone walls which flowed perfectly into the floor. Immense paintings of a long line of monarchs produced by the current dynasty hung among the tapestries. Suits of armor and chainmail stood against the walls.

Several cabinets displayed a wide variety of weapons of both current and past ages. A large, intricately carved stone rectangular table occupied the center of the room. The surface of the table was inlaid with panels of richly stained wood in elaborate geometric patterns, surrounded by a dozen richly upholstered chairs. The one at the end sat on a raised platform and had a tall back, decorated with all the symbols of the royal family. Tall windows filled the space between the bookshelves, providing ample light for study. The upper portions of each window contained historic scenes depicted in brightly colored stained glass. A menagerie of maps and documents, scattered in no particular arrangement covered the table. The monarch, in his usual attire of blue shirt and black slacks when in private, sat at his desk on the far side of the room rummaging through more papers. His gold and silver crown sat squarely on his head.

"Have you seen these reports, General?" the monarch asked, still studying the papers before him. "Somebody, possibly several somebodies, is attempting to influence members of Parliament. Many of the votes we use to consider solidly in our control have begun to stray."

"Yes, Sire. While the votes have predominantly been on minor matters of commerce, they are most troubling in their implications."

"This news is very disturbing, General. Why wasn't I informed about this activity before now?"

The General snapped to attention as he replied. "We have only just now discovered the information, sire. They hid their tracks very skillfully. The efforts appear to focus on reducing regulations concerning corporate mergers, elimination of penalties on certain monopolies, and land acquisitions. The name GenCore has come to our attention, but we haven't been able to verify anything. It's all just speculation so far."

"I need to find out what is going on and who's behind it all. We can't afford any interference with our plans now. Get to the bottom of it and report back to me within the week."

"Yes, Sire. Whoever is responsible for these matters is meticulous at covering their tracks. We are lucky to have noticed the disturbances at all. I am continuing to work on the problem and have set several of our best agents into the field to see what they can learn."

Brach thought about this for a bit while the General remained at attention, his uniform glowing in the sunlit room.

"Have you been able to determine how long this has been going on?"

"Not precisely, Sire, but it does appear that the trend has been occurring with increasing frequency for several years at least."

Brach threw the papers on the table and slammed his fist on top of them. "Keep on it, General. We cannot afford to be caught unprepared if this turns out to be more than just an innocent set of coincidences. Matters are much too fragile right now and a slight alteration could bring all of my efforts crashing down around us."

"Yes, Sire," the General turned and marched out of the room.

Once the door closed behind the General, a curtain opened on the opposite side of the room and a figure emerged from the hidden alcove. The man wore a short, simple, brown hooded robe and trousers with a homespun shirt. The only visible ornamentation being the iron Eye of The Eternal, symbol of The Faith, hanging from a leather necklace.

"This news is most disturbing, Your Majesty," said the man. "We hope this meddler is not going to interfere with our arrangements."

"Not at all, Bishop," said Brach. He bowed to the clergyman and kissed the ring on his raised hand. "The Faith has nothing to be worried about. Our cooperation will ensure enough placement of your faithful to control Parliament in just a few years. We can handle this inconvenience."

The Bishop was a tall man so thin and pale that he appeared almost cadaverous with dark, sunken eyes and protruding cheek bones. Being second in command of The Faith, and one of the few true believers, he commanded unquestioning obedience of his followers, but the monarch was of special interest as a potential convert and had to be treated carefully.

"We hope you are correct, Your majesty. The Eternal commands us in this task and we cannot fail. We need to be confident that our alliance with you is no error. Your own brother cautions us to be wary around even you with constant reminders of how politicians are swayed as easily as leaves in the breeze." He watched the monarch closely for any sign of infidelity.

"Do not concern yourself, Your Grace. I have been playing this game all my life. I know how to control Parliament. We will not fail."

"Very good then, Your Majesty. I will leave you to handle matters. Here is The Prior's latest proclamation and his wishes for Parliament's next session." He handed a sealed case to Brach and turned to leave.

"Thank you, Your Grace," Brach said, accepting the case. "Give my regards to my brother."

Brach tossed the case negligently on his desk once the Bishop left. His crest flared red as he yanked on the cord summoning the General.

"Yes, Your Majesty?"

"I want you to set up and train a special division within our spy network," Brach said, leaning heavily on his desk, drumming his talons sharply on the wooden surface.

"This will be a particularly dangerous task and you must take extra care in choosing only those whose loyalty is beyond question."

"Yes, Your Majesty. May I ask who will be the target of such men?"

"My brother.

Chapter Twelve

"Is everything satisfactory, Dr. Rocker?" asked Dr. Contor, the lead geneticist.

Rocker could only nod. Entering the laboratory felt like the first time he saw the Eternity Festival celebrations since childhood. He saw his guide shift his feet and glance toward the door. Dr. Rocker cleared his throat.

"Yes, this will do very well," he said, and motioned for his new colleague to continue the tour. *Feathers! I hope I didn't sound like a pompous ass. I'm going to need all the help I can get here if I want to hit the ground running.*

GenCore's facilities proved to be without equal and a far cry from the dingy basement make-shift lab he was accustomed to at the university. Rocker marveled at the equipment that he now commanded. Sterile biohazard rooms glistened behind large windows. Four long lab tables filled the center of the room under banks of lights, providing near daylight conditions. State of the art equipment occupied the surface of the lab tables, some of which Rocker read about only recently in the journals. Liquid nitrogen storage tanks, electrophoresis gels by the score, digital microscopes, two electron microscopes, and computers at each lab station. Everything a cutting edge laboratory required. *Back at the university I had to beg for every petri dish and test tube. I must have died and gone to...*

"If there is anything you require, just tell your administrative assistant. We are here to make sure that you lack for nothing."

"I see," Rocker replied, gesturing around the room. "I can't imagine anything has been forgotten here, but I will keep your offer in mind. This is incredible. It must have cost a fortune. Even your Rings courts in the gymnasium are high tech. Worthy of any pro team."

Dr. Contor smiled, nodding in agreement. "It's nice having a fairy godmother. Seriously though, our benefactor, The Director, has very deep pockets and takes pride in his facilities being the finest anywhere."

The older geneticist grabbed Rocker's elbow and guided him toward a group all dressed in lab coats. "Our staff geneticists and lab techs have been recruited from the finest facilities in the world. We have been steadily raiding corporations, labs, and universities for a couple of years now."

Rocker hooked talons with the men as they were introduced.

"This is Dr. Kintar Rishman and Dr. Ponan Shigmer," said Contor. "They're the geniuses who developed everything we have accomplished so far here at GenCore."

After exchanging a few pleasantries, Rocker pulled Contor aside so they could speak privately. "Are you sure I'm the right guy to tell them what to do? I'm just an associate professor of genetics. Will they accept me as their department leader?"

"Oh, yes, sir. Everyone here has read your work and we are excited about how it has expanded our thinking into areas nobody had anticipated. You are, without doubt, the right man to lead us to the next level in clone animation."

"How have you read my work? The university only published my more mundane research. Certainly nothing that would inspire the likes of these geniuses."

"As I said, Dr. Rocker, the director has very deep pockets and a great deal of influence. I don't think anything is beyond his reach if he puts his mind to it."

Before Rocker could respond, the door to the lab swung open and a young man entered, handed the guide a paper, and left.

Dr. Contor's eyes darted over the note and pursed his lips. "Hmm. It appears that the boss wants to see you before we continue our tour. Follow me, Doctor."

"Okay, I guess I do need to meet him at some point or another. Can you tell me anything about him that might help make a good first impression?"

"Oh, this won't be his first impression of you. The director personally directed your vetting process." Contor pointed up at the ceiling. "I'm sure he's been observing you as we have toured the facilities."

Rocker looked up and noticed the security cameras at regular, strategic intervals along the hallway, feeling his neck feathers prickle realizing he was under constant surveillance. He turned to Contor and said, "Man, you guys take your security measures pretty seriously."

"Yes, we have a great deal of proprietary work going on here a lot of people would love to get their hands on. Access codes are changed weekly. ID badges are encoded and updated monthly and a number of other precautions nobody but those who need to know can actually confirm." He got a conspiratorial grin on his face and leaned in close to Rocker. "We even heard rumors that they are going to install a moat, complete with flesh-eating sarts, next month."

Rocker laughed and clapped Dr. Contor on the back. "Lead on, then," Rocker said. With a flourish of his hand and a slight bow to his guide, they headed to the executive offices on the top floor of the building. All along the way, Rocker looked for signs of hidden security measures. He noticed the smooth narrow ceiling length panels in the wall curving gently into the walls and thought they might be metal or electronic detectors of some sort. *Bet there's plenty more I'm not seeing. Oh well, with what they are paying me, I guess a lack of privacy just comes with the territory.*

"Welcome to GenCore, Dr. Rocker," said Kirta as the two geneticists entered the outer office, "he's waiting for you. Go right in." She pointed toward the doorway on her right. Emblazoned on the door was a bronze plate that read:

Karm

Director

GenCore Inc.

The only decoration was a large map of Dyan'ta, lit by two sconces on either side. Dozens of multicolored pins decorated various locations on every continent. The long table in the center of the room was stacked with books and littered with folders and loose papers. A desk sat by the window, small, wooden, also piled high with additional papers and books. A tan-shaded lamp sat precariously on top of one of the stacks. A large monitor hung on the wall nearest the desk. It displayed multiple images from numerous locations within the building. Rocker looked more closely at the monitors and recognized some of the hallways they passed through on their way to the Director's office.

The man who sat reading through a folder at the desk appeared elderly, but still gave the impression of great vitality. Though not physically impressive, his presence commanded respect. The office was not the typical setting of a man in such a position of authority. Other than the large wall map it displayed none of the expected symbols of power and authority Rocker had grown accustomed to in the military and at the university.

"Good afternoon, Doctor," the director said as he stood and reached out his hand to hook talons with Rocker.

"Good afternoon, Director," a strange sense of familiarity struck Rocker as he hooked talons with his employer. "May I first express my gratitude in your selection of me to head up GenCore's clone research department? It's a great honor."

The director waved off Rocker's modesty as he advanced. "Nonsense, I only hire the best, and everyone here tells me you have already surpassed all others in the field of cloning research." He continued shaking Rocker's hand without saying anything and then broke off the contact with a nervous laugh. "I make it a point to welcome all of my department heads, but I must admit I was exceptionally excited to meet you in person. After all, your work is charting a new course for our future."

Rocker wanted to ask the director what he meant by "our future", but a concealed door opened and in walked the small woman he met in the Chancellor's office. She wore a stylish business suit, but her efficient movements across the room made it look more like a uniform. After handing the director a binder marked, CONFIDENTIAL she took a position next to the secret doorway.

Rocker smiled at her and said, "I want to thank you for rescuing me from the Chancellor the other day. That was quite some achievement. I've never seen him take orders from a..."

"From a what?" she asked, shifting her feet a shoulder's width apart, clenching her left fist. "A woman?" The crest feathers on her head changed color to a threatening red.

"From ahhh...from anyone," Rocker laughed and put his hands up to surrender. "Sorry, I meant no offense. I was just expressing my gratitude." Despite the initial impression, his chest gave a slight flutter, reminiscent of the ones he felt when watching his wife approach. A rush of guilt surged through him.

The director looked up absently from the binder and said, "Dr. Rocker, may I introduce Maripa, my personal assistant. Maripa, of course, already knows you."

Rocker took a step forward with his hand extended, but Maripa's scrutiny discouraged him from proceeding. He stepped back and placed his hand to his shoulder in mock salute. "Nice to see you again, Maripa is it?"

"You will have to excuse Maripa, Doctor," the Director continued when Maripa did not reply. "She is not one for pleasantries, but, as you have witnessed, she is very effective at what she does."

"That I have, sir. The likes of which I have never seen before. But, as I said, I appreciate the rescue," Rocker said with a sideways glance at Maripa. "And I am also very pleased to see the quality of the labs you have provided for my research. Your staff and your facilities here are unmatched anywhere on Dyan'ta."

"Anything worth doing, Professor," the Director responded before drawing his attention back to the confidential binder.

Rocker could not hold back any longer. "Excuse me, sir, but have we ever met before? I cannot get over the sensation of familiarity I am feeling here. I do not mean to be impertinent, but I just have to ask."

A dark cloud shadowed the director's face, but it quickly vanished behind a polished smile and dead eyes. "If I had a dorket for every time I hear that, I would be a rich man. Wait... I am a rich man!" He laughed at his own joke and smacked his hand on the binder. "I guess I just have one of those faces that blends into a crowd and looks like everyone's favorite old uncle or something."

"That is probably it then. I am sorry, Director. Again. I meant no disrespect or undue familiarity."

"None taken, Doctor," the director responded as he closed the binder and set it aside. "Now let's get down to business. Maripa has brought in all of the necessary paper work: security codes, medical forms, stock option opportunities, and your official clearance badge and employee handbook. Everything you need to get off on the right foot here at GenCore." He passed the binder over to Rocker who looked inside and took out his holographic photo ID badge. He winced at the hologram, and clipped it to his shirt pocket.

"Now, I know you've had a busy day and I don't want to keep you any longer. I just wanted to welcome you personally and assure you that everything you need will be provided. After all, we do have a vital job to accomplish here and not much time to do it in."

"And just what is that vital job, sir?" Rocker asked, tilting his head, crest feathers lifting in confusion. "Why is there not much time? My work is theoretical. There's nothing time sensitive about any of it. With the growing influence of The Faith, I doubt seriously the government will allow any research that results in producing a viable clone. Not when they have more pressing research dedicated to preventing our extinction."

"I thought you understood, Doctor, we are going to save our world," the director said, and slapped Rocker on the back. He escorted the silent professor to the lobby outside his office and shook his hand again. "I have to rush off to another meeting, Professor, and I'm sure you're anxious to get started in the lab."

Rocker robotically shook the director's hand with an unsteady, "Of course, sir." He watched as Karm strode back into his office. Before the door closed completely, he saw Maripa and the director exchange worried glances.

Inside the office, the director sat behind his desk and laced his fingers behind his head. "No need to fret, Maripa. Dr. Rocker knows nothing more than he did when we hired him. He's an insightful and intuitive man who is gifted at analytical reasoning, but he will only know what we allow him to know."

"If you say so, Karm, but I intend to keep an even closer eye on him for a while. He is still not out of danger and we need him."

"Yes, yes, of course you are right. He has already begun to notice and ask about our normal security measures. Just don't let him discover your team's surveillance of him. We don't want to scare him off at this delicate time."

"I know how to conduct a discrete surveillance, Karm," Maripa glowered and returned to her office to make the necessary calls.

As the door closed, Karm pressed the intercom button on his phone. "Is that call to the Prime Minister ready, Kirta?"

"Yes, sir. On video line two."

Karm pressed the button and an image of the Prime Minister appeared on the screen.

"Strixo, Karm," said the Prime Minister putting on his most diplomatic smile, "What can I do for you today?"

"I want to know why that pharmaceutical bill is being stalled," said Karm. "You know how important that piece of legislation is to my interests. I have put too much time and effort into it for anything to go wrong now."

"Don't worry, Karm. We had a bit of trouble with some of the new members of the ministry, who were attempting to block it, but we have that solved now and there should be no further delays."

"What happened? There wasn't supposed to be any opposition." Karm sat up straighter and furrowed his brows in concern at this news.

"It seems The Faith has been able to influence a number of new ministers. They have been coerced into signing some sort of anti-cloning pledge and they were refusing to compromise on the issue. We were able to get enough votes in spite of them and get the bill moving."

"Send me some more information about this pledge and who is signing it. I may need to take steps to counteract The Faith if they start gaining more strength." He hung up and sat back in his chair rubbing his eyes as he contemplated his options.

***

On his way home, Rocker reflected on the events of the long day. The drive was not much longer than from his old job at the university, but instead of bumper to bumper traffic, he now commuted along a tree lined countryside dotted with small farms. The levicoach maintained a constant ten centimeter suspension above the pavement regardless of speed and conditions. He appreciated not having the brightness in his eyes during the drive home. The annoying glare from the dying orange sun had been a daily reminder of the impending end.

Rocker wondered how his clone research could possibly be anything so vital to the current situation. The experts were saying the planet still had about 100 years before the sun goes nova. Too much just didn't add up. Turning absently into his driveway, he barely registered the dark blue coupe parked across the street. As he got out of his levicoach, a reflection from the driver's side of the unfamiliar vehicle caught his attention. His heart skipped a beat and he quickly surveyed his surroundings. *Okay, big fella, slow down, now. You're not in the desert anymore. It's just someone waiting for the neighbor to go out to dinner or something. GenCore's excessive security paranoia just has you spooked.* He closed the front door behind him, turned on the porch light, and a few more lights than necessary inside the house. After one quick glance out the front window, he proceeded to look for something to eat.

While nibbling distractedly on his meal, Rocker absentmindedly began twirling the ring on the chain around his neck and gazed at the worn photo he still carried. *I wish you were here to help me figure this out, my love. This Karm character seems just too good to be true. I should have done this before accepting the job, but a bit of recon on Karm and his assistant are definitely in order.*

The large man down the street, hidden in the shadows, returned his energy pistol to its holster as his talon pressed the contact to disarm the weapon. He noted the arrival of Dr. Rocker in his log book, as well as the departure of the unrecognized blue vehicle and its two occupants, shortly after the doctor's arrival home.

"I need a check on a dark blue Alpha Dotson, registration ID 822BL4. Possible security risk to Gen One."

"Roger that, Gen One Eyes," came the response over the earphones. "Next check in four hours."

"Roger that. Out." And he settled down for his watch.

***

In the middle of the third triad the game was still too close to call. Rocker had joined the company Rings club at GenCore and in just a few days was earning the reputation as a leading contender for the individual championship trophy. Standing at mid court he flicked the hard rubber coated ceramic ball in his net. A quick double juke and a hard slam of his shoulder into his opponent gave him the open lane to the small center ring on the back wall. Rocker leaped high, extending his net as high as he could reach and deftly tossed the ball through the ring. An orange light lit up above the ring adding five points to Rocker's score on the electronic board.

"Good move, Jontar," said Dr. Contor, his regular Rings partner. "See if you can stop this one."

Contor scooped up the ball from the floor and bounced it hard so it ricocheted off of the corner and back to mid court behind Rocker. Using the foot long stick of his net to knock Rocker's net aside, Contor drove his shoulder into Rocker and circled around him just in time to catch the ball in his net as it descended.

"Cute move," said Rocker as he raced up behind Contor, then darted around him with a body block to cut off his lane. "Got ya now!"

"Nice try, but not in time to stop this," taunted Contor. He spun quickly to his left and stepped into the bonus area where he jumped and shot his ball into the larger left side ring. "Yes! Double points!" He shouted as the orange light, plus a blue one next to it both lit up, increasing his score another six points.

Back and forth they went over the next seven minutes, each taking over the lead as they made shots that drew appreciative cheers and applause from the small after-work crowd watching them. When the final buzzer sounded, Rocker won by only three points.

Both men stood, breathing hard with hands on their knees dripping sweat. "Good game," Rocker said as he reached out to shake talons with Contor.

"Almost had you there," Contor smiled back. "Where did you learn those moves? I've never seen anything like it outside the pros."

"Join me for a drink after we get cleaned up and I'll tell you."

Half an hour later, doctors Rocker and Contor sat at a table in the local tavern sipping their drinks. Sitting at the bar had become nearly impossible since the news of the supernova. At least this crowd seemed more peaceful than in other regions. Their conversation drifted from Rings strategy and techniques to the office and briefly onto family before Rocker broached the topic he planned for this evening. Taking a long sip on his brew, he looked Contor in the eyes and lowered his voice.

"So what's the story behind Karm?" He asked conspiratorially, his eyes glancing around the room. "I've never heard of him before that Maripa showed up at the university and recruited me."

Dr. Contor placed his mug on the table, leaned in and lowered his voice. "Not much to tell, actually. What I hear is that he made his fortune as some big wheeler dealer buying and selling companies and real estate. He saw the market for research opportunities in genetics and built GenCore as a new division in his empire. He recruited the best and brightest minds on the planet and the rest is history."

Rocker frowned and shifted in his seat. "Is he connected to the military or the government in any way? Aren't you nervous about what might come of all this new technology we are developing?"

"Not at all. That's exactly why I left my previous employer. I found out he was looking for ways to earn some new military contracts. Haven't you read your employment agreement?"

"I skimmed it through. Probably not as thoroughly as I should have," said Rocker lowering his eyes toward his mug feeling a little embarrassed to admit this oversight.

"Well, if you had, you would have seen a clause stating that any individuals having any connections with the government or military, even responding to interview requests without notifying GenCore management immediately will be terminated on the spot and all of their research confiscated and reassigned. Karm is absolutely adamant about this facility, and all of his holdings, being absolutely under his, and only his control. He is almost paranoid about that sort of interference. We had one lab assistant who failed to put down on her application form an uncle who is some minor official for the roads and transportation division over in the capital. When security found out, she was interrogated by Karm himself, as they all are, and escorted off the grounds before anyone even knew what was happening."

Rocker frowned, his crest twitched nervously. "That does sound extreme. I'm not so sure it reassures me though.

He sounds like some sort of control freak. Does he ever interfere with your research?"

Dr. Contor shook his head in response. "Absolutely not. The old man gives us the freedom to take our research in any direction we think is necessary. He always says that those who know most about the work should determine the process and procedures. All he demands is regular reports on our progress."

Rocker sat quietly for a while, contemplating this new information. *Nobody is that altruistic. There must be something he's hiding. I'm going to need to keep my eyes open on this one. I don't want to be remembered as the father of some genetically enhanced group of super soldiers.* A loud uproar from the bar interrupted his internal reflections.

"Looks like the Raptors just clinched the division title," Contor said, pointing to the monitor. "Kak, I was hoping the Nationals would go farther this year."

"Not a chance," replied Rocker as he recovered his wits. "The Raptors have too good a defense. So you're sure about Karm and his intentions?"

"Absolutely. I wouldn't be here if I wasn't. You're not the only one who hates to have his work controlled by some bureaucrat with delusions of godhood. As long as he leaves me alone to do my research and isn't looking for government contracts I'm happy."

Rocker smiled and lifted his mug in salute. "OK, thanks. Being the new guy on the block I was just looking for some insight into the boss and what he's like. Sounds like a pretty sweet deal here. It helps to know more about the company's history." *But it still doesn't sit right. I need to keep digging.*

In the back of the room, seated at a small wooden table, sat a small woman, her head covered in a plain brown scarf. Her rough clothing and quiet demeanor gave the impression of a mid-grade working girl, probably a seamstress or clerk in some office, just stopping in for her evening meal. Her head turned as Rocker stood to leave. She quickly placed a few coins on the table, waited for him to exit out the front door, and headed out through the kitchen.

Chapter Thirteen

The clear night sky sparkled with stars winking on and off in the blackness. A beautiful evening for a stroll to clear one's mind. Rocker often used these quiet moments to organize his thoughts and ponder new combinations of the chemicals he knew were the key to stabilizing the somatic cell nuclear transfer, commonly called the SCNT. *We've made more progress in the past few months than I made over two years of research at the university.*

Rocker walked with a bounce to his steps these days. He no longer felt concern about the unusually high levels of security, chalking it up to private industry concerns over patents. He rarely even noticed the ever present cameras and guards in the labs. Even so, he always seemed to be aware of Maripa's presence whenever she was around. His crest always gave a slight twitch when he noticed her nearby. The security measures never interfered with his work, so he, in turn, ignored them.

*It's only a matter of developing the correct proportions and dosages to fully stabilize the process. It may be just a matter of…*and then everything went black.

The pain in his head was something he had not felt since being wounded in Alpha Corp's fire fight against the Latonian desert rebels. He tried sitting up and opening his eyes, but the vertigo proved to be overwhelming. *Better not try that just yet.* He laid still to let the world stop spinning. *What the strix happened?*

"Dr. Rocker, I see you are awake now," an unfamiliar voice commented, as if no more concerned than asking about the weather. "You probably have a concussion, so you don't want to move around too quickly yet."

Rocker tried to speak, but his throat was too dry. He swallowed and tried again. "Where am I, and what the strix happened? Was I in an accident?"

"No, Doctor. No accident," the voice answered. "We…invited you here for a polite conversation."

Rocker opened his eyes a bit more carefully this time. Everything blurred, but at least the spinning was subsiding and his eyes slowly regained their focus. The room sounded spacious, like the inside of a warehouse. Voices and machinery echoed through the space. As his vision cleared, Rocker noticed aisles of metal shelves filled with various containers and boxes filled the large room. He lay on a cot with a blanket covering him and he felt a bandage around his head. He winced as he touched the large knot beginning to grow underneath it. The voice speaking to him came from a man behind a small wooden desk. There was a light behind the man, shining in Rocker's direction so he could not make out any features, only a shadow against the light.

"And a simple 'Please come with us' was out of the question, I suppose?" Rocker sat up slowly and placed his feet on the concrete floor. He stretched and rubbed his neck as he tried to survey the room, but it was too dark to see anything, and the throbbing in his head made it impossible to focus on anything else.

"I'm afraid not, Professor."

"Okay then, suppose you tell me why I am here. And can you get me an aspirin or something? My head is killing me."

"Certainly, Doctor." The shadow picked up a phone, spoke into it quietly and hung up. Before long there was a knock at the door. A woman in a blue uniform walked in with a tray, placed it on the shadow's desk, and left. The shadow brought the glass of water and pills to Rocker, then returned to his desk.

Once Rocker swallowed the pills, the shadow continued. "How is your work progressing, Doctor? Have you solved the imbalance problems yet?"

Rocker paused and looked toward the shadow. His back straightened as he brought his hand to feel the knot on his head. "You know I can't answer that."

"Yes, we know, and it really doesn't matter anyway. We just need you to stop what you are doing and end this line of research. You are here so we can discuss this matter."

"Sorry, I don't believe we have anything to discuss. I never have taken kindly to bullies." He placed his feet more firmly on the floor, and tried to stand. Off to one side, back in the darkness, he heard a brief shuffle of feet and the electric hum of an energy weapon being armed.

"Now, Doctor Rocker, please stay seated. It should be clear to you by now that we are willing to go to extremes to get what we want. This is merely a polite warning. Next time, well...no need to discuss those messy matters, now is there?" The shadow never moved or changed the matter-of-fact manner of his voice. There was a cold deadliness to him. Rocker became nervous.

"And just how am I to manage this?" Rocker asked. "There will be a lot of tough questions if I suddenly stop everything, especially after..." He stopped before going any further, cursing himself for almost revealing too much.

"You are an intelligent man, Doctor. I am sure you can come up with some clever method of convincing your superiors that your research has hit a dead end."

"Not very likely," Rocker said as he looked around the room, trying to locate a weapon and the exits.

"Oh, I think you..." The shadow gave a sudden jerk and reached for his neck. He stiffened, and slumped over onto the desk without further sound. A small, hooded figure appeared from nowhere, spun and tossed a silvery object into the darkness. Rocker heard the thump as another body hit the ground.

"Are you alright, Dr. Rocker?" a feminine voice laced with steel asked. A definite contrast to the caress of a soft hand on his forehead.

"What's going on? Who the strix are you?"

"It's Maripa, Dr. Rocker. Sorry it took me a while to get here. I was across town when word came in that you had been taken. Can you walk?"

"I can damn well run to get out of this place. Let's go."

The young woman made no sound as she crept ahead of Dr. Rocker through the aisles. One hand held beneath her cloak, eyes aware of everything. Near the door they were approaching lounged two workmen. Rocker noticed, however, they did not appear to be doing much work, only watching.

"Wait here," She turned and scurried up the shelves as easily as a six legged dinter up a tree. Rocker watched as she effortlessly lifted herself into the rafters. He marveled at her grace and skill as she ran along the narrow beams. Upon reaching a point directly above the two workmen by the door, she dropped from her perch, landing a solid kick to the head of the one on the left. She rolled to one side, leaped, and landed another kick to the face of the second man. Neither had a chance to raise an alarm. She signaled for Rocker to come along. "Help me move these two out of sight."

They hid the unconscious men behind some boxes and opened the door.

"Drem, that you?" came a voice from outside.

Before Rocker could even think, the woman reached inside her cloak, and tossed a small dart at the man in the doorway. The man fell to the ground before he could say or do anything. Maripa grabbed the unconscious man by his wrists and dragged him toward where they hid the other two. Rocker leaned against the wall to steady himself. As he watched Maripa, he noticed another man appear in the doorway aiming a weapon at Maripa's back. Rocker reached down to a pile of bricks and hefted one of them. He struck at the man's head with the brick, but missed and hit him in the shoulder instead. The man dropped his weapon and swore as he turned to face Rocker.

"Oh, mutes!" muttered Rocker as the man approached.

Gathering all of his strength, Rocker hit the man square in the face with a second shot. The man's face exploded in a spray of blood and he collapsed to the floor just as Maripa returned.

"Nice work, Doctor," she said looking at the man on the floor and the gun beside him.

"Let's just get out of here," He dropped the brick and they ran through the doorway.

Rocker stumbled after the woman toward the security fence. She led him to an opening. They escaped into a waiting levicoach just as an alarm rang out.

"GO!" she commanded to the driver. She reached into the small refrigerator and pulled out a bottle of water. She then retrieved some pills from another compartment.

"Here, Dr. Rocker," Maripa said as they settled into their seats. "This will help reduce the swelling and dizziness." Her voice seemed somehow softer, and more anxious than usual.

"Maripa," he began as he swallowed the tablets and took a drink of the water. "What are you doing here?"

"I thought that would be obvious by now, Dr. Rocker."

Feeling a bit chagrined, he avoided her gaze by examining the interior of the mag-lev. "Thank you. I was beginning to think I might not get out of there in one piece. Nice getaway coach."

"Karm will want to talk to you right away," was her only response as she removed the hood of her cloak. She preened her crest to settle it comfortably, her eyes never leaving the road behind them.

"You were pretty remarkable back there. Ex-Military?"

Her look was uncompromising. Conversation was not part of the rescue. Her demeanor returned abruptly to her more familiar detached persona.

Rocker sat back, took in a deep breath and gave a long, relaxing exhale. Then he drifted off.

Only then did the man next to the driver speak. "Are you okay?" he asked Maripa, gentle concern in his voice.

She looked up at Darkon, unable to contain a brief smile. "Always worried about me. Yes, I'm fine. Nothing we couldn't handle."

"We?"

"Yeah," Maripa said, pointing at Rocker. "Turns out he's pretty good in a fight."

The debriefing with Karm and Darkon proved to be relatively painless, but Rocker was not about to let this slide by. "I don't like being kept in the dark, Karm. You need to tell me why my project is worth somebody kidnapping and threatening me." He paced back and forth pointing his finger at Karm.

"We don't know for certain who kidnapped you yet," said Darkon. "Our best bet is on some faction of The Faith, but we haven't ruled out government interference yet."

"Maripa is investigating it as we speak," added Karm.

"Those people certainly acted like some para-military organization," Rocker said, still pacing angrily. "Much too good for a bunch of down-heads. If you have any ambitions about weaponizing my research, turning clones into some sort of super soldiers, think again. I'll be out of here and talking to everyone I can find so fast it'll make your head spin."

"Calm down, Doctor." Karm   stood now and walked around to stand in front of his desk as he spoke. "I promise you, I have nothing of that sort in mind. I am as opposed to using clone research for something as unthinkable as that as you are. This is precisely why I am working so hard to keep the government out of our crests and in the dark as to our true purpose."

"And just what might our true purpose be? It obviously isn't anything as simple as clone research."

"All in due time, I assure you. Surely, you can appreciate the need for tight security. For now, you will have to be satisfied with my guarantee nothing immoral or unethical is going on."

Rocker paced again, but felt his anger fading. He stopped in front of Karm and faced him, pointing a talon at his chest. "There better not be."

"You have my word," replied Karm. "And one more thing, Professor. Your research may be closer than you think to becoming not only practical, but in all likelihood the most important scientific development in history."

An hour later, Rocker reached up and rubbed the painful lump on his skull. His head continued to throb as he tried to adjust his pillow to a more comfortable position. He still could not shake the odd feeling of familiarity whenever he met with Karm. The lab nurse assured him there was no permanent damage and that he could return to work after a couple of days rest. For security reasons they were relocating him to a new house on the grounds of the GenCore campus. He understood the need for security, but objected to being watched 26-10. Although having Maripa as his new babysitter was not altogether unpleasant. She was a very pretty young thing, at least when she didn't scowl at him. She definitely was not one for conversation, but he could tolerate her shadowing him everywhere so long as she did not interfere with his work. Still, there was something about her that he couldn't shake. He finally drifted off to a disturbingly erotic dream involving himself, Maripa, and a deserted warehouse.

***

The General stood in the warehouse, watching the man struggle back to consciousness lifting his head from the desktop. As his eyes began to focus, he saw his prisoner had escaped. Then he saw the General.

"Care to explain what happened here?" the General asked. His gaze never wavered, and only his inner eyelids blinked.

"I can't, sir. One minute I was interrogating the prisoner, then nothing until now." The man sweated profusely and looked toward the body of his partner by the doorway.

"I see." The General raised his hand. His talon pressed the firing contact twice. A beam of charged ions split the air with an orange beam. The man fell over onto the floor, a pool of blood spread out from under the body.

The General pulled a communicator from his pocket and hit the first button. "No, sir, the incompetents we hired let him escape." He listened impassively to the irate response on the other end.

"Yes, Your Majesty, I know. That makes things more difficult now."

***

After double checking her security patrols around Dr. Rocker's house, Maripa returned to her private quarters. She ate a few leftovers she scrounged from the refrigerator, gave up on the book she tried to read, but couldn't quite focus on and headed off for a shower and bed. She tossed and turned, unable to turn off her brain. For some inexplicable reason, thoughts of Dr. Rocker prevented her from drifting off to sleep. She kept revisiting her surveillance of his Rings games. Watching his agility and skill at the game always impressed her. *What the strix am I doing? Knock it off, girl. You have a job to do. Focus on the job.* She fluffed the covers around her and gave her pillow another thrashing, then began her meditation routine to settle her mind and purge Rocker from her thoughts.

Chapter Fourteen

A few days later, Maripa sat at her desk when the computer screen flashed a warning box.

SECURITY BREACH. LEVEL FIVE FIREWALL ATTACKED.

She picked up the phone and dialed the number for security. "Darkon, what's happened?"

"Someone attempted to break into level five secure files. The firewall appears to have held so only some of the lower level files were compromised."

"Are you tracking it?"

"The tracers kicked in automatically. We should have something for you in a couple of hours."

"Good. Keep me informed." She hung up and went to the door allowing her direct access to Karm's private office.

"We have a security breach, sir. Someone just tried to break the level five files. Security protocols held up and we are investigating the problem."

Karm dropped the papers he was reading onto his desk and lifted his gaze to Maripa. "This is serious. Level five is supposed to be unbreakable."

"Yes, sir. The higher level files are still secure, but some non-critical information was accessed. We need to find out who has the ability to get as far as they did."

"Do what you need to do. Keep me informed."

"Yes, sir," she said, turning to leave. "I may need to use the unregistered coach tonight."

Later that evening Maripa sat in the back seat of the levicoach with Darkon. She wore dark, tight fitting apparel, soft soled shoes and a dark hooded cloak. She pulled the hood forward to completely hide her face in its shadows.

The name UNIVERSAL CHARITY shined brightly above the main entrance. "You sure this is it?" she asked her companion.

Darkon nodded in the darkness of the vehicle's interior. "No doubt about it. They attempted to cover their trail, but we were able to trace the signal to this location. Examination of the building blueprints indicate the most probable location is on the top floor."

"Wait for me here. I won't be too long." She slid silently out of the transport and disappeared into the night.

The night watchman was not a problem. She pulled out the hollow metal tube from a hidden pocket in her cloak and loaded it with the small dart. With perfect aim, the dart hit the guard in the neck. He dropped his cigarette, grabbed for the dart, and slumped to the ground. Relieving the guard of his keys and pass card, she dragged the man around to the back of the building. Slipping on a pair of gloves equipped with razor sharp metallic talon tips, she scaled the side of the building and pulled herself onto the roof. Tossing a small metal star, she knocked out the solitary light plunging the roof into blackness. She glided noiselessly across the roof to the access door and used the keys to enter the stairwell.

Upon reaching the fifth floor, she pulled out a small disk, unlocked the door, and cracked it open. She pressed the button on the disk and tossed it inside. *Let's see how their cameras handle a magnetic pulse.* A bright flash shone through the crack in the doorway. Maripa entered the hall and saw the cameras had gone dark. *Now for the fun part.* Sticking to the shadows, she moved silently down the hallway and used the guard's pass card to enter the nearest office.

Once inside, Maripa went straight to the computer and turned it on. She plugged in the security bypass drive and watched the screen as the proper passwords and codes were deciphered and input. She pressed a few keys and bypassed the local security network, allowing her access to everything the organization had on file. *Now let's find out why Universal Charity is so interested in us.* Ten minutes later she found the incriminating files showing someone in the organization was gathering information about Karm's empire and his work with the adult DNA cloning process. Maripa downloaded the information, then inserted a second drive and downloaded the virus. She watched as the files vanished from the screen. *That should take care of their system for some time now.* She removed the card, shut off the machine, and left the office.

An orange light flashed in the hallway and a sharp pain erupted in her thigh. Maripa was thrown to the ground from the impact of the beam. She spun as she hit the floor and reached into her cloak. She tossed three metal stars at her assailant and watched him fall back, firing once more, harmlessly into the ceiling. "Kak!" she swore as she reached down to examine her leg. "Feathers!" *Should have checked more closely for another guard. I'm getting as careless as Karm.* She clenched her teeth, forcing herself to ignore the pain, and saw blood flowing freely from the wound. Using her cloak, she pressed against the hole to staunch the bleeding. Her head was spinning and her eyes were unfocused as she stood. Leaning on the wall for support, she headed to the stairwell and down to the main floor. Locating the loading dock doors, she exited the building as fast as her legs allowed and returned, limping heavily, to the waiting levicoach.

"What happened?" asked Darkon. "We heard shots."

"I got careless. There was a second guard. I never saw him until he shot me." It was hard to focus now, her mind drifting. She forced herself to stay conscious.

Darkon's face paled when he saw her wound. "We need to get you to a hospital."

"No, no hospitals. Get me back to the house. Call Karm and have him get the doctor. He can handle this. Just help me stop the worst of the bleeding until we get there."

"Alright, lie down and let me get a look at it, Squirt." Forcing himself to sound calmer than he felt, Darkon grabbed the first aid kit from its compartment and pulled out his knife. Quickly slicing up the leg of her pants, he revealed a deep gash, scorched at the edges. He used one portion of the torn clothing to wipe away the pooling blood.

Maripa gripped the edge of the seat, inhaling sharply through gritted teeth. "Careful! That hurts like a quetzel! Is this your way of getting back at me for all the times I beat you at tuttles, old man?"

"Don't be such a baby," Darkon said as he ripped open several gauze pads, placing them on the wound. "You know I let you win most of those games." he said, giving a wink.

Maripa laughed, but tensed suddenly as new waves of pain shot through her leg.

"Here, press down on this hard so I can get it wrapped." He grabbed her hand, placing it on the reddening pads. Pausing briefly, he looked up to see her face contorted in attempts to control her pain.

"Nothing to worry about, Squirt." He bound her leg with more gauze wrapping, pulling it tight. "I've seen you with injuries worse than this before. Just lost a bit of blood is all." He forced himself to smile as he continued to wrap her leg. "Remember that time you fell out of that Tark tree? We thought you broke your neck for sure. I knew you would try climbing that damned tree as soon as you were able, so I ordered the gardener to cut it down. Karm reamed me good for it, but I couldn't risk another fall like that one again. There! All patched up and ready to go. Let's get you to the doc."

He looked up and saw Maripa had slipped into unconsciousness. A quick touch to her wrist confirmed a steady, but weak pulse. "You'll be fine, Squirt," he said gently squeezing her hand. Sleep is what you need now. I'll get you home safe."

Darkon released his grip on Maripa's hand and, securing her to the seat, hurried to the driver's seat and gunned the engine.

***

Karm paced the hall outside Maripa's quarters. He wore a long blue robe and leather slippers, both covered in blood from when he took Maripa from Darkon and carried her to her room. The doctor was waiting for her and had ordered Karm out of the room. An hour later, the doctor opened the door and quietly closed it behind him.

"She is out of danger now. I've given her a transfusion and a few stitches. She'll be fine in a few days. She does need to rest, so keep her in bed for at least a couple of days."

Karm exhaled in relief and grabbed the doctor's hands. "Thank you, doctor. Can I see her now?"

"Yes, but only for a few minutes. The sedative will be taking effect soon and she needs sleep more than anything right now. I'll send a nurse over to sit with her and take care of the I.V."

"Thank you again, doctor," Karm said as he released the doctor's hands and turned to open the door to Maripa's room. As he entered, he saw the pile of bloody clothes on the floor. With an effort, he averted his eyes from them and looked toward the bed. Maripa lay there, her leg bound with bandages but otherwise uncovered. She sat propped up on several large pillows. She opened her eyes and watched as he approached.

"Well, that was a royal cluster kak," she said weakly, trying to fight the effects of the sedative.

"Don't worry about that now. Darkon tells me you got the information we needed and destroyed their entire system. I'm just glad you weren't more seriously injured."

"We're both getting sloppy," she said, wincing as she adjusted her position on the pillows.

Karm lowered his head and sat gently on the foot of the bed, placing one hand on her leg. "I know. You tried to tell me, but I wouldn't listen. Now look what I've done. You could have been killed." He carefully squeezed Maripa's leg and stood to leave. "Get some sleep now. We'll talk later."

"Karm," Maripa called after him. "This was not your fault, but we do need to talk."

Karm nodded and left the room. Darkon stood waiting in the hall. He had not changed out of the blood soaked clothes he'd arrived in. "She's a tough little gal, sir; she'll pull through in no time," he said.

"I know. Nevertheless, I never should have let things go this far. There are going to be a few changes around here, Darkon. Come to my office first thing in the morning."

"It is morning, sir."

"It is?" Karm looked out one of the hallway windows into the soft light of dawn. "Well, go get yourself cleaned up, get some breakfast and come see me in a couple of hours."

"Yes, sir." He turned and left for his own room in the north wing.

***

The monarch leaned on the table in front of him, fists clenched, gritting his teeth.

"Anything new on that break in yet?"

"No, sir," responded the General, snapping to attention. "They managed to trace our connection.

Everything at Universal Charity was destroyed before we could analyze it and one of our people was killed."

"How did this happen?"

"We don't know, sir. All security cameras were disabled and the other guard rendered unconscious. He never saw anything. They discovered a virus planted into their system wiping out all references to Karm and his interests. Any proof we may have had is gone."

"Our friends in The Faith will not be pleased with this. They think Karm has been the one responsible for blocking their attempts at enacting certain legislations they have been supporting."

"Yes, Your Majesty." The General stood at full attention. "There is one small matter needing investigation though."

The monarch waited.

"We have a photograph of Karm leaving a fundraiser a few weeks ago. The photographer was attacked, and his camera destroyed by someone who was with Karm. The photographer was smart enough to have a partner with him who caught the entire incident on film."

"And…?"

"The assailant was a young woman. We cannot find any record of her prior to a few years back when she attended The Academy. She seems to be his personal assistant, but there are some anomalies warranting further investigation."

"Find out everything you can. We need to know more about Karm, his plans, and this mystery woman."

Chapter Fifteen

Maripa felt the tension in the lab immediately. Rocker sat with two of his staff geneticists examining the data on one of the view screens.

"Another failure, gentlemen," Rocker said. He arched his back and rubbed his eyes. "It's still falling apart at the amino group bond. We need to rethink our entire approach."

"Perhaps, if we attempted something out of the heavier Halogens…"

Rocker shook his head. "No, too volatile, the reaction would be too rapid,"

"We seemed to be so close… but now?" The younger man looked to his boss for encouragement.

"We were wrong, gentlemen. The data doesn't lie. We just need to rethink what the data is showing us and see where it leads us."

"That could take months, maybe years."

Rocker pounded his fist on the table and stood up. "It will take what it takes. It isn't helping anything sitting here wallowing around in frustration. Let's just drop all of this, start acting like scientists, and get back to work." He pushed past the men and headed toward his office. He grabbed a folder off the top of a precariously balanced stack, flipped it open and rifled through the pages, examining the series of calculations it contained. With an angry growl, he threw the folder across the room, scattering the papers like confetti fired from a popper. Not satisfied with this small bit of chaos, Rocker kicked at his desk, toppling the remaining folders to the ground, adding to the debris field. Standing in the midst of this bedlam, Rocker grabbed his top crest with both hands, closed his eyes, forcing himself to regain his composure. After a few moments, he began to feel himself again and attempted to gather the papers into some resemblance of order again, only to surrender in defeat almost immediately. Returning to the doorway, he leaned his head against the frame and hesitated before opening it. "Sorry, gentlemen. I'm just frustrated and tired. You're doing a great job. This is just a difficult nut to crack." He turned to face them. "Go home, it's late. See you in the morning."

He noticed Maripa at the door and waved to her. "Be right there."

The slightly rounded hallway echoed their footsteps as Rocker and Maripa walked toward the exit. "I could use a drink," said Rocker, turning to Maripa. "Looks as if you could use one, too. Let's get away from here for a bit. How does Barto's sound?"

She stopped and looked at him, narrowing her eyes suspiciously.

"What, after all these months you think I don't know you, at least a little?" He smiled. "C'mon, we both need to get out of here and kick back a little."

She continued to scrutinize him a bit longer and then her face relaxed. "What the strix, I do need a drink tonight. But it's too dangerous to leave the compound. Let's just go to your place."

"Alright. I think I can rustle us up something to take our minds off our troubles."

Maripa was surprised to find her heart suddenly thumping somewhat harder in her chest.

A couple of hours, a little food and a few drinks later, they both started to relax.

"You know, Dr. Rocker, your actions with Alpha Corp during the Latonian uprisings were admirable," Maripa said, taking another bite of her sandwich as she nursed her third glass and brought her bare feet up under her on the sofa.

"Admirable enough to get me discharged," Rocker said swirling the ice in his drink. He was on his fourth Golden Talon, savoring the thick fruity taste of the intoxicating liquid sliding down his throat, and picked at the remaining crumbs on the plate in his lap, and caught himself noticing how green her eyes were.

"You saved the lives of one third of your unit under conditions nobody should have survived. You deserved the Royal Medal of Honor instead of your CO. If it were me, I would_have fragged him when no one was looking." She finished her drink and held it out to Rocker, shaking it for a refill.

He took her glass and filled it from the pitcher. He poured another for himself and said, "That's not quite how the court martial court saw it." He sat in the chair across from her, watching as she finished her sandwich, and kicked off his shoes. The drinks relaxed him and Rocker noted how pretty she was. A sudden feeling of guilt rushed over him and he hoped it did not show on his face, fearing another relationship might destroy him.

"There really is much more to you than one sees at first glance, Doctor."

"I do have a name, you know. Do we have to be so formal here…now?"

"No, I guess we don't. Jontar it is, then." She raised her glass to him and took a drink. "What I mean is how many Special Forces soldiers can even spell geneticist, let alone even dream of the ground-breaking research you are doing here?"

Rocker took a long drink and sat back closing his eyes. "Thanks, but if we don't start getting results soon, Karm may want to get somebody to replace me. With all of the recent set-backs, and The Faith putting more and more pressure on Parliament to cancel our permits, I can't imagine him being patient much longer." He reached up with one hand and rubbed his neck.

Maripa looked at him for a moment; she seemed to be trying to come to a decision. After a brief hesitation she stood and walked around behind him. She reached down and began to massage his temples. "Trust me, Karm will not replace you. He has faith in your abilities. How's that?"

"Mmmmm, feels good. Thanks. I hope you are right. I know we are close. All we need is just one break." His mind drifted and the nerves unknotted. *I could really get used to this. Wonder what other talents she is hiding. Oh feathers! What am I doing? It's only been a few years since her death, but why don't I want to stop?*

"And don't you worry about The Faith, Parliament, or any of the rest of the nonsense going on out there. Karm has more than enough resources to handle them." She worked her way down to Rocker's shoulders and began to dig into a particularly large knot she found there.

"Even Karm can't stand against the world forever." Rocker winced as her knuckles dug into the knot. "There's a lot of pressure to pass some very restrictive legislation on our work. The politicians won't stay loyal when the voters turn against them." He hesitated before continuing. "This is precisely why I am so concerned about Karm's intentions. Everyone I have talked to reassures me of his grand ideals and altruism, but I can't shake the feeling that something here is just too good to be true." He took another sip from his glass. "Can you honestly tell me he has no ulterior motives in all of this?"

"No wonder you are stuck. You worry too much. I have known Karm all my life. He may not be perfect, and he is probably the most secretive and mysterious person on the planet, but I have never known him to be cruel or have any ambitions beyond this grand scheme of his. Trust Karm to deal with those matters and focus on the lab. He is the perfect SOB to handle all of them." She gave one final twist into the knot and ruffled his crest.

She hopped back into her place on the sofa and sat on her knees. She took another long drink and smiled. "What you need Doctor, I mean Jontar, is a good workout every morning. It's just the thing to get the blood flowing and the mind charged. You haven't played a good game of rings in months. How about you join me at the gym starting tomorrow?"

"You play Rings?" Rocker eyed the tiny girl up and down, trying to judge her ability. "I've never seen you on the court."

"I usually practice when you are in the labs. Not much chance of anything happening to you there, so I can grab a quick work out then."

"But against me? I must be twice your weight and a good foot taller. Wouldn't be much of a game."

Maripa's eyes narrowed dangerously. "You're probably right, but I'll try to take it easy on you,"

Rocker noticed her glare and swallowed his laugh before it escaped his lips. His actual response was more nonchalant, or at least he hoped it was. "Sure, why not? I'll try anything at this point. My workouts have been pretty sporadic ever since I moved on campus. If you're sure I won't get in your way or anything."

"No problem at all. I'll reserve a court for us. How's six sound?"

"Great. Looking forward to it."

"It's settled then. I'll see you there." She set her glass in the sink and grabbed her valise. "Don't be late," she said as she opened the door.

Rocker stood to lock the door behind her. "Good night, and thanks, Maripa," he said as she walked down the path to the waiting levicoach.

He watched as she turned to wave, and then tripped on a loose stone in the path, catching herself quickly despite her slight intoxication. He laughed quietly as she slapped herself on the forehead, increasing her speed toward the waiting mag-lev.

As Rocker closed the door, he unconsciously reached up with his left hand and held the ring still hanging under his shirt. He shut the door, locked it and then headed up to bed, realizing he was looking forward to seeing her in the tight fitting Rings attire.

The game proved to be as one sided as Rocker had thought it would be…just not in the direction he had thought. Maripa's speed and agility outmatched him at every encounter. Even by the second period after he decided to forget she was a girl and half his size she always outmaneuvered him and avoided his attempts at any blocks or slams. During one of his attempted blocks she landed an elbow into his sternum. The blow was not particularly hard, but an electric shock shot up his chest, paralyzing his breath for a second or two. Streaming sweat and breathing hard at the end of the game he leaned against one wall downing a bottle of water.

"Okay, I surrender and admit defeat. Where did you learn to play like this, and why don't you own every trophy the company games give out?"

Maripa smiled up at him as she slowly sipped from her own water bottle, not showing any signs of having given him one of the toughest games of his life. "Oh, I don't compete. I use this game as one of my workouts to stay sharp." She took another sip and gave a sly wink. "You're good, though. I normally have to train against two or three others to make it competitive.

"Thanks. And on behalf of all my fellow male players, we appreciate your concern for our fragile egos. He performed an elegant bow in mock respect.

Maripa smiled again and walked off to the locker room. "See you out front. The car should be here by now."

Rocker finished his water as he watched Maripa walk away. She definitely looked good in Rings gear.

As the next several weeks passed, their games of Rings continued to end mostly in Maripa's favor, but Rocker found his own skills improving and the scores were not so embarrassing lately. They began to spend more time together, mostly having lunch or an occasional dinner.

**

Rocker leaned back in his chair, stretched, rubbed his eyes, and ran his talons through his crest. The data on his monitor continued to be a frustrating mass of seemingly conflicting information. "Enough is enough," he said aloud to himself as he rose to his feet. Grabbing the jacket off its hook on the wall, he opened his office door and called out to Dr. Contor. "I need to get out of here for a while and clear my head. Be back in a couple of hours." Dr. Contor raised a hand, waving, without looking up, intently peering into a microscope.

He borrowed the keys to a mag-lev from the motor pool and headed into town. Finding a parking spot next to the town square, he locked the vehicle and paid a street vendor for a sack of Tormund and a bottle of Kral juice. The sticky-sweet mixture, his go-to guilty pleasure, contrasted well with the sour drink. As he walked along the path, an angry voice intruded into his thoughts. Looking around, he noticed a crowd surrounding a young, grey-robed cleric. The man was gesturing wildly as he berated the onlookers. Just as he was about to turn and walk the other way, he recognized something familiar about the speaker and continued to approach.

"You are all witness to The Eternal's wrath!" shouted the cleric, wide eyed, pointing manically at those gathered around him. "He has condemned this world to oblivion because of your heresies!"

Rocker's eyes shot wide open as recognition flooded his awareness. *Crebot? Yes, of course. Feathers he's changed. By The Eternal what happened to him?*

"You have closed your eyes to the TRUTH!" Crebot continued to shout. Some in the crowd began calling back in agreement, others in disgust. "I know! I was once a sinner like you! Worse than that. I was a willing participant in the heresy of clones. My wickedness helped lead us all into damnation!" Crebot's eyes suddenly locked onto Rocker, recognizing his former professor on the edges of his audience. "And there, among you, is one of the unrepentant! Beware of his false teachings!" Crebot leveled his gaze and both arms, palms upward, toward Rocker. All eyes turned to see him, some just stared, mouths open, as though they were seeing the cursed one himself. Others took on a more menacing posture. Responding to the mob, Crebot continued. "No, my flock, do not harm this poor deceived wretch. Vengeance and retribution belongs to The Eternal. Pray instead for his salvation that he may turn from his wickedness and come to see the TRUTH."

Not waiting for any further development, Rocker turned and walked quickly back to his vehicle and returned to the lab. Shaken by the experience, he sat in the garage for a few moments, trying to reconcile the Crebot he once knew with the fanatic he witnessed today. Combing talons through his crest, Rocker exited the mag-lev, returned the keys and calling in to inform Dr. Contor he was taking the rest of the day off, and walked home.

Chapter Sixteen

"**H**urry up you two," called Darkon from the mag-lev, checking his pocket timepiece for the third time. "Karm is expecting us at the new sampling facility and we are late already and this storm is only going to get worse."

Rocker and Maripa hurried down the path from his main lab huddled together under an umbrella and climbed into the vehicle.

"Relax, old man," chided Maripa. "We have plenty of time. Just sit back and enjoy the ride in the mountains." She flashed a smile at the security chief who grunted excessively before turning around to face the front of the transport, barely concealing his own smile.

The new facility was located three hours away in a secluded valley in the Montar range, some of the highest peaks on the planet and a favorite vacation spot for the famous and ridiculously wealthy. Rocker sat, hand-in-hand, with Maripa gazing out the window as the car wound its way next to a shimmering creek. The grey sky, spitting bits of snow, contrasted beautifully with the orange foliage of the trees. Grey mountain dintars climbed and swung among the branches over the heads of grazing, spiral horned Quol. A new blanket of snow weighted heavily on the bushes along the icy stream. Occasional views of snow-capped peaks in the distance added their majesty to the scene.

Their inspection of the facility, a beautiful building constructed of native stone and designed to blend into the surroundings, proceeded as expected. The personnel proved to be highly skilled and only minor alterations to a few components and procedures were ordered.

"I think I hear a stream calling me. It won't be long before the river freezes over so I want to get in a few casts while I still can," Karm said stretching his long arms above his head, gazing longingly down the hill and the sound of rushing water. "I'll catch up with you back at The Citadel tomorrow."

Maripa laughed gently and rolled her eyes. "Alright, Karm. It's not too late for us to head back now and I have some work piling up back in my office."

"Sure you don't want to stay and rest a bit?" asked Rocker as he surveyed the surrounding mountains. "I could stand a few more hours relaxing up here, maybe spend the night if this weather gets any worse."

"Wish I could," she replied turning to walk back to the corporate mag-lev. "But there are some time sensitive matters I need to attend to. Go collect Darkon so we can get started will you?"

The drive back down the twisting road proved almost as beautiful as the ride up, even if the increasing snow did hide some of the trees. Out of the corner of his eye, Rocker caught a glimpse of something large and brown leaping in front of their vehicle, and everything vanished into a chaos of noise, flashing light, and then darkness.

As the darkness slowly grew into brighter shades of grey and the sound of running water became recognizable in his ears, Rocker opened his eyes to a world turned upside down, and an uncomfortable pressure on his hips and shoulders, not to mention the ache in his head and left leg.

"Maripa, are you okay? I think we hit something."

He heard a soft moan from somewhere nearby and, turning to locate Maripa, he realized the mag-lev was upside down, its front end dug into the creek. Maripa hung suspended next to him by her safety restraints, her crest hanging over her face, as her hands searched her body for injuries.

"I'm okay. How about you?"

"I think I cracked my head and knee a bit, but nothing too bad. Let me see if I can get out of these restraints." He struggled with the clasp, finally releasing it, allowing him to crash head first into the crumpled roof. Twisting himself around, he worked to free Maripa, catching her as she fell free. Kicking out the remains of the window, they crawled out of the wreck and fell onto their backs on the rocks of the streambed.

"Darkon!" Maripa, sat up suddenly, looking for the security chief. "Jontar, where is Darkon? Help me find him!"

Jontar fought to stand up and began searching the area. "The driver seems alright," he called out, feeling for his pulse and listening for breathing. "Just unconscious." Then he noticed the figure lying face down in the water just beyond the sandbar a few yards away.

"Maripa! Over there!" He pointed in the direction of the still form as he ran toward it.

Maripa arrived, splashing the freezing water as she ran, just as Rocker pulled Darkon's body onto the sandbar. Looking up at the frantic face of the girl, he saw panic rising inside her.

"I don't feel a pulse."

Maripa shoved Rocker aside, gathered Darkon's head into her lap, running her hands over his face and chest. Without warning, she began to scream.

"No! Not like this, old man! Not like this!" She grabbed one of Darkon's hands and held it to her face, her eyes welling up in tears she fought to keep in check. "Not some senseless accident! You were supposed to grow old and play with my children! You promised me!"

Rocker knelt behind her, gently rubbing her back as she held the body, her eyes and wordless expressions a confusion of anger and loss. He dug the communicator from his pocket, and called GenCore's emergency number.

Hours later, after the doctor's cleared them, dressed in the dry clothes one of the nurses located for them, Rocker escorted Maripa, his arm securely around her waist supporting her, up the walk to her house. Once inside, he helped her upstairs to her bedroom and, after removing her shoes and jacket, gently helped her lay down, the doctor's sedatives beginning to take effect.

"Don't leave me," she pleaded quietly. "I don't want to be alone."

"I'm not going anywhere. As long as you need me, I'm right here."

Maripa curled up next to Rocker, her head resting in his lap as sat on the bed beside her.

"Why did he have to die like that? Why him?"

"Only The Eternal knows. Sometimes there is no sense to make of it."

Maripa shivered in his arms as silent tears fell down her cheeks. "Did you know, when I was a little girl, it was Darkon who I was most comfortable with? He always seemed to have time for me. Karm was always too busy." She shifted her position to bring Rocker closer, tightening her grip. "I even discovered it was he who actually bought my birthday presents and reminded Karm of the date. He was always there for me."

Rocker softly preened her feathers with his talons as her breathing gradually subsided into the soft, regular rhythm of sleep.

The morning sun glowed warm in her room as she stirred. A sudden awareness of not being alone shocked her into full alert mode. "Feathers and Quills!" She bolted upright from her sleep, knocking Rocker off the bed. "Why are you still here?" She jumped to the other side of the bed, eyes searching for something sturdy to swing.

Struggling up from the floor, he raised his hands, palms out defensively. "Easy, Maripa," he said calmly.

"Nothing happened. You needed me to stay, so I stayed. That's all."

Noticing for the first time they were both fully clothed, and the bed was still made up, she relaxed her posture and tilted her head as she studied him, memories of yesterday's tragedy returned.

"Okay, good," he said, also starting to recover his wits. "You were so distraught over Darkon I couldn't leave you alone. I know what it's like to lose someone close, so I wanted to be here for you." He rubbed his eyes to remove some of the sleep still left over. "You want some narl tea?"

Maripa sat back down on the bed, still studying Rocker, trying to understand. "Yes, please," she said quietly, leaning back onto one elbow. "I definitely need some caffeine this morning. And thank you. I was just startled to find you here when I woke up. Sorry."

Rocker laughed, shaking his head as he left to start breakfast. "I'm just glad you didn't break my neck."

After a shower and putting on her most comfortable sweatshirt and leggings, Maripa stood quietly in the doorway to the kitchen, watching Rocker as he puttered about the room. He looked up to see her standing there, an unfamiliar expression on her face. "I was just about to call you," he said, smiling and handed her a steaming cup of the pink tea. "Breakfast is served."

"You are a puzzle, Dr. Rocker. A very curious puzzle."

"Is that good?"

"Only time will tell."

***

In the months following Darkon's funeral, Maripa became a regular visitor in the lab, this time casually leaning on Rocker's shoulder as they viewed some new data on the screen.

"Thank you for dinner last night," she whispered in his ear. "I do enjoy our talks."

"Me too," replied Rocker squeezing her hand briefly.

She watched the monitor as Rocker fed data into the computer. "I still don't completely understand what you are looking for, Jontar," she said.

"Here, let me show you something," he said, reaching for a device on the counter.

He took her hand and brought the device up to her fingers. "What are you doing?" Maripa jerked her hand away.

"Trust me," he said, holding out his hand for her.

"I don't like needles," she said, hesitantly placing her hand back in his.

"This isn't a needle, just a sampling probe. All I need is one drop of blood. You won't feel a thing." He pressed the probe against her finger and pressed the button. "All done."

"That's it?" she examined her finger. "Now what?"

"I just set the probe into the slot here and the computers do the rest. Let's take a look at your DNA." He typed in a few commands and the computer screen flashed a series of responses. After a brief exchange of prompts and commands, the screen displayed a long sequence of letters, the representation of Maripa's genetic code.

A-A-G-T-C-C-G-T-T-A-C-C-C-T-T-G-A-A-G-G-T-G-T-C-C-A-G-T-A-A-C-

Page after page of code flashed by. Millions of purines and pyrimidines, or organic compounds which make up all DNA linked together in the code representing the individual.

As Rocker watched the screen, he explained how the DNA strand worked to code for the proteins which are responsible for life.

"The sequence is the key," he told her. "Any changes to the sequence result in completely different organisms, mutations, or any number of genetic diseases. The wrong mutations in the sequence can be fatal. The problem is in the replication process. Traditional methods have relied on electricity to stimulate the mitotic processes. I believe that the electric shock is responsible for the degradation of the amino bond to the nitrogenous bases, all those letters you see here on the screen." He looked up to see if Maripa was following.

"So far so good. Keep going," she said, looking back at him and then up at the screen.

"My theories involve combinations of certain chemicals instead of electricity to stimulate mitosis and preserve the forces linking the compounds."

"Is this the Somatic Cell Nuclear Transfer process you've mentioned before? That SCNT thing?"

"Yes, exactly, very good," he said, smiling as she leaned in closer. "The problem is we haven't been able to isolate the right combination of chemicals to do the job. Every time we get close, the bonds just fall apart. Not as catastrophically as with electricity, but they still fall to pieces. It's driving us all crazy."

"And what is this here?" She pointed to a blinking portion of the sequence on the monitor.

"What?" Rocker asked as he looked where she was pointing. "Wait, that's impossible!" He grabbed the keyboard and typed in a command, watching as the monitor gave a new view, showing much more of the gene sequence at once.

"Now there are several parts blinking. What does that mean, Jontar?"

"This is just impossible." Rocker continued to feed commands to the computer and examine the data displayed on the monitor. "It can't be." He turned to face Maripa, his eyes wide with astonishment.

"You're starting to scare me, Jontar. Tell me." She sat down in the chair next to his.

Rocker took her hands in his, leaned forward and looked deep into her eyes. "You are a clone, Maripa." He paused for her to register that information. "The indicators are undeniable. I rechecked every parameter and there are no mistakes. You are a clone. How is that possible?" He let go of her hands and pulled back realizing the magnitude of what he had just said, his fears suddenly re-emerging in full force.

Maripa's mouth dropped open. He saw the confusion in her eyes.

"You're the great geneticist, you tell me!" She reached out to him, but he pulled back further.

"What's the matter, Jontar?" She hesitated, and then reached for him again. "Don't you dare do this to me…not now!"

"Maripa, you're a clone," was all he could manage.

Maripa jumped up, knocking her chair over. Her crest flamed red and her eyes hardened. *How could I have been so stupid! I knew this was a mistake!*

"Karm!" she whispered. Turning to leave she felt Rocker grab her arm.

"I'm going with you."

"Oh, no, you stay right here. I need to deal with that old man myself."

"Not on your life. I need to find out what's going on here as much as you. I'm going."

She held up her hand, blocking him. Rocker did not flinch.

"Suit yourself," she said as she turned and marched from the room. Rocker stayed just out of arm's reach as he followed her to the executive offices.

Maripa slammed open the office door, storming into the room ready for battle. "Alright, Karm, we need to talk,"

"Sit down, Maripa," Karm said as he stood looking out his window. "We do indeed need to talk."

Rocker entered the office behind her and saw the two of them locked in place. As he surveyed the room, he noticed the monitors were all showing his station in the lab. The central monitor displayed a close up of his terminal s flashing bits of genetic code.

"Is it true, Karm?" Maripa asked as stood toe-to-toe glaring up at her uncle, her fists clenched.

Karm looked at them both as he considered his options. "Yes," he replied. "Sit down, both of you. This will take some time and probably several drinks." He motioned to the chairs by the window. Shot glasses and an open bottle were already set out on the offices mini-bar.

"Well?" asked Maripa. Her eyes never left Karm's face as she sat. "I'm waiting."

"It all began about seventy-five years ago…" As he began his tale, Karm held out his left arm. His palm began to glow and an image began to form in the air above his hand.

Chapter Seventeen

Karm poured Rocker and Maripa a drink and brought them their glasses as they sat speechless.

"You can probably use this about now," he said, looking at the two of them. They took the glasses, but did not drink.

Dr. Rocker looked at Maripa, then back at Karm. He was a scientist. He knew none of this was possible. Rocker took a drink from his glass without moving his eyes from Karm's face.

"What is that device there?" asked Rocker pointing wide eyed to Karm's palm. "Are you some sort of living computer or something? What are you?"

"I told you, this is merely an implant given to me by the Skae..."

"And who, exactly, are the Skae?" asked Maripa, curling her feet underneath her as she sat.

Karm smiled patiently as he explained again about how the Skae found his DNA in the lost ship. "I realize this is difficult to take in. I will answer whatever questions I can."

"How does that device of yours work?" asked Rocker, peering at the images projected and the glow from Karm's hand.

"It's called a biocomputer and is connected to my central nervous system. I operate it by thought."

"And Bolt is what...your mentor or something?" asked Maripa.

"Much more than a mentor," said Karm smiling fondly at his memories. "He was my friend."

"This is ridiculous, Karm. How can she be a clone? The technology doesn't exist yet. And if it does, why do you need me? If you already have clones working for you, then you don't need my research. What is your game here? I've seen what Maripa can do. Are you trying to build yourself an army of super soldiers? Is she one of your prototypes? By The Eternal, Karm, what are you up to?"

"You are correct, Dr. Rocker," said Karm as he sat in a nearby chair facing them. "The technology does not exist. At least not in this time."

"Rocker shook his head and held his hands out in front of him. "What do you mean, 'not in this time.'? Either it exists or it doesn't."

"The Skae cloned Maripa, just as they cloned me, from our surviving DNA. I realize this is confusing, but some of my past is actually still far into your future."

Rocker opened his mouth to respond, but then closed it and simply stared at Karm.

"So these Skae," Maripa interrupted, eyes downcast, "have the ability to make clones. Then why didn't they just tell you how to do it instead of going through all of this?"

"They didn't invent the technology. Bolt told me they learned how after going through the wrecked ship's databanks. I don't really understand this either, but he explained that since we, actually you Dr. Rocker, are the ones who developed the technology in the first place, we are the ones who have to do it, but here in the past so they can discover it in the future. As a result, I was not allowed to bring any of the cloning technology with me and my biocomputer will not access any meaningful information on the topic. We need you to develop the technology for us now. Not for building armies, but to save our species."

Rocker dug his knuckles hard into his temples. "Do you really expect us to believe this nonsense about time travel?"

"For now, yes. Can you really offer a better explanation for all of this, other than what I have revealed? There is only so much I can disclose without changing the future to irreparable proportions. I know this is a lot to ask, but you do need to trust me on this."

Maripa dropped her glass on the floor, its contents spilling over her shoes. She stood and hit Karm with a right cross knocking him back a few steps.

"How could you? How could you not tell me any of this before now?"

She ran from the room.

Rocker stood to go after her, but stopped halfway to his feet and fell back into his chair. He took another drink and stared at the door.

"We need to talk, Jontar," said Karm as he rubbed his chin and returned to the chair behind his desk.

"Haven't you said enough?" Rocker turned to face Karm, his crest streaked with red.

"Not yet. You have a lot to think about right now. Take a few days to process it all. I will be here to answer as many of your questions as I can. "

"And what if I decide this is all some sort of colossal hoax?"

"I've read your files, Jontar. I have followed your life and your career very closely. It's no accident you wound up at the university when you did." He paused and took another sip of his drink. "I know about your mistrust of the government and your fears about the potential exploitation of your research, and I know what you have just learned has set you reeling. You and Maripa have gotten very close over the past months and now you learn the truth about her. Anyone would be conflicted and confused over it all."

"You think so, Mr. Time Traveler?" Rocker stiffened and stared threateningly at Karm.

"There is a lot you still don't know, Doctor; there is still a great deal I cannot tell you yet. Don't be too quick to judge. I am well aware of your hesitance to become involved in another relationship since the tragic death of your wife. I can't imagine how difficult it is for you to risk starting over again with Maripa, only to discover this, especially given your fears. Please believe me when I say I never anticipated you testing her blood and discovering this secret. Now you know. But what you know is only part of the truth."

"Then tell me the rest."

"Not now," said Karm. "When the time is right, but not now. You will just have to trust me for the time being."

Rocker leaned forward and the two men locked eyes. "That's asking a lot, Karm."

"I know, but you have to believe my intentions are for the best. Not only for you and Maripa, but for the entire Brin species."

"Go on."

"You're a scientist, Dr. Rocker. You believe in the evidence of your research, despite what your personal prejudices may tell you. You have a unique ability to suspend your personal beliefs and accept the data you collect. Can you do that now?" He sat on the edge of his desk and looked at Rocker, raising his brows in question.

"What do you mean? What evidence? What data?"

I know you have been asking questions about me and what people think about me and my intentions. Doesn't everything you learned from your investigations convince you of my goals for your work? I am not the monster you fear, and neither is she."

Rocker slumped, his eyes glazed over. "I just don't know."

"Trust the evidence, Doctor. Trust your instincts and I think you will discover the answer. Take a few days to think it over, then get back to the labs and continue your work. We are too close to stop now. I know you will come to the right conclusions."

"Alright, Karm, I'll admit I wasn't able to find anything wrong with what you are doing here, and I was beginning to trust you, but your story is a bit much to swallow. Do you really expect me to accept all of this?"

Karm stood, placed his hand on Rocker's shoulder. "For now, yes. There will come a time when I can tell you more, but right now I am asking for your trust. But I am probably not your biggest concern, Maripa does not give her trust easily. I doubt she has ever opened herself up to anyone as she has to you. Your reaction has been quite a blow to her, one I hope the two of you can overcome." He patted Rocker's shoulder and left him alone in the office.

The trail of destruction preceded Karm through the halls to Maripa's quarters. Overturned tables, statues, and glassware littered the carpet with the occasional tapestry ripped from its moorings. Several servants peered cautiously from behind half opened doorways. The sound of breaking glass, shattering furniture, and swearing grew louder as he approached her rooms.

Karm took a deep breath before turning the knob and entering Maripa's quarters. He saw her sitting on the floor amid the rubble staring blankly. "Care for round two?"

"Get out of here, old man, before I decide to take you up on your offer." She pulled her knees up tight, her head buried in her chest.

Karm waited silently, closing the door behind him.

"What the strix am I? Did you make me from spare parts just to be your personal assassin squad? Who are my 'parents'? And who the strix are you? You're obviously not my uncle." She stood and shook her talon at him as she faced Karm. "What gave you the right to play The Eternal with my life? Do I even have any rights, or am I just something for you to use and toss aside when you are done with me like one of your companies?"

Karm looked directly into Maripa's eyes. "I have never thought of you as anything less than my own daughter. Yes, you were brought up and trained with some very unique skills, but that was necessary. I wish it could have been different, but I am bound by history and the future and I cannot always do as I wish."

"You're not making any sense. Just go away before I decide to use some of those skills you created me to use."

"Not until I know you aren't going to do anything stupid. You know there are a great many things I cannot reveal yet. I cannot risk that, even for you. I've been saying this a lot lately, but you need to find some way to trust me."

"Ha! What gives you the right to tell me I have to trust you? You have betrayed me and everything I thought I knew." She turned her back to Karm walked to her window. "You know as well as I do about his anxiety over his work being used to create Brin with precisely my skills and abilities, not to mention his nervousness about being in a new relationship. Things were going so well. Did you see the look on his face? How can anything ever be the same again?"

"Don't underestimate him. I think he will prove to be more than his dossier. I know this has been quite a shock for you. Take a few days and think things through. If you want to continue then come back and we can pick up where we left off. It would be a terrible shame to give up on him without giving him a chance." He reached over and rubbed her shaking back.

"I saw the look in his eyes. Do you honestly believe he can get passed his beliefs on this or ever be able to feel the same way about me again?" She looked up at Karm, her eyes wide and pleading.

"I do," he said. "You just need to give him a chance. I think I know Dr. Rocker a little better than most and I trust him. Don't judge him based on his immediate reaction to such shattering news. Give him time to adjust and think things through. He will probably surprise you."

Maripa turned to face Karm, leveling her deadliest glare on him. "I do hope you are right, but don't get any ideas that I will ever trust you again, old man. I have a lot to think about and I'm not even sure I want to be part of this anymore. Just try not to get yourself killed while I am gone. Now get out of here." She shut the door behind him and went to pack her bags.

Chapter Eighteen

In the months following her time away, Maripa continued her duties as Rocker's body guard. They saw each other daily in the labs. Their conversations, polite at first, gradually grew more comfortable and they began to relax around each other again. While still far from their previous closeness, a mutual, but carefully guarded friendship grew in strength as they helped each other face the facts of their new realities. Then the results for Batch 821-b4 came in.

Batch 821-b4 began as just another promising variation of the chemical soup their current research had guided them toward. They applied it to the prepared cells the day before and left it to incubate overnight. In the morning, the lab tech recovered the petri dish from the incubator and set it into the microscopic analyzer. She then went about the rest of her work to prepare the lab for the day. An hour later, Dr. Rocker entered with Maripa close behind. She took up her post by the door.

Rocker went to his office and read the seemingly endless string of emails that had accumulated since yesterday. He watched as the rest of the staff arrived and got to work.

"Are the results from the last batch in yet?" Dr. Contor asked the lab tech.

"Yes, Doctor. I set them in the analyzer first thing. You should be able to see the analysis on your screen by now."

Dr. Contor turned on his monitor and clicked on the file labeled Batch 821-4b results. His excitement grew as he read the analysis. As soon as he finished reading, Dr. Contor leapt out of his chair and ran to Rocker's office.

"Dr. Rocker, you need to see this," he blurted out as he swung open the door.

"What's up?" asked Rocker.

"Come and take a look for yourself."

Rocker got up and followed his department chief to his station.

"Sit down and read this," said Contor, pointing to the monitor.

What Rocker saw on the screen took a moment to fully register in his brain.

METABOLIC PROCESSES: STABLE

CELL GROWTH PARAMETERS: STABLE

SCNT: STABLE

MITOTIC RATE: STABLE

DNA EQUILIBRIUM: STABLE

"Has this been verified?" Rocker asked the chief.

"Starting verification now, sir," said Dr. Contor, already on his way to the incubator to get a second sample.

An hour later, the results of the second sample confirmed the original readings. The room erupted into cheers and shouts, the geneticists hugged each other, and threw papers in the air. Tears streamed from a few eyes. Maripa could not contain herself any longer and she approached the celebrating group.

"What just happened?"

Dr. Rocker turned, saw Maripa and grabbed her up in a twirling bear hug. "We did it! It worked!"

"What worked?" she asked as he landed her on the ground again.

"Batch 821-b4. It worked; the process is stable and growing normally. There is no sign of degeneration."

"Your process works? Does Karm know?"

Rocker stopped dancing and kissed her. "Guess I better tell him." He pulled out his pocket communicator to make the call.

Maripa stood, mouth open in shock, staring after him. A smile gradually appeared, but she shook her head to help gather her thoughts.

Karm burst through the door out of breath after running all the way from his offices on the top floor. "Show me the results!" he called over the bedlam in the lab.

"Over here, Karm!" shouted Rocker.

Back in Rocker's office, they shared a bottle of Ophlam, brown and very strong, Rocker had been saving for this moment. "Of course, we need to retest an entirely new batch and send out the results for internal review, we can't risk letting the world know just yet, but the data is solid. We did it." He held up his glass to the others and they all toasted their success.

"Congratulations, Dr. Rocker. Dr. Contor, please extend my gratitude to your entire team. You might also let them know I intend to see they get a healthy bonus this month." Karm raised his glass in salute noting that Rocker and Maripa were sitting next to each other.

"I will leave you all to your celebrations now, Dr. Rocker. But will you and Maripa please meet with me in my office tomorrow morning at 10:00?"

"Yes, sir," they said in unison.

That night, as Maripa again escorted Rocker to his home, he turned to her before getting out of the levicoach. "I know things have been rough for you these past few months, and I haven't been helping matters much, but I am trying to work through it all."

She shifted her position to face him. "I know you have been and I appreciate that."

"Would you like to come in and talk?" He looked into her eyes, searching for something.

"Not just yet. Let's just take this slowly and see how it all develops."

"Alright, see you in the morning then?"

"Nine-thirty sharp." She smiled at him, took his hand and held it for a moment, but then turned away.

Rocker got out of the coach and entered his house. When the door shut, he set the alarm system and watched through the front window as Maripa drove off, his fingers absently reaching once again for the ring still hanging under his shirt. He headed off to bed, feeling a little unsteady from the celebrations and too exhausted to stay awake any longer.

The next morning at exactly ten, Maripa led Dr. Rocker into Karm's office.

Kirta looked up from the computer screen as they entered. "I understand congratulations are in order, Dr. Rocker."

"Thank you, Kirta," said Rocker, smiling through a slight headache.

"There's been a slight change in plans. He's waiting for you on the roof on the executive patio." She smiled and returned to her work.

They took the elevator to the top floor and headed down the hallway toward a large glass wall. Using her pass card Maripa unlocked the door and the two of them stepped out into the fresh air. Karm was standing by the rail looking out over the grounds of his headquarters. Nearby stood a table containing an assortment of fruits, breads, and breakfast sweets, along with three choices of juice.

"Come join me. I hope you haven't eaten yet."

"Just some juice, sir," said Rocker. "And a little food might be good, thank you."

"Maripa?" Karm looked toward his assistant. "Join us, please."

"Thank you, sir. I could use a bit of food, too."

They both sat at the table and loaded their plates with several items from the tray. After further congratulations and small talk about the cloning process, Karm cleared his throat and began to talk more seriously.

"I think it is now time to let you both in on the rest of my plans." He picked up the remote and aimed it at the glass wall of the building. The partition turned opaque, but remained blank. He pressed a couple of the other buttons, but the wall remained blank.

Maripa reached for the controller. "Let me, sir." She pressed the top button and the view came to life. "Just use the arrow keys now, sir," she told Karm, returning the device to him. The interior of a vast factory appeared. In the center of the view, the framework of a large oblong metallic vessel came into view.

Rocker stared at the image, his hand frozen halfway between his plate and mouth. "What is that?"

Karm beamed broadly. "This is the Hegira. Isn't she beautiful?"

"Hegira? Isn't that the name of the mountain where Tokal supposedly brought all those animals and a number of the ancients deep into the caverns there to save them from the comet that wiped out almost all life back then?"

Karm laughed appreciatively. "Very good, Jontar. Yes, the Brothers teach that story from the Book of the Eternal. The name is appropriate, don't you think?"

"I don't understand, sir," Rocker said, his face still contorted, trying to work out the puzzle.

Maripa's face lit up in sudden realization. "It's a rescue ship."

"Good girl, Maripa. Yes, it is! This is how we are going to save the Brin from total annihilation."

Rocker shook his head, not sure he was getting the full implication of what he was hearing. "Maybe you better start from the beginning, sir. I'm still not quite following you."

Karm stood and started to pace around the patio as he spoke; his hands waving and pointing to emphasize specific details.

"This whole planet and everything on it is doomed. We have known this for some time now, but have been unable to get Parliament to support any one strategy to save us. They believe the next one hundred years before the sun goes nova is plenty of time. They hope to pass the dilemma along to future generations. I've decided to venture out on my own to build this ship and equip it with the resources necessary to at least save our species and as many other species as we can manage."

"Keep going," said Rocker.

"A number of years ago, astronomers located a planet in a relatively nearby system so similar to Dyan'ta they think it could support life. Spectral analysis indicates an oxygen and nitrogen atmosphere as well as the presence of water."

Rocker frowned and shook his head. "What good is that? You're talking about something requiring thousands of years to reach. It would necessitate generations and a ship far larger than what you are showing us here."

"Your lab is not my only investment. While you have been trying to solve your problems, others have been developing a new method of propulsion. They call it Hyper-Ionic Drive. This new drive can get a vessel from Dyan'ta to the new planet in only eighteen years."

Rocker waved a hand toward the projection, shaking his head dismissively. "That's great, but your ship can't possibly hold all the supplies and equipment for more than a few dozen people at best. It's just not enough people to ensure enough genetic variability for long term survival."

"And that is where your cloning process comes into the picture. I don't intend to send more than sixty people on this voyage. In addition to the crew, there will be DNA samples for tens of thousands of individuals placed into storage. Once the ship lands on the new world, we named it Raince'to, those sixty can use your technique to awaken the samples and grow whole cities of people. The sixty will act as surrogate parents, educators, and government for the developing civilization. Even the crops and animals they'll need can be sent as DNA samples."

Rocker and Maripa just looked at each other in silence, unable to move as they absorbed everything they just heard.

Finally, Rocker shook himself out of his stupor. "Are you sure this will work?"

"Some of the greatest minds on the planet assure me it will. And what alternative do we have? Even if the engines fail or the planet turns out to be uninhabitable nothing is lost that wasn't doomed already."

Maripa stared wide-eyed at her 'uncle'. "It's amazing, Karm. How soon will it all be ready?"

"There is still a lot of work left to do. We still have some final testing of the engines before they are installed. There are all those DNA samples to collect and you, Dr. Rocker, need to work on reducing the size and weight of your equipment so they can be carried in the Hegira. Then we have to notify Parliament and allow them to help select the crew so we can get the launch permits. And let's not forget logistics and loading all of the supplies the crew will need during the flight. I anticipate at least three, maybe five, more years before we can launch."

Maripa's eyes scrunched in thought, one hand cupping her chin, a taloned finger tapping her cheek. "Eighteen years is still a long time. How will the crew stay sane being stuck inside such a confined space for so long?"

"I have one of my engineering and pharmaceutical divisions working on a cryogenic suspended animation process. The entire crew of sixty will not be needed to operate the ship en route so most of them can sleep in rotating shifts of a year or so."

"Looks as though you have thought of everything," said Rocker. "I'm speechless."

"Not quite everything, Doctor. I haven't been able to stem the growth of The Faith, and their growing influence poses a real threat to the project. That is why I have been operating under such tight security all this time." Karm stopped pacing and looked at them both directly. "You are now my co-conspirators. Nobody else knows what the others are doing, and each group is operating under the impression their work is for something entirely different. If anything were to happen to me, it will be up to the two of you to see this thing through. Are you with me?"

Rocker and Maripa looked across the table at each other. They each gave a nod in silent agreement. "We're in," they said together. "Just tell us what we need to do."

Chapter Nineteen

"**W**elcome, gentlemen." Dressed in the more casual outdoorsman attire he preferred when staying at The Citadel, Karm greeted the members of Parliament as they arrived. He kept this castle as a place to impress people when he called them to meetings he considered particularly vital.

"I am sure you are all tired from your journey, so I have had rooms prepared for each of you. We will not meet until tomorrow, so make yourselves comfortable and enjoy the facilities here."

Maripa met Karm as he re-entered the castle. She dressed in her usual business suit and flat shoes. "Scans completed, sir," she said. "There weren't any weapons, but a couple of them did have hidden recording devices. We neutralized them so everything is secure."

"Thank you, Maripa. Shut down the cell tower to eliminate phone connections to the outside and we will be ready to begin. And have your investigations completed by tomorrow afternoon. I will want to meet with you once our guests leave."

"Already done, sir." Maripa proceeded to walk the guest wing of the castle ostensibly to check on the welfare of the guests, but always alert for security risks.

At the evening gatherings, she took up her station in her office and monitored the cameras. Seeing nothing more than the usual small talk and occasional Parliamentary maneuverings, she called the security chief. "All yours now, chief. Call me if anything happens."

"Yes, ma'am," he replied. She retired for the evening.

The new day dawned warm and clear. The grounds behind The Citadel, what Karm referred to as the backyard, was filled with large white canopies. Servants carried dozens of trays of food to the waiting steam tables under two of the awnings. Folding chairs, good enough to be used in most homes as fine furniture, were assembled under the main shelter, ten to a table. A podium stood at the front, flanked by loudspeakers. Microphones placed on each table allowed anyone wishing to speak to be heard by all in attendance. A large screen hung from the ceiling behind the podium. The support poles all contained electronic dampening devices guaranteed to prevent any discussions held inside the main tent could not be overheard even a few feet away on the outside. Nevertheless, storm clouds brewed as the meeting started.

Karm strode to the lectern and raised his arms as he addressed the assembly. "Welcome again, gentlemen. We have vital business to discuss today so let's get to it."

Gardak, the Prime Minister, stood, approached the podium, and addressed the gathering, "It has come time to address the threat we are all facing from The Faith and their constituency."

There was a general buzz of agreement, but a few members sat silently. One of the elder statesmen present rose to speak.

"We have never encountered anything like this, Karm. Only four years ago The Faith was a back country fringe group with no real organization. Three years ago, after the announcement of new brain cloning technology, they suddenly gained a following. Pareth was able to unite people behind the belief that science, cloning in particular, was threatening to destroy belief in The Eternal. He was able to have enough of their followers elected to office so they could disrupt the progress of some of our bills."

"Yes," Karm interrupted, "but that was only a minor inconvenience. We were able to control those who opposed us"

"That was then, Karm, but no longer. The movement has grown in popularity among the people and a significant number of Parliament is being swayed by it. There is even a new effort to have members of parliament sign a loyalty oath obligating anyone who The Faith supports to oppose all legislation not approved by them."

Karm waved his hand in dismissal. "A loyalty oath? Nonsense!"

"Not at all, sir," continued the elder statesman. "If they don't sign the oath, and follow through with their votes, The Faith will remove their support and replace the uncooperative representatives in the next election. Many of our members have discovered just how powerful The Faith's followers can be. We lost a dozen members to them in the last election with several dozen more threatened next year. Some of us have been around long enough to resist them, but we will be powerless before long if The Faith is allowed to continue."

Karm surveyed the room and saw most of those present nodding in agreement. "So, you all feel this way? I will have to call in some of these junior members and assure them of my support so that they won't have to fear re-election."

Another representative stood to speak. "That won't work. The Faith controls voters in too many districts now. The masses are afraid for their souls. Since we released word of the supernova, many Brin who never put much stock in such beliefs have found solace in rediscovering religion. The Faith has convinced them that joining is the only way to gain the protection of The Eternal when the end comes. All of your money and power cannot overcome the blind belief of these individuals."

"So it is their way or nothing? What do they want so we might be able to come to a compromise with them? There must be something they need that we can use to gain the upper hand."

"No, sir. Nothing," replied the first statesman. "We are dealing with matters of faith here. They are so convinced they are guided by The Eternal, that any compromise is seen as a denial of their beliefs. This is a sort of holy war for them and they intend to win at all costs." He spread his arms, palms upward, in a helpless gesture, and sat down.

"Rather than allow for any other opinions or values, they would risk a holy war which threatens the extinction of the entire Brin race? Karm slammed his fist on the table. "That is insane."

"Not to them, sir. It is strictly a matter of faith. The security of their souls being with The Eternal in the afterlife trumps any losses here in the physical world. Besides, time is on their side. Dyan'ta's destruction is not likely for another one hundred years. However, changes in solar radiation output will rise to lethal levels even sooner. All of us will be long gone by the time Dyan'ta is destroyed."

Karm walked to the podium and pressed a button on the control panel. Kirta retrieved a stack of papers from her table at the back of the tent. She distributed these to each of the legislators in attendance and left. As each man read the information before him they turned to Karm in disbelief.

The Prime Ministers hands trembled as he read the document. "What is this? Where did you get this material?"

"My people have access to much more accurate equipment than any government facility, gentlemen. I have employed the best minds on Brin for many years now and given them essentially unlimited resources. They are developing some amazing devices. What you see is the end result of an exhaustive study I initiated two years ago. We don't have a century. There are only ten years left before our sun explodes and destroys everything. I can provide the raw data for you and your own experts to examine if you wish."

The assembly erupted in confused and angry shouts. Many of the dignitaries reached for their communicators, only to discover all communications cut off. Their offices, loved ones, bankers, whomever they attempted to contact, impossible to reach. Others gathered in small groups, arguing over the best means of dealing with this now imminent disaster. He let them process the shock and then continued to address them. "This information does not leave these grounds, gentlemen."

The Prime Minister raised his hands and asked for quiet. "Of course, we will want to examine the data more thoroughly, but let's suppose for now that your analysis is correct. Wouldn't it be better to openly enlist the resources of the entire planet to try to find a solution?"

"You know how the public would react," replied Karm, scowling and grasping the lectern with both hands. "If news of this were to ever leak out the resulting panic would be global and devastating. We cannot allow that to happen."

"But the populace has a right to know!" shouted one of the officials.

"No, actually, they do not," said Karm. "The public cannot be allowed to know any of this. Think about it. Do you really want to live out the last ten years of your lives with global rioting and chaos? Why should anyone follow the laws if the consequences no longer matter? Look at what happened in the aftermath of the revelation we had a hundred years left. However, I do have a plan. Now if you will all sit down and listen, I will tell you what I've been preparing." He pressed another button on the control panel and the screen behind him lit up with a series of images detailing each point as he spoke.

"As you know, Dr. Rocker has solved the problem of cloning individuals so there is no longer the trouble with DNA degradation."

"Releasing that information was foolish," shouted another of the council members. "The protests against cloning were bad enough before, but now we may all lose our jobs. I've had to hire extra security to protect my home from the mobs."

"The next elections are the least of our concerns now. As I was saying, Dr. Rocker is now perfecting the equipment for that process to make it more portable. Once this is accomplished, we will collect DNA samples from as many Brin as possible in the next five years."

"And just what good will collecting DNA samples do us?" asked one of the representatives. "The DNA will be destroyed along with everything else. The whole damn planet is going to be incinerated."

"Not if we are no longer on the planet. My engineers and manufacturing plants have been constructing a spaceship to take the samples to Raince'to. You all remember the news a couple of years back, about the planet that was discovered only twenty light years away? We will send the DNA samples there, to be reanimated and the Brin will survive."

"And just who would reanimate them?" asked one of the legislators.

"I propose we choose a group of sixty individuals based on the requirements for developing a colony. The ship can only carry so many together with the supplies and equipment they will need. We will enlist construction workers, farmers, ranchers, engineers, medical personnel, teachers, and scientists...all those who would be essential for organizing and building colonies on the new world. The only individual I must insist on is Dr. Rocker. Nobody understands his process better than he does. If anything were to go wrong then he will be the only one able to fix it. Otherwise the entire operation will be a waste."

"Lies!" Came a shrill cry from one of the tables near the front. "The Prior is right! We cannot listen to the scientists and their supporters any longer!"

The delegates erupted in pandemonium. "Sit down, sir!" "Who let this maniac in?" "What is he talking about?" Some tried to restrain the legate, but he shoved them away and continued to yell. Security pushed their way through the crowd attempting to reach the deranged individual before he could disrupt the gathering any further.

"Only The Faith tells us the truth of things!" The wild-eyed representative reached inside his belt and brought out a long thin blade. He raised his arm as if to throw the weapon at Karm, who stood less than fifteen feet away. There was a quick flicker of reflection and the would-be assassin screamed, grabbing his hand and dropping the blade. A silvery metal star protruded from his bleeding wrist. Maripa appeared as if from nowhere, subduing the maniac onto the ground. As soon as the other guards reached them, she handed the offender over and helped escort him from the area. The entire incident was over almost as quickly as it began.

Karm called out to his panicking guests. "Please! Everyone, please listen to me!" A faint blue glow radiated out from Karm, encompassing the entire gathering, and then fading before anyone could notice. The delegates slowly calmed and listened. "Everything is under control now. You can all resume your seats now. It's all over and nobody is hurt."

"You expect us to stay here after what just happened?" asked one of the dignitaries when his composure returned.

"Yes, I do," Karm said as calmly as he could manage. "The matter before us is too important to allow a brief incident to bring us to a halt." He looked over his audience and reassured them as best he could. "We have all faced dangerous situations before. That is the nature of our jobs. Let's all remain calm, take a moment to take a deep breath, and continue."

The Prime Minister rose to speak. "I agree. If what we have just learned is true then we cannot waste another second." His look dared any of those gathered to contradict him before continuing. "You seem to have been at this for quite some time already, Karm. How do we know you can accomplish all of this in time?"

Karm tilted his head, touched one talon to his temple and smiled. "We are ahead of schedule actually. The ship will be ready for launch in four years if necessary."

"Be that as it may, how can we possibly keep all of this under wraps for so long? And how can we hold off The Faith long enough to accomplish everything in time? You know how strong they will become in the next election. You may have bottomless pockets, but even you are not above the law. They will see to it that all of your work on cloning is stopped and destroyed."

"Leave The Faith to me," Karm said, pointing his finger at each of the men in turn. "All you need to do is overlook what you now know about the sun. Keep the government running and keep those anti-cloners out of mischief as long as you can. The survival of our species depends on this."

"What do you plan to do, Karm?" asked the Prime Minister.

"Nothing you need to worry about, Gardak. Everything is strictly legal, but the less you know the more you can deny later." Karm gave the head of Parliament his most politically correct smile, and then addressed the entire assembly. "Gentlemen, I think we have covered everything we needed to. You all know your jobs. You are welcome to stay for the dinner being prepared. However, your bags have been packed and brought out to vehicles that will take you back to the airport after you have eaten. Unfortunately, I will not be joining you. I have another pressing engagement to attend to. Please return the information sheet to my secretary as you head out." Karm left the room and servants entered to direct the guests to the awaiting meal in the adjoining canopies. A few moments later, Karm joined Maripa in the security office where she was watching as his guests talked over their meal. "We will discuss the attack later," he said. "In the meantime, how's it going out there?"

"They are understandably disturbed, but I don't think we will have any trouble with them. They definitely do not want worldwide anarchy erupting so they are clamping down on anyone who they think might leak the information." She pointed to a small group on the monitor huddled together in a heated discussion.

"Good. Monitor them until they leave and then join me in my office." He satisfied himself with one more look at the monitors and then left.

Two hours later, Maripa caught up to Karm in his third floor office. "All of the guests have left. I don't think we will have any trouble with them. The Prime Minister had private words with each of them to reinforce everything you told them. He also made sure nobody will gossip about the incident either. The last thing he wants is for more rumors about The Faith to get out."

"Alright then, what do you have for me? How could that idiot have gotten past you?"

Maripa stiffened and refused to lower her eyes. "I have no idea. He must have been keeping his alignment with The Faith a secret. It may even be something he has been only on the fringe of, until he broke under the strain of what you told him today."

What about the knife? People just don't walk around carrying concealed weapons."

Maripa let out a quick smirk. "You'd be surprised. Many in power carry just that sort of thing in case of an attack, especially with the turmoil on the streets these days."

"If this is such a common thing, then how did he evade your security searches?"

Her scowl deepened and her voice grew strained. "I take full responsibility for that breech, sir. It would seem my staff needs a refresher course in their technique and a long talk about diligence in their duties."

Taking a deep breath, Karm let the tension ease from his body. "No matter now. At least nobody got hurt. Is he still here on the grounds?"

"He's being held under guard and in restraints in the cellar. I didn't want to call the police until we had a chance to talk. I know how sensitive the information he now has is and I didn't think you wanted to lose custody of him just yet."

"Good. I can arrange it so he forgets everything that happened to him over the past two days. He'll simply wake up in the hospital and have no idea why he is there, or how he got there." He held up his hand and a deep orange glow hovered in the air above it.

"One more item though, sir." Maripa place a folder on his desk. "It is much worse than we had thought, sir." She began to pace the floor as she talked. "It appears His Majesty is being recruited by The Faith."

"Are you sure about him? If they join forces they could upset things badly."

"Yes, sir. We have confirmation from several of our insiders indicating one of The Faith's bishops visited the Monarch and is a frequent guest at many of their functions since that initial encounter. Brach and Lerit, sorry, Pareth, have also met privately on at least two occasions we know of. The Faith's bank accounts have substantially increased in value since this meeting as well."

"Brach is not the most religious man on the planet, Maripa. He and the Prior are still brothers after all."

"Possibly, he's being very accommodating to them so the two of them could be collaborating. They are accomplished politicians and very intelligent so it would be hard to tell their real motives. I will want to maintain surveillance of His Majesty just to be sure."

"Of course. Do what you need to do to find out what they are up to. We need to know if this is just a ruse or a real alliance." Karm flipped absentmindedly through the report Maripa gave him. "What is this about a possible military faction?"

Maripa stopped her pacing and approached Karm's desk. "That's the most disturbing part of it all. It appears the Monarch's 'conversion' has had a profound effect on the military. Entire regiments are, under direct orders, joining The Faith. Some, however, appear to be joining willingly. No indications yet if The Faith's leaders intend to use them as enforcers, but why else would they recruit so many so quickly? We need to keep a very close eye on this."

"Well, so much for my little vacation down by the stream." He sighed and threw his arms up in disgust.

***

His Majesty sat at his desk stamping the royal seal to a series of documents he had just signed when his seneschal entered the room.

"The General has arrived as you commanded, Your Majesty."

"Good, good, send him in," replied Brach as he continued to press the stamp into the soft wax.

The General, in the red and gold uniform he always wore for an audience with the monarch, marched into the room, clicked his heels to attention, and saluted. "Your Majesty. "You summoned me?"

"Yes, General. I have a rather unique request of you."

The General's eyebrows rose slightly, "Request, Sire?"

"Command actually."

"Yes, Sire."

"You will need to resign your commission immediately, General." Brach looked up from his documents and watched the General's reaction.

He hesitated only a moment, his stance wavered slightly, and then he recovered. "Of course, Sire. May I be permitted to ask why, Sire?"

"You are going to join The Faith, General." Brach paused to allow the impact of this statement to take full effect. "The prior and I need to keep open our lines of communication and you will serve that need as our liaison. To convince my brother of your neutrality, you will need to sever all official ties to me. You can tell him your honor requires you to be completely neutral if you are to perform your new duties to the best of your abilities. After some time has passed, you can begin to develop an interest in The Faith and eventually become a devout follower."

The General frowned as he thought this over. "I believe your brother would accept my honorable decision to sever ties to you in deference to my duties as a liaison, but I sincerely doubt he would ever believe my conversion to his religion."

"A lot of Brin are doing many things out of character these days, my old friend. You could always claim to succumb to the inevitability of our fate and a desire for peace at the end."

"I suppose that would be at least reasonable, Sire, but I still have my reservations."

"I have complete faith in your ability to be convincing," Brach replied with a dismissive wave of his hand. "Within the next year or so you will fully convert to

The Faith, join the ranks of the clergy and, in time, become the cause of my final conversion and rise to the rank of Archbishop." Brach watched the General's face carefully as he said this.

"Forgive me, Sire, but I am a military man. I have no interest in religion. I would make a very poor follower and unlikely to rise at all in their ranks." He maintained a stance of rigid attention, but his eyes mirrored the questions in his mind.

Brach smiled and gave a laugh. "Don't worry General, this is a special assignment and I believe only you can pull it off. All of my other attempts have failed, but I don't think they will be able to resist having you as a convert. Especially when you tell them that you have my ear and should be able to complete my conversion as well."

The General paused briefly to consider the matter. "I would be more inclined to believe your brother would see me as too great a risk."

"True, but his bishop's might be persuaded and, if we are lucky, they might not be able to resist the publicity of me becoming one of the faithful, despite his reservations. And we really do need your services as our go-between. You are the one person we both can trust to be honorable and trustworthy in this position."

"Of course, Sire. I would never betray such a confidence."

"There is no doubt of the extreme danger in this ruse, so while this is officially a command, I would feel better knowing you are willing to put yourself in such a position."

The General's eyes brightened and he stood at full attention again. "I see, Sire. I understand. When do I begin this campaign?"

"I will let my brother know immediately, General," said Brach. "But, give it a few weeks, then start spreading some rumors about your growing interest in The Faith.

Maybe you should start having a few religious visions and hear some voices compelling you to convert. Let one of them approach you first and then you can begin. In the meantime, we will need to work out a way to communicate secretly while you are among them. Any further questions?"

"No, Sire." The General snapped another salute, turned on his heel and marched out of the room.

Chapter Twenty

Rocker and Maripa stared dumfounded at Karm. "What do you mean you are going to meet with The Faith?" asked Rocker. "You can't seriously want to surrender yourself to them like this." The sound of the river flowing by was the only disturbance as the three accomplices sat under one of the pergolas Karm had built near his favorite fishing holes. The lunch prepared for them remained only partially eaten as they argued.

"At least demand that the meeting be held at some neutral site, not in the palace," said Maripa. She stalked around the structure flailing her arms in frustration. She bent down, picked up a stone and hurled it into the water. The plunk startled several birds downstream sending them noisily into the air.

"You both know how powerful The Faith has become in the past year," said Karm. He sat calmly chewing his sandwich, as he watched the pair vent at him. "My support has become inconsequential in the past year. Those fools have the power to demand whatever they want now. And once the elections are over they will be in a position to severely threaten our project. We need to switch strategies."

Rocker leaned up against one of the support posts and shrugged. "What strategies do we have left? They know they have us by the crests. Why even bother calling you in for this meeting?"

Maripa moved next where Rocker stood, took his hand, and leaned against him. "They are probably just waiting to arrest you on some trumped up charges. Or worse yet, have you assassinated. I need to go with you."

"Oh, you are going with me," said Karm, "but not for the reasons you think. You're simply going as my personal aide. I still have appearances to maintain." He gave them both a wide grin and winked. "Besides, I might still have a trick or two up my sleeve."

"What are you planning, Karm?" asked Maripa.

Karm grinned from one auricular to the other. "Patience, my dear."

He stood and walked over to join his co-conspirators. "I wouldn't want to spoil the surprise." He turned to watch the river. A slight breeze rustled the leaves of the trees above them.

"I hate surprises." She frowned and tensed her grip on Rocker's hand.

"Dr. Rocker, I believe you have some important work to get back to in your lab. I would not want to keep you from it any longer." He shook Rocker's hand, and slapped him on the back. "Don't look so glum. We have them right where we want them."

Rocker shook his head and tried to smile. "Whatever you say. Just don't get yourselves killed with whatever you've cooked up."

"You just go back to your lab and get that equipment down to size in time. You let me worry about the politicians." He turned to Maripa. "Shall we head into the bertal's den?" He helped them pick up the remains of their lunch and led them back across the open field to The Citadel.

In a matter of hours, Karm and Maripa arrived at the palace. The sun beat down from overhead in a clear teal sky, casting only the shortest of shadows. The white marble exterior of the palace gleamed in the bright daylight. The beauty went unnoticed by Maripa as she stepped out of the levicoach. Her attention was riveted on the crowd gathered in the plaza before them. "Oh, strix," she muttered. "We don't need this right now. Where are the palace guards? Why don't they clear these idiots away?"

"Clones are an abomination to The Eternal!"

"The Faith is the only way to salvation!"

Several dozen individuals marched back and forth on the plaza shouting and waving their signs while dozens more watched the spectacle from afar, including, as Maripa now noticed, five of the palace guards.

"I don't like this," she warned, taking Karm by the elbow. "We need to get out of here right now."

"Don't be so worried, my dear," said Karm. "I don't think we are in any real danger here and I absolutely must attend this meeting. I have no doubt you will keep me perfectly safe if the need arises."

Maripa stared at Karm, unable to think of anything to say as he started toward the protesters. The crowd grew louder and closer as they approached, but only continued to shout their slogans. She led the way through them, occasionally needing to elbow a pathway through the mob. They soon exited the throng without incident and continued to cross the plaza leaving the protest behind them.

"You see," beamed Karm. "I told you there was nothing to worry about. That was just a show put on for our benefit by our hosts."

Maripa rolled her eyes and stalked on ahead, muttering a great number of curses under her breath.

As she and Karm mounted the stairs, guards opened the massive doors to allow them entry. Servants took their cloaks and showed the visitors to a waiting room. Karm helped himself to a plate of fruit from the table already prepared with a variety of drinks and foods for them. Maripa was not hungry.

He sank into one of the large overstuffed chairs and ate silently as they waited to be summoned. She sat in her chair watching the doorways.

An hour later, the door to the back of the room opened and a retainer dressed in the red and gold silks of the palace officials, walked in. "His Majesty will see you now."

Karm and Maripa rose, straightened their clothes, and followed the functionary down a long hallway. He stopped before a door about two thirds of the way down the hall and opened it for them. Karm squared his shoulders, put on his best politician's expression, and entered the room. Maripa followed, scanning every face and corner in the room.

A large rectangular conference table dominated the room. A dozen men dressed in plain brown and grey robes sat around the table with the Monarch at its head. All eyes turned to watch the pair as they took their seats at the foot of the long table.

"Thank you for the opportunity to meet with you today, Your Majesty," said Karm as he sat.

"Silence, heretic!" shouted one of the younger robed figures. "We have summoned you here. This is no opportunity for you to exploit." He shook his pointing finger at Karm.

Pareth raised his head and turned to the young man. He said nothing, but all those present grew deathly quiet. The young man sniffed and lowered his hand.

"No need to be disrespectful, brothers," Brach said as he turned to look directly at the young enthusiast. "Civility is the hallmark of intelligence and breeding. I am sure we can all agree to handle matters without shouting and insults."

Karm nodded his head in agreement and waved for the Monarch to continue.

"As you know, we of The Faith disapprove of what you are doing in your work with cloning." Several of the robed men murmured and thumped the table in agreement.

"We have called you here to ask you to stop this unethical and immoral experimentation."

Karm's eyes widened in perfect innocence, his arms spread in supplication. "I am a bit confused here, Your Majesty. Have I broken any laws? Mine is a privately run corporation. I take no government money. I have no bank loans. The way I see it I can do as I wish with my money and my businesses."

Another of the robed men jumped to his feet and pounded his fist on the table. "You have broken The Eternal's laws, heretic! The laws of decency and Brinality! You are creating abominations in His eyes and will burn for it unless you repent and cease immediately."

"That will be all, brother Crebot," said Pareth with deadly calm. His grey eyes burned into the zealot.

"I apologize, Prior," he said between clenched teeth as he sat back down. His crest continued to blaze red.

The monarch allowed a moment of quiet and then proceeded, "No laws have been broken as of yet, Karm. However, once the next elections occur, The Faith will control a majority in Parliament. With my support we will pass legislation that will outlaw cloning of anything other than replacement organs. If you do not cease immediately, you will find yourself in front of a magistrate."

"Do you realize how many Brin I employ? Hundreds of thousands would be out of work if you pass those laws. How long do you think you can remain in control with that many angry voters?"

"Acceptable losses," said one of the robed men. "As more of the masses join The Faith, the more they will see the necessity of eliminating this abomination. We will stand behind those who support us."

"I see," said Karm. "I guess I have no choice then." He looked at each of the men at the table and lowered his eyes. He placed his hands in his lap and his left palm began to glow.

"No, you do not. We will give you two months to dismantle your operations that deal with the cloning of individuals and…"

Karm's voice was calm and quiet, yet reverberated with authority. "You misunderstand me, Your Majesty. I mean that you have left me no choice but to do this the hard way." He turned to Maripa who opened a blue folder and handed the papers inside to each of the men at the table.

The monarch bolted upright in his chair, sputtering in astonishment. "What is this?"

"Information you need to know before you pass final sentence on my work." Karm gave the men a few moments to read the paper.

"This is heresy! Scientific trickery!" shouted Crebot, the young zealot. "I was once deceived by the spell of science. I understand their treachery. Only the Eternal can reveal the truth to us, not the unbeliever scientists. We cannot trust them."

"Abomination!" shouted others as they tore the paper into pieces.

"Brothers," said Pareth in a calm, but firm voice. He looked directly at Crebot. "We will listen to all voices here. Be still."

The young zealot did not reply, but his face contorted in anger as he returned the Prior's stare.

"I assure you it is not a trick. You are welcome to share the data with any of your scientists if you wish. We have less than ten years, not the one hundred or so as we had previously believed. Life on this planet will become unsustainable long before the sun goes nova." Karm stood and leaned on the table in front of him. "You can see the data regarding the alarming rise in cancer rates as well as severe changes in our climate. The data I undeniable. Matters are accelerating more quickly than previously thought. Time is running out. I caution you, however, be careful what you do with this knowledge. Revealing this to the world will cause nothing but panic and rioting. Nobody will have any control over anything."

The monarch looked up from his paper. "How is it you have discovered this when our best scientists have not?"

"My equipment is much better than anything the government has access to. All of your funding cuts to scientific research have left you far behind recent developments in the private sector. You are welcome to send some of your best men to my facilities to check the validity of the data."

Pareth then raised his hand for quiet and spoke. "Then it appears your experiments with cloning are a wasted effort after all, Karm. Why continue with them now? Why not join us and save what is left of your soul?"

"I have no intention of discontinuing my work, Pareth. I have nothing better to do in the years we have left and I think it is better to keep everything as normal as possible. As long as the people are kept busy they're less likely to lose control."

"Then if, as you claim, we only have ten years left, I believe our time is best spent fulfilling the wishes of The Eternal. Our duty requires us to stop your experiments. The people are sure to turn to us out of need for comfort in their final years. We will provide for their souls. You have nothing they want."

"I was afraid you might come up with something along those lines," Karm handed a red folder to Maripa and she passed out the documents it contained.

"Now what?" asked the monarch. He picked up the paper and began to read.

As the figures at the table absorbed the incriminating facts in front of them, many began to stir and shift their gaze from one to another.

"My staff has been busy for the past several months collecting data on The Faith. We have gathered quite a bit of information about your finances, political connections, investments, even background on your entire leadership. It appears many of you are in for a great deal of explaining about your personal finances. Not to mention the lesser known doctrines of your so-called religion regarding concubines, tax advantages and special privileges allowed your leadership." He paused to look at each of the robed men around him; none of them returned his scrutiny. "This is only a sample of what I possess, gentlemen. Do you really think the society will turn to you once this is leaked?"

"This is blackmail!" said the young zealot, but he remained seated and did not look up at Karm.

"Yes, it is, young man. Have no doubts about my intentions or willingness to follow through with it if I am interfered with in any way. Moreover, that includes any threats on my life, or the life of anyone in my employment. Any attempt to disrupt my efforts in any manner will result in the automatic and immediate release of everything you see before you. All of your hypocrisies will come crashing down right on top of your heads."

"Come now, Karm," said the monarch. "A simple pre-emptive public act of contrition and purging of the ranks of The Faith will only instill greater admiration in the masses for our cause. We can lay the blame on a few sacrificial scapegoats, revealed by our own efforts. The people will love us even more for keeping our own house clean. What else do you have, Karm? We are shepherds of the hipi and you are the ulfur stalking in the shadows. Who will they believe?"

"Perhaps," said Karm. "That might work for some, but what if your charade leaves shadows of doubt in the rest? I'll take my chances and go right on with my work, Your Majesty, but I will let you in on a little secret." He smiled and sat back down in his chair. "Maripa, are you ready?"

"Just a moment, sir." Maripa opened her case and removed a small holoprojector. She pressed a few buttons and the machine beamed the image of a silvery spaceship to the center of the table.

"This is why I cannot allow you to interfere with my work, gentlemen. I am going to save the Brin." Karm proceeded to outline his plans for the spaceship and the clones. He told them of the sixty crew members required to man the ship and set up the colony on Raince'to. He explained about the new type of propulsion system powering the ship and how it could reach another planet in a matter of four decades rather than centuries. The holoprojector flashed images and data related to each of the areas he discussed. Then the images dissipated.

"In summary, gentlemen, if left unmolested, I can complete this project and be ready to launch in four or five years. If you try to stop me, you condemn our race to extinction."

The young zealot looked up at Karm. "What you propose is not salvation. You want to send abominations to the new world and not True Brin."

"That is your doctrine, not mine, and certainly not one belonging to most of Brin. Especially if I release the information I just showed you."

Pareth turned to Karm and raised his hands spreading his arms wide. "If what you say is true, then what is in it for us? What is our incentive to agree to your plans? Why should we not take our chances and see just how strong our influence over the populace is rooted?"

Karm smiled as he leaned back in his chair. "I am prepared to make one small concession, Pareth. If I am allowed to continue my efforts without interference of any kind then I will set aside one twentieth of the crew slots for members of your clergy. You will have the opportunity to be the only religion on the planet."

"A planet of soulless abominations," said the zealot.

"Now, brother," said Pareth, waving his hand at the younger man, his eyes narrowing, studying Karm. "Let us not be so blinded by doctrine. We are open to new instruction from The Eternal. If we do not attend to the needs of this new flock then who will? Perhaps by our ministrations we can bring souls to the soulless. But I do not see how we could possibly manage such a feat with such a small percentage of the crew. I believe one third to be a more acceptable number for our holy work."

Karm raised an eyebrow and brought his hand to his chin. "A third of the crew seems a bit presumptuous to me. I will agree to ten percent."

The Prior folded his hands, clacking two talons together, and surveyed his brethren with a glance. "Yes, ten percent would be acceptable to me as well."

Karm smiled at the men around the table and raised hands to the monarch. "You see? New opportunities for everybody. Are we in agreement then, gentlemen?"

"I think we have no choice, Karm," said the monarch. "You will keep us informed of your progress and allow periodic inspections of the ship and supplies?"

"Of course, Your Majesty, but on my terms alone. This is, after all, still my money and my organization. Let's not forget that I also control the largest manufacturers of military hardware and software. Do you think for one minute that I would forget to put in place a means of controlling all of your forces? With one call I can either shut down or take complete control of your entire army."

"Very well. We are in accord." The monarch rose and left through his private entrance followed by his brother. The others remained in their seats as Karm and Maripa exited the room.

The sun cast much longer shadows now as it sunk lower in the sky. The protesters confronting their arrival were gone. Karm and Maripa walked down the stairs outside the main palace entrance. The melodies of songbirds competed with the cacophony of those carrying out the affairs of state. Karm stopped as he reached the levicoach waiting for them and looked around.

"My, what a beautiful day," he said as the chauffeur opened the door for them.

"How does it feel to be the smat who ate the kedi?" Maripa said once they were on their way.

Karm smiled at Maripa and reached into the refrigerator for a bottle of Champagne and two glasses. "You didn't think I was going into that den of thieves to surrender, did you? I thought you knew me better than that." He popped the cork and poured them each a drink.

"You planned all this?"

"Of course. I have been five moves ahead of them for the past two years. Go ahead and call your boyfriend and tell him to stop worrying." He reached into his pocket to pull out one of his violet pills and downed it with a quick gulp.

"Boyfriend? We're getting along at this point, but I'm not so sure I am ready for anything more just yet. I know he is still trying to come to grips with his feelings for me while dealing with the guilt he feels over the death of his wife." She took a long drink and looked out the window.

"Give him time, Maripa. He'll come around. Have a little faith." He winked as she looked back at him.

"And what makes you so sure they won't double cross you?"

"You forget my advantage." He held out his glowing palm. "I tapped into their brainwaves and electronics. If any of them makes the slightest move to cause us problems I can make sure he is removed and kept quiet. The Brothers of The Convocation do not want to risk their positions so they will keep everyone in line."

"You can do that? Access their thoughts?"

"Yes. I only did it as a last resort, but it was necessary. Now, make that call."

***

Back in his offices Brach could release the seething hatred he forced himself to control during the meeting.

"How dare that insolent, egotistical, blackmailer! How dare he threaten me!"

Rampaging through his private office, waving his arms, shouting at the portraits of his esteemed predecessors, sweeping everything from the surface of his desk, he raged on.

"How could you let Karm gain the advantage like that?" demanded Pareth, grabbing his brother by the shoulders, bringing them nose to nose.

"This is not over. I will see Karm rotting in the deepest dungeon I can find."

"Don't let stupidity compound the mistake," said Pareth, disgustedly shoving Brach away. "So long as Karm holds the upper hand, we must at least appear to go along, while we search for a weakness we can use to our own advantage."

Brach stormed over to the decanter nearby, poured himself a goblet of wine, and downed it in one swift gulp, spilling large portions on his shirt in the process. "I know that, you idiot," he grumbled, wiping the excess wine from his chin. "It galls me to have to play this role in the game. Rest assured I will find his sstrix's thin point and crush him with it."

Pareth studied his brother for a moment before coming to a decision. "Just don't let your emotions get the better of you again, brother. Karm is a dangerous adversary. We cannot afford any more blunders. Let him have his moment for now. His fall will be that much more satisfying in the end."

Three hours later, their plan to bring down Karm was complete. Brach went to his desk and pulled the cord to summon The General. "Alright, Karm," he muttered to himself. "You threw the gauntlet and have the first blow. We will see who is still standing at the end."

Chapter Twenty-One

*This is ridiculous. I can't keep going back and forth like this. I love her, but...*Rocker shook his head and rubbed his eyes again. The clock told him it was three in the morning and he was staring into the refrigerator. He grabbed a juice carton and a container of two-day-old left-overs. Drinking from the carton he stumbled to the kitchen table and sat looking out into the darkness. He was startled by a loud knock at the door.

"Good, you're still up," said Karm as he walked past Rocker into the kitchen.

"What the strix are you doing here? It's the middle of the night!"

"And we're both wide awake. We need to talk," Karm said as he produced two bottles of whiskey. "Where are the glasses?"

Rocker opened a cabinet and pulled out two large tumblers and added some ice from the freezer. Karm filled both glasses with an unsteady hand and handed the one with less to Rocker as he sat himself down in the rickety chair.

Karm took a long sip. He spilled some of the drink onto the table as he set it down. "I'm getting tired of waiting for you to grow up, Jontar. What is wrong with you? Don't you realize this was an even greater shock to her than it was to you? She's been trying to get her life in order but keeps stumbling over you and your damn issues with clones."

Rocker's eyes widened and he took a deep gulp of the amber liquid. "I don't see what business this is of yours. You may be the boss, but this is personal."

"The strix it is. Things are starting to move faster now and I need Maripa back at her job without all these idiotic distractions. I can't afford to have her wondering about what you think about her in some critical situation. One mistake at the wrong time could get us all killed." He refilled both of their tumblers, spilling even more in the attempt.

Rocker swallowed half of his drink in one quick gulp and, BANG! Slammed his glass back onto the table. "So, that's it. You don't really care about her, or me, or anybody. It's always just the mission and the plan. I've finally accepted the fact that you aren't going to use my research for some nefarious plot to take over the planet, but you're just a clone so maybe you can't really feel anything for others, at least not the way us non-clones do. But I'm flesh and blood, a TRUE Brin. I can't just ignore my feelings."

"Alright then, explain those feelings to me," said Karm, tightening his grip on his glass as he took another drink and topped off the glasses again.

"What do we really know about clones? Do they love or feel commitment to others the same as the rest of us? How long will they live? How resistant are they to disease? Can they mate with a true Bin and have children or are they sterile? You two are the only samples in existence. We don't know anything about your kind at all."

Karm leveled a steady glare at Rocker, as if measuring him. "Come now, Professor, you don't expect me to buy that, do you? You're too good a scientist for that to be what's really bothering you. Out with it! The truth this time!"

Rocker jumped out of his chair, knocking it to the floor behind him as he stalked off to the other side of the room. He stood shaking and silent before making his final decision. "Alright," he shouted. "If you really need to know…I'm afraid!"

Karm studied him a bit longer, then softened his tone and replied. "Afraid of what?"

"You know how she is," said Rocker waving his arms around him. "Always jumping out of one fire into another. She's already been shot once from what I've heard. What if she gets killed trying to protect one of us next time? How do I live with that? I don't know if I would survive another loss like that."

He gripped the edge of the sink and stared out the window into the dark night.

"What if she wakes up one morning and decides she is no longer interested in this little 'experiment' with a real person and leaves? How could I survive being rejected like that again?" He stopped suddenly and stared at Karm, his body shaking.

Karm reached out and gently placed his hand on Rocker's shoulder, leading him to a chair by the table. "Your wife didn't reject you, Jontar. She died. There's nothing you could have done. Your research has saved hundreds of lives from a terrible disease, but it came just too late to save her. It's a horrible reality of medicine. You cannot keep condemning yourself for it."

"I should have worked harder. We were so close to the cure."

"Nobody could have worked harder. You may be the finest geneticist on the planet, but you're not omnipotent, Dr. Rocker. We both know your difficulties over her being a clone are just a cover-up for the real issue. You lost one love to disease. Do you want to lose another to ignorance and fear?"

Rocker covered his face with his hands and leaned on the table. "No, I don't."

Karm finished his drink and stood to leave. "Maybe you should consider that as well during your self-examination." He closed the door and left Rocker alone with his thoughts.

The sun was just starting to light up the horizon as he sat pondering this dilemma. Unable to settle his mind on the issue, he stood up and went upstairs to shower and dress for the day. At the mirror he noticed the gold ring hanging on the chain from his neck. He held the band in his fist for a moment, then removed the chain from around his neck. He laid the ring inside his top drawer, patted it gently, and slowly closed the drawer. He finished dressing and met Maripa at the waiting levicoach out front. She smiled as he walked up to her.

"Good morning. Sleep well?"

"Yep, the full four hours. Pretty good these days." He bent down to give her a kiss and got into the coach. "You're looking lovely today."

Maripa rolled her eyes and laughed as she got in behind him. Then she looked closely at him and noticed the missing necklace. "Did something happen last night?" She asked, pointing to his neck.

"Karm paid me a visit," he said, nodding his head. "He helped me come to grips with a few things I've been struggling with and I think I've come to some decisions… about us…and a great many other things. We need to talk."

She hesitated before continuing, knowing this was shaky territory. "I know you have been struggling with your feelings for me and the guilt over your wife's death. All your agitation over me being a clone was just a convenient excuse. I've been willing to wait for you to figure it out, but I was starting to worry about you." She patted his arm and waited as he gathered his thoughts.

"I need to exorcise some old ghosts before I commit to anything more. Can you be patient with me while I do this? He sighed and turned to face her. "It may take a while."

"I know, and yes. I believe you will work it out. At least Brach and Pareth are keeping their side of the bargain and have left us alone." She turned away to look out the window and sighed. "Just don't take forever. We really don't have much longer, you know."

Later that afternoon, Rocker visited the engineering labs to check on the progress of their latest designs for the miniaturized electrophoresis equipment. The lab was a typical engineer's playground. Several lab benches were scattered with electronic gizmos that flashed and made all kinds of noises. Other benches held robotic arms of various sizes and designs being tested to grab, lift, turn, drill, and virtually any other motion imaginable. One had to watch their step in the lab because of the various robotic vehicles skittering across the floor performing their intricate pirouettes.

Rocker scanned the room and located the lead engineer. "Nebitt, strixo!" he called out as he crossed the room carefully, stepping over one of the maneuvering robotic carts. "Looks like you have a few new toys here to play with."

Dek Nebitt was monitoring one of the electronic devices, adjusting some dials to alter the read out, which Rocker saw only as lines on a wiggling graph. He quickly looked up and waved, but returned his focus to the screen and dials.

"I suppose you want to see the latest designs on your gel things?"

Rocker knew better than to correct Nebitt concerning the name of his equipment. He purposely said such things just to annoy others. It was one of the engineer's joys in life. Nebitt was a genius and had multiple advanced degrees in Chemistry, Physics, and Electronics. Engineering allowed him to put his genius to practical use. It was what he often referred to as "The only game worth playing."

"Yep. How are we on the Mark 5? Did you solve the connectivity issue?"

"We'll know in a minute," replied Nebitt. He set down his gadget and turned it off. "Let's go take a look." He led the way to another bench where other engineers were stationed. As usual Nebitt was frequently distracted and veered off in random directions to check on several other projects under way. "You can see the progress with our coolant system here," he said, adjusting a handle to reduce the cloud of vapor escaping from one of the containers. "Watch yourself here, that stuff is pretty cold."

"You've overcome the timeframe problem? We can keep the samples cold for the duration of the journey?"

"Absolutely!" Nebitt replied. "Solved that one a few days ago. I was going to send you a report today."

A loud whistle and a mechanical clang caused both men to jump. "Feathers and Quills! Not again!" cried Nebitt. "I thought we had it this time."

"Should I ask?"

"Just a problem with stabilizing the water purification system. As you know, we're trying to shrink it down another thirty percent. There's still a few technical glitches to work through, but nothing we can't handle." They watched as two other technicians ran over to the offending equipment and began flipping switches to turn off the mechanism.

After making inspections at a few other locations they finally arrived at their original destination. Nebitt approached one of the men at the bench and asked, "Are you finished testing the Mark 5 yet?"

"Just now, boss," said the man. "Everything looks good. Moving the connections to quadrant 4 solved the problem as we thought. We should be good to go on the final reduction now."

"That's great. How about the pressure tanks?"

Nebitt waved his arm indicating another corner of the lab. "Oh, we figured them out yesterday. We got them down to specs and they're holding just fine."

"Wonderful! Looks like we will make it after all. I should have known better than to worry. You are the miracle man."

"Tell that to Karm and get me a raise," replied Nebitt, "I could really use another lab and a dozen more engineers. "Oh, mutes!" he shouted. He took off running back to his bench and grabbed his machine, madly turning dials.

"Just send me the prototypes when they are ready for field testing," Rocker called out to Nebitt as he left the lab.

Rocker had to hurry. He was nearly late to his weekly briefing with Karm. At least the jog across the commons helped clear his head. He bounded up the stairs to the administrative offices and headed to the elevators. He reached the top floor and Karm's office with five minutes to spare.

"Welcome, Dr. Rocker. You're just in time." Karm waved him over to the mini bar and poured them both a cup of tea. "How's your work coming?"

"Just fine. We've solved the connectivity problem and the coolant tanks are ready for final trials. Those were the main difficulties left to overcome so we should be ready in plenty of time."

"Good…good. Exactly what I wanted to hear. Come over here and sit down." Karm led the way to the fireplace and sat on the sofa. Rocker followed and settled into the heavy chair. Karm pressed a button on the control panel in the arm of the sofa and Maripa entered through the connecting door to her office.

"Good afternoon, Jontar," she said as she handed Karm a folder.

"Hi, Maripa." The two exchanged smiles and then she turned to return to her office.

Karm smiled as he observed the not-so-subtle body language between the two of them and started to comment, but changed his mind and opened the folder instead. "Good news on all fronts. The ship is a week ahead of schedule and the collection of DNA is gaining steam across the globe." He tossed the folder down onto the sofa next to him and reached for his tea.

"I just had my DNA collected a couple of days ago," said Rocker. "I told them mine wouldn't be necessary since I was going to be on the ship in person, but they said something about wanting to use my DNA to help calibrate their system. I'm not an engineer, but that makes sense, I guess. The CAT scan surprised me though. Since when are scans part of DNA sample collection?" Rocker sipped at tea and watched Karm for any reaction.

Karm waved his hand as if brushing away flies in front of his face. "Just taking precautions, Doctor. We need to be sure we don't miss any genetic defects that could cause problems later on. The scan is set to look for flaws in the neuro-pathways indicating potential genetic diseases of the nervous system. It is an experimental device cooked up by one of the divisions so we are field testing it."

"Why wasn't I informed of this? I will want to see the specs on it as soon as possible."

"Of course, Doctor, I will have them sent to your office. No need to worry about it, though. It is a harmless procedure and we just want to see if it can be of any practical benefit."

"I still want to see the specs."

"You will have them on your desk tomorrow. Now, about those coolant tanks…"

Chapter Twenty-Two

The monarch had little time to indulge in falconry these days, but this particular morning he woke up with a complete apathy toward paper work and a burning desire for fresh air. He pulled the cord by his bedside summoning his seneschal.

"Yes, sire," said the servant upon entering the room. "How may I serve you this morning?"

"Cancel my morning appointments and have my Tal readied. Tell the royal falconer to meet me in the stables immediately after breakfast and tell the cook to prepare a traveling lunch for us."

"Shall I notify the Captain of the royal guard as well, Your Majesty?"

"Yes, but tell him to join me without any additional guards. I need to get away from all of this for a while. The last thing I want is a crowd of noisy guards blocking the view and scaring off any prey."

The servant bowed and left the royal bedchambers. Two hours later Brach was pounding through the forest on the back of his prized Tal, a large black animal specially bred for hunting. The beast covered miles of terrain without tiring, using long, powerful strides, claws on all four legs chopped at the hard-packed dirt of the path they followed. Its scales shone bright in the morning sun, golden eyes with the deep red vertical slit irises, a sign of champion breeding lines, flashing brightly as he ran.

"I had almost forgotten what this felt like," he said happily to the royal falconer who rode beside him. "I can almost feel the pressures melting away." Brach held a large hooded grey and black striped bird with a broad speckled tail on his heavily gloved left arm. "Let's see what we can stir up over the next rise." He spurred his mount into a lunging gallop, removed the hood and launched his raptor into the air. The Captain following behind at a discrete distance.

As they rode, Brach and the royal falconer discussed various techniques of training different species of birds of prey for the hunt, new trends in the sport, and pros and cons of different styles of equipment. The monarch particularly enjoyed the heated discussions of their preferred species of birds, and his own ideas for new breeding combinations, most of which the older, more traditional falconer discounted with something approaching derision.

As the morning drew on and approached the lunch hour the trio found a clearing to make camp and prepare lunch.

"A good hunt, Your Majesty," said the falconer. He pulled this morning's catches out of the sack he carried them in and laid them out on the grass.

"Yes," agreed Brach admiring the day's catch as he rubbed down his Tal. Six Blue-Frilled Smats, the four winged birds that migrated through this region every year, three Mot-Mots, a common yellow striped burrowing rodent with dark grey fur, and even one large Red-Tongued Grek, prized for its iridescent scales and savory meat.

"They'll make a fine supper for tonight." With great skill, he skinned and gutted the game, cutting off several small pieces for the falcons who had done the actual work.

As they sat eating their lunch, the Captain abruptly jumped to his feet and grabbed his sword. "Men approaching, Your Majesty."

"How many?"

"I count three, Your Majesty. Looks like the new Archbishop."

"Well, there goes a beautiful day," Brach sighed. He stood up and brushed off the grass sticking to his trousers and shirt, trying to make himself at least somewhat presentable.

The Archbishop arrived astride an only slightly less magnificent Tal, most likely bred from the same stock as those in the royal stables. He wore the red and gold colors appropriate to his station. Somehow, even the muted colors and simple fabric looked regal on the man. He always reveled in the ribbons and medals decorating the uniform he wore when he was known as The General, so he contrived to have the garments fitted in such a way that they displayed subtle refinements, yet conformed to the rules of The Faith.

"Good afternoon, Your Majesty," he said as he dismounted, handing the reins to his companion.

"Congratulations, Archbishop," he called out as his co-conspirator reigned in beside him under the trees. "I never doubted for a minute you could do this." They dismounted to stretch their legs and walk the animals a while. Come, tell me what our 'friends' in The Faith are up to."

"Thank you, Your Majesty. I think you will be pleased by what I have been able to learn."

Brach removed the hood from the bird of prey on his gloved hand and launched it into the air. "Tell me, then, are our partners in crime really behaving themselves after Karm's ultimatum?"

"For the most part they are, Your Majesty." The new Archbishop adjusted his riding habit and removed the golden skullcap signifying his rank. "Even with the majority in Parliament since the last elections they are too afraid of Karm. They definitely will not propose any legislation that interferes with his endeavors. They do keep discussing strategies for increasing the number of their followers on Karm's escape vessel. And there is still the matter of a small group of extremists within the organization trying to push for legislation outlawing cloning in any form, even organ replacement."

"Should we worry about them?"

"No, Your Majesty. We should probably keep a close watch on the young zealot named Crebot. He seems to be the most radical and outspoken of the group. But the Brothers have been able to curtail him so far."

"As long as they are still under control and just sit around discussing ideas we have nothing to worry about. We should speed up our own efforts to get our people on Karm's ship in greater numbers. Maybe we can..." The arrival of a messenger diverted his attention. The courier handed an envelope to the Captain of the guards, their only companion.

"Sire," the guardsman rode up beside them and reached out to hand Brach a sealed packet. "I am sorry to interrupt, but you told me to let you know as soon as the messenger you were expecting arrived."

"Send him over here right away." Brach said, examining the papers. "You probably want to see this, Archbishop. This might be just what we have been waiting for."

"Are you sure it is wise for this man to see us together, Your Majesty? What if word of the true purpose behind our hunts leaks out?"

"Don't worry, my friend. This is no mere messenger. He is one of my most secret agents and knows his life is forfeit is he reveals anything."

After looking through the stack of photos and other papers the messenger delivered, the monarch passed them over to The Archbishop. "Are you sure this is accurate?" he asked the messenger.

"Without a doubt, sire. My men have been using the new QK4300 system to recover the data and enhance the images from cameras surrounding the Universal Charity buildings. This is unquestionably what we suspected all along."

"Excellent. Leave these with me and go pick up your voucher from the seneschal before you return to your assignment." He picked up several of the papers and tossed them in the air. "We have him, General! We finally have him!"

"Is this who I think it is, Your Majesty?"

"Karm's mysterious young attendant caught in the act!" He whistled, summoning his falcon to return. Once the bird was safely hooded and tethered again the party returned to the palace. Once back in his quarters Brach summoned his seneschal. "Get Karm in here first thing in the morning." When the servant departed, Brach poured himself a large goblet of wine, sat behind his desk and smiled as he swirled the golden liquid in the glass. "Now it's my turn to make him squirm."

Chapter Twenty-Three

"His Majesty will see you now," the doorman said and stood beside the door that led into the monarch's most impressive reception hall.

The palace reception hall was a showcase for all of the trappings of royal status. Clear crystal cases displayed numerous jeweled ornaments worn only during the highest of ceremonial affairs. Grand portraits of the past seven hundred years of the royal lineage hung on the walls, appearing to judge all who passed before them. Tall windows of intricately designed colored glass depicted the great historical moments of the monarchy. Karm strode nonchalantly down the passage, apparently unimpressed by the show of opulence. Maripa followed close behind, watching warily for any sign of threat. A thick, heavily embroidered carpet muffled their footsteps. At the far end of the room sat the royal monarch on a tall back chair, reminiscent of the throne, behind a grand wooden desk, heavily carved with the symbols of his office, all raised on a two tiered marble dais. Two small simple chairs sat empty in front of the desk. Brach himself wore a military uniform with a deep green and gold-bordered sash showing off perfectly the multi-colored ribbons and jeweled badges displayed there.

He motioned for them to sit.

"What can I do for you, Your Majesty?" asked Karm.

"Do you remember the break-in and murder at Universal Charities a few years back? Terrible thing. One guard injured and another killed. All of their files sabotaged." He watched Maripa for any sign of nervousness, but she remained cool and reserved.

Karm rubbed his chin with two talons, his eyes searched the ceiling as he appeared to think. Maripa sat motionless. "I seem to recall something about it. But, as you said, it was a few years back."

"I think you should look at these." The monarch handed Karm a folder filled with papers and photographs.

One of the photos Karm examined showed images of Maripa pulling a man's body alongside the Universal Charities building. Another showed her on top of the roof next to the roof access door. The images were highly pixelated and dark, but her face was unmistakable. The papers provided time notations and code references linked to the various photos. Karm closed up the folder and placed it back onto the monarch's desk. He looked up at the monarch, but there was no defiance in his eyes.

"So now what?" Are you prepared to shut down our last hope for survival?"

"Nothing so dramatic, Karm. After all, since our scientists confirmed your findings I have no choice but to accept our fate. I do not, however, need to accept your choice of who travels on your rescue ship."

"What do you want, Brach?"

"It's really very simple. I want total control over the sixty members of the crew. I decide who goes and who stays behind." Brach placed both hands on the desk and leaned forward. His face was hard and his eyes cold.

"And just what is your plan? Have you let your brother, the Prior, in on your discovery?" Karm dropped his hands into his lap. His left palm glowed.

Brach smiled conspiratorially. "No, Karm, why don't we keep Pareth out of this for now. You and I are in agreement as to how dangerous too many members of his phony sect could be to this mission. So I want half of the crew to be my people. My name will top the list as will several of my family. The remaining half, other than a small handful of representatives of The Faith, will be the necessary scientists and technicians. You will supply me with the dossiers of your top people and I might even be persuaded to accept some of them." Brach paused for a moment and sat back, crossing his arms. "You, this young lady here, and your Dr. Rocker will definitely not be going anywhere."

"And what is to stop me from halting all work on the ship?"

Brach pointed at Maripa. "Any delays or falling behind schedule will result in this saboteur's immediate arrest, trial, and execution for murder. I will also expose your complicity in the matter ensuring that the public's trust in you vanishes." Maripa sat rigidly in her chair. Her face held under strict control. Her eyes bored straight into the monarch.

"You will allow my inspectors on site and they will have access to all of your data. Any interference or attempts at subterfuge and she suffers the same fate."

"We're going to all die anyway. What difference does it make if she, or any of us, die now or in a couple of years? You're going to have to give me more than this if you want my cooperation."

"And what will it take for you to play along?" The monarch's jaw stiffened, his crest bristling at the affront to his ultimatum.

"You need to agree that the three of us get on the ship."

Brach considered the options before him, then a cat-like grin grew as he extended his hand. "All right. If I allow you and your friends on board, I control the entire operation. Agreed?"

"Agreed. How do you intend to keep this from the Convocation?"

"You let me deal with them. They have been valuable pawns, but they are losing their usefulness lately. I am still the monarch here and even they are not immune from my royal decrees."

"So it was a scam after all? Another one of your political maneuverings?"

"As they will soon find out to their displeasure. I think this session is over. I will send my people in a few days. Be certain they are well informed and supplied. I will send for you if I need you again." He reached for the cord and summoned the seneschal.

Back in their coach Maripa finally spoke. "I fouled up. I not only got myself shot, but I endangered the entire operation." She sighed and turned to look out the window. "I trusted you, Karm. You told me you had them all under your control. I thought you could see their plots and protect us. Guess I was wrong."

"Don't be so melodramatic." Karm was smiling. "I am amazed that this took so long. I had to practically spoon feed them everything."

"What?" Maripa jerked upright and snapped to face Karm in the seat next to her. "You planned this? You wanted them to know what I did." Her jaw dropped.

"Of course. You don't think those cretins could actually outmaneuver me at this point, do you? Everything is going exactly as planned. I need them to feel in control so they won't snoop around too much." He reached out and took her chin in his hand, turning her face to his. "As long as they feel they have won, they won't be plotting anything too extreme. This was always part of the plan."

"All right," she said, raising her hands to rub her face, then turning again to stare out the window. "But remember, you're pushing the limits with all of us."

Chapter Twenty-Four

Two months later, Rocker decided he was ready for their talk. "Do you think Karm will give us a few days at The Citadel?"

Tilting her head, Maripa greeted him with one raised, questioning eyebrow. "Good morning to you, too, Dr. Rocker."

"Sorry, my thoughts are pretty scattered today. Good morning," he leaned over and gave her a hug and resisted the urge to give her a kiss, not wanting to startle her with such a move. "What do you think? Can you get away? Is The Citadel booked for anything the next few days?"

"I don't think there would be a problem. What's going on?"

Rocker turned and held her small hands in his. "Not here. Talk to Karm and see if we can get out there tonight. We need to escape and be alone for the things I need to say."

Maripa felt a cold chill run up her spine and she shivered. "Is everything okay? You're making me nervous here."

"No, it's all good. I just think we need to talk in private and The Citadel is about the most secluded place in the world. Is that all right?"

"Fine, I'll play along. I can arrange it for the rest of the week. Have your bags packed and ready to go by six tonight."

"Good. See you then." Rocker gave her a quick kiss and jumped out of the levicoach as it stopped in front of his labs. He turned to wave as he entered the building and then disappeared inside.

Maripa raised her hand and touched the cheek where Rocker's lips had been. Her brows furrowed, her head tilted, as if trying to decide something. She exited the coach as it arrived in front of the executive building.

Later that day, Rocker left the lab early so he would have time to pack and prepare himself to finally vanquish the last of his demons. Maripa grabbed a quick bite to eat and packed her own bags before calling for a driver to take them to the airport. She had one last drink to settle her nerves.

"You sure everything is good between us?" she asked as Rocker climbed into the mag-lev. "You're killing me with all this secrecy."

"Absolutely. Don't worry. I just really want us to be alone when we talk." He put his arm around her shoulders and tried to reassure her.

When they landed on The Citadel's airfield Maripa saw a levicoach waiting for them. The mansion windows glowed warmly in the night and servants appeared at the door as they arrived. A dinner was prepared and ready for them in the smaller dining room often reserved for intimate meals. Their conversation remained on the safe topics, a recent Rings match, progress in the lab, the weather, anything to avoid what they both wanted most desperately to discuss; their current relationship status.

"Would you join me for a walk?" Rocker asked when they finished eating.

"It's a nice night. Why not?" She searched his face for some clue to the mystery of what he was thinking.

Rocker and Maripa walked along the path that led back into the woods along the stream. They paused in a small meadow, enjoyed the warm air, and watched as the full moon rose over the tree tops. "I want to apologize to you for being a first class quetzal," said Rocker as he looked up into the night sky. "I got so paralyzed by my own fears I …I don't know how exactly to explain it, but every time I tried to talk with you, all I could think about was how hard it would be to lose somebody I cared about again. I know it was all in my head …"

Rocker hung his head, shoulders slumped, hands stuffed inside his pockets, "I know you have every right to walk away, but can you ever forgive me?"

Maripa stopped and faced Rocker. "You hurt me, Jontar. You abandoned me when I needed you most. It's not easy to get over something like that. It took me a long time before I even felt comfortable being in the same room with you. But now I have come to grips with the situation and I think I can."

He turned his back to her as he spoke. "Her death nearly killed me and I didn't know if …well, let's face it; your job here is not exactly the normal routine of a personal secretary. I guess I used the clone thing as an excuse and took it out on you."

She walked around to face him and looked into his down-turned eyes. "Tell me what you want to say."

He hesitated for a moment, arguing with his own thoughts, then with a deep sigh, made his decision. "I love you." He grabbed her hands and looked back into her eyes. "It took me far too long to finally…oh, feathers! Can you forgive me? Do you still want me?"

Maripa threw both arms around his neck, pulled him tight and kissed him, tears welling in her eyes, her heart pounding in her chest, nearly toppling both of them to the ground.

Breaking the kiss, Maripa gave him a straight right to the shoulder sending Rocker off balance. "You had me scared muteless!" she yelled at him. "I convinced myself you wanted to try to end it all between us. I wasted hours trying to come up with all sorts of arguments to convince you how wrong you were." She moved slowly into his arms and planted another long deep kiss lasting for several minutes, then stepping back, punched him in the shoulder. "Does that answer your stupid question?"

Rocker grabbed Maripa and lifted her off her feet in a bear hug, returning the kiss. They fell to the ground still in their embrace.

"I have been waiting for this for a long time, Jontar," she said as she gasped for air. "I do love you. I have for a long time now. I don't know what I would have done if you decided to leave me. I am a trained killer, you know."

Maripa's crest ranged through an array of colors, mirroring her unfamiliar jumble of emotions. She shivered at his touch. The two lovers reveled in each other as they became one.

"That was worth waiting for," Maripa said as she gazed into his eyes. Her fingers played in his crest which turned a deep blue. The cool night air washed over them, distant sounds of the night creatures echoed in the forest around them.

They spent the next few days at The Citadel exploring all of the ways the two lovers could enjoy the many different rooms of the mansion.

The time soon came, however, when they needed to return to the real world of the labs and their duties. When the plane landed back at the airport they saw Karm waiting for them standing by the coach.

"Welcome back," Karm said as they approached. "Just looking at the two of you I don't think I need to ask how things went." He smiled and shook Rocker's hand then placed his hand on Maripa's shoulder.

"Everything went just splendidly," Maripa said as she slid into the levicoach.

"So, you two solved your problem?"

She smiled at her surrogate father, taking one of his hands in hers. "Yes, we did. You don't have to worry about us any longer."

Karm gave Maripa a hug. "I never doubted you for a moment. I'm just glad everything worked out. I may be your boss, but I'm also your 'uncle' and, though it may not always seem like it, I do want you to be happy."

She simply smiled in response and took Rocker's hand.

Maripa suddenly wrinkled her brow and, with squinted eyes, turned to Karm. "Why are you meeting us out here at this late hour? Is everything alright?"

"Oh, yes, everything is just fine. You two aren't the only ones who can take time off now and then. I just flew in about a half hour ago and decided to wait for you to arrive and give you a ride home."

"Where did you go?" asked Rocker.

"Back out to the desert. The accommodations in the cabin are not as splendid as The Citadel, but I didn't want to disturb you two, and I can completely get away from it all out there."

"How do you stand it? I would go crazy out in the middle of that miserable sand pit with nothing to do and no place to go. What's the attraction?"

"I enjoy the solitude. The Citadel has become far too public and accessible lately. The land out there is beautiful in its own way, and remote enough to avoid any distractions. I do miss the river though."

"To each his own, I guess," replied Rocker and he turned his attention to Maripa.

"Don't listen to a word he says," she chided. "The cabin, as he refers to it, is more rustic, but still a mansion by most standards. Fully staffed and very comfortable."

Karm's face took on its more normal stern and business-like demeanor as he changed the subject. "This may be a bad time to ask, but is everything ready for an inspection? The monarch sent a message telling us his team of inspectors will arrive here tomorrow morning. We want to impress them, but not allow them to see anything we don't intend for them to see."

"Everything should be fine, Karm," Maripa replied. "I've been anticipating an inspection for some time now and directed our people to set up the networks to hide anything of real importance. Fake files and menus are in place and populated with a heavy mix of reality and imagination. Security measures are set to prevent any intrusions, but without looking as if they are blocking anything. Some of the software the network people came up with is phenomenal. Far superior to anything the inspectors could possibly anticipate. Everything should look absolutely real to the monarch's men. I will check with my people as soon as we get back just as a final precaution."

"Excellent," Karm said, relaxing back into his seat.

Maripa turned her attention back to Rocker. "It's late. The labs are probably shutting down now so why don't we drop you off at home and I will join you for dinner after I check in with the office. It shouldn't take long."

They spent the night together for the first time without fears or doubts about their future. However long remained for them would be spent together.

The next morning, Karm waited in his office. He watched through his window as the inspection team arrived. "Time to begin the games," he muttered aloud while downing the last of his juice. "Let's see who blinks first." Grabbing another pastry, he went to the wall map of his empire and removed the gold pin from the Latonian Desert just as the intercom lit up.

"Your ten o'clock appointment is here, sir."

"Send them in, Kirta." He stood to greet the inspectors as the five of them walked in. Each was dressed in the latest business fashion and carried a briefcase.

"Welcome gentlemen. It's a pleasure to have you here. How would you like to proceed? We are at your service today." Karm shook their hands and directed them to waiting chairs.

"Thank you, Karm," said the lead man. "My name is Belcor. I have an agenda here that lists everything the monarch wishes us to see today."

Karm accepted the paper and read it carefully. "This is quite a lot for one day, gentlemen. We should probably get started." He pushed the intercom button on his phone again. "Kirta, send in the guides for our guests."

The door opened and in walked five more men dressed in somewhat more expensive, impeccably tailored suits. Each was wearing badges identifying them as GenCore security personnel.

Karm directed his attention to the guides. "Gentlemen, you are to answer any and all questions these men have for you. Please conduct them to wherever they wish to go and grant them access to anything they need. I have provided you with all the necessary passcodes and access cards. Withhold nothing, interfere with nothing. Do I make myself clear?"

"Yes, sir," each of the men replied in unison.

"I hope that is satisfactory," he said turning his attention to Belcor. "My staff is preparing lunch for you back in this office at 1:00 so you may ask me anything you want at that time. If you need me before then, simply tell your guide and I will be contacted immediately. Have a good day, gentlemen. I know you will find everything in order."

Karm shook their hands again and opened the door for them as they left. He returned to his desk and activated the monitors on the wall. Maripa entered through the door to her connecting office. She set her computer on one of the tables and started up the security scan programs.

"We can watch them and keep a record of everything they access from here," she said as she settled down into her cushioned chair. "The IT people are in the security office just in case anything needs to be fixed on the fly."

"Everything will be fine. Just relax and enjoy the show." Karm settled back into his favorite chair, set his hands on top of his desk, and turned his left palm up as it began to glow.

***

The monarch bounced in his saddle as his Tal galloped over the top of the hill. The falcon hunts had proven to be highly successful as a means of conducting clandestine business with the former General. They could easily discuss matters far from prying ears and eyes. Their common interest in the hobby was well known and served well as a cover to disguise the true nature of their regular excursions.

After exchanging a few pleasantries Brach asked his entourage to leave them alone for a while to eat their lunch and discuss their secret agenda.

"How did the inspection go?" asked the Archbishop once the others departed to a reasonable distance. "Anything we can use to hang that arrogant quetzal with?"

"No, Your Grace, nothing at all. The inspectors report everything went smoothly. They were able to access everything we told them to look for. Our best people cannot find any discrepancies or faults with the information they brought back." The monarch sat down on the grass and stretched out his legs comfortably as he spoke. "It appears our 'friend' is cooperating. We will of course continue to watch him and send in surprise inspectors from time to time."

"I still don't trust the man," said the Archbishop as he continued to stand. He would never presume to sit next to his monarch on the ground, even if asked.

"Neither do I, my good man, but so far we have been unable to find anything wrong with any of his operations. We accessed thousands of terabytes of documents and data covering every aspect of his operations. Everything is exactly the way we expected. There were the usual tax issues and attempts to hide large corporate assets, which they wanted us to find. However, after some high level digging with our new decryption software we did locate a few concealed files leading us to some illegal title transfers involving several mining facilities and banking operations in the eastern province. The security people became most unhappy when we discovered those hidden attempts to deceive us."

The monarch grinned as he lay back to watch the clouds pass overhead. "I am sure they did not expect us to have access to such sophisticated technology. We will have to deal with Karm on this matter, certainly. Enough of this, though. How are things over at The Faith? Are our people keeping matters under control?"

"So far, Your Majesty. There are still a few hotheads wanting to publicly condemn Karm and announce to the world the new date of Armageddon, but The Convocation still seems to be on top of things."

The monarch's brow furrowed as he leaned toward the Archbishop. "Make sure they do. We can't afford to lose control to a bunch of idiotic fanatics at this stage of the game. If they gain the upper hand there's no telling how far the panic will spread. This is one area I think Karm underestimated: the capacity of the people to wreak havoc."

"I agree, Your Majesty. There would not be enough time for faith to overcome the terror. A terrified populace may not stop long enough to worry about their souls."

"Has the Convocation fully accepted you into their inner circles yet?"

"I am starting to gain some headway in that regard. The few who do not fully trust me yet are protesting on grounds of age and years of service. None of them suspect my true purpose there."

"I knew you were the right man for the job, Your Grace."

"There is one further matter, Sire. Your brother requests a personal audience."

"What does he want now?"

"He would not tell me his reasons, Sire, only to bring you this urgent request."

Brach sighed, scanning the skies for his falcon, but only heard its plaintive screeching reverberating off the hillsides. "Very well. Tell him I will receive him tomorrow morning."

***

"**D**on't think you have me fooled for a minute," Pareth said as he slid regally into his chair opposite Brach. His assistant remained standing by the door. "Your spy, The General, may have fooled some of my bishops, but did you really believe I would be deceived by this charade? Do you truly consider me such a dullard?"

Brach raised his hands in supplication, eyes wide in mock sincerity. "Not at all, dear brother. Nevertheless, I must have my little games. And you certainly have profited by the public's acceptance of his conversion, not to mention my own." He plucked a red berry from a bowl, wincing at its tartness as he bit into it.

"And that is the only reason I have put up with his presence in our order," Pareth said pointing a talon at Brach. "And, since I have been so understanding, I feel it is only right to expect some recompense for the inconveniences you and your spy have caused me."

Brach sat up straight, narrowing his eyes as he inspected his brown robed visitor. "Just what do you mean, 'recompense'?" his voice lowered dangerously.

"Oh, come now, brother. You know you cannot intimidate me. All I ask for is an increase of twenty-five percent to my share of the personnel onboard the ship, plus a guarantee that whatever new world we find will be ruled as a theocracy."

Brach laughed as he responded. "You can't be serious! What makes you think I would ever let you take the throne anywhere? Have you lost your mind?"

"Oh, you would still retain your position as monarch, but subject to my authority as the representative of The Eternal. Surely, you understand by now the power of my influence over the people. I thought I was being…"

"Have you gone mad? You don't believe in The Eternal any more than I do. I will not surrender the throne to the likes of you."

Pareth sighed and leaned back, folding his hands in his lap. "I thought not, but we did need a starting point for our negotiations, didn't we?"

"I wasn't aware we were negotiating anything. Now if you'll excuse me…"

"Sit down, brother. If we are to succeed in this little gamble to take control from Karm, we need to work together. And, since you have so obviously tried to deceive me, I require something to convince me you will not be so foolish in the future. We must have absolute trust in each other…or at least as much trust as we can both agree on." Pareth paused as he appeared to think over his demands. "It occurs to me, dear brother, you still do not understand the nature of true power and who controls it. Perhaps a small demonstration is required."

Pareth sighed, rose to his feet and strode nonchalantly to whisper in his assistant's ear. The man paled, but a look of ecstasy grew on his face. As Pareth returned to his seat, the man reached into a pocket, pulled out a small round case, opened it, removed a red capsule and swallowed it. Within seconds his eyes rolled back in his head, he began to spasm, and then dropped to the floor, lifeless eyes raised to the heavens.

Brach jumped to his feet and pulled the cord calling for his aides. "What have you done?" He sputtered in amazement, unable to turn away from the body. The door opened and he signaled for his servants to remove the inert figure.

"Merely a demonstration of true power, brother dear. I simply told him of a recent vision in which The Eternal called his name, showed me the place reserved for him, and told him it was his time to join The Eternal. Would your soldiers be so willing to do the same for you?"

The monarch, unable to find words, sat dumbly, finally turning his gaze back to his brother.

"Don't worry, though. I am willing to be reasonable about this. If you insist on resisting a complete rule by theocracy, then it occurs to me the planet is bound to have more than one continent. What would you say to sharing the new world?"

"You mean we each control our own continents?" Brach, emerging from his shock, stroked his chin as he considered the suggestion. "We would need a treaty on non-aggression between us. After all, it would be several generations before we could even begin to civilize an entire continent, much less a planet. Our descendants could deal with the issue in their own time. But, how do I know you won't be back in a month with more demands?"

"You don't," Pareth said rising from his chair, extending his hand. "For the same reasons I am compelled to trust that you won't send your soldiers to block us from boarding the ship at the last minute. I have taken precautions against that, by the way."

"What do you mean, precautions?"

"Now, Brach," chided the Prior, waggling a talon at his brother, "you don't suppose the Latonian peace treaty has been maintained through the military alone, do you? It really is amazing how tractable some fanatics can be when you take care to fill their souls along with their bellies. So long as we are in agreement that our shared enemy is Karm and we must work together to remove him from the equation as soon as possible."

Brach hesitated, deeply troubled about how he could have so greatly misjudged his sibling's ruthlessness. When at last he pulled his mind out of its depths, he stood and extended a hand to his brother. "Agreed."

Chapter Twenty-Five

Karm enjoyed his dinner as he watched the snow falling outside his window. The first snow of the season always signaled a special treat for him. *Time to dig out the winter waders and fingerless mittens. Those fish are getting hungry now.* His fingers twitched at the thought of a wet line humming through his reel with a hooked trout on the other end. *I hope our trout DNA takes to the water of the new world. I can't imagine...*

"What the...?" The alarm tingled through his left arm as a holographic image appeared of a young cleric, robed in purple, standing on the steps of The Faith's central church. The man, Karm recognized him as Crebot, was gesturing at a crowd gathering in the plaza before him, visibly angry at the reporter shoving a microphone in his face.

"Yes, you heard me! You only have eight years to save your souls and join The Eternal when our world ends." The young cleric's eyes were wild and his voice trembled with righteousness as he shouted into the camera. "You are listening to lies and heresies. Your worldly leaders have kept the truth from you. Only by renouncing them and joining with us can you be saved." He returned his icy glare to the reporter. "You and your smug condemnation of our teachings will be the first to suffer the wrath of The Eternal. You mock our beliefs, but have none of your own. Well, hear me now. This world is about to die and all of you with it. Heed my warning and tend to your souls or perish for all eternity."

Karm was on his video phone and in direct contact with the Prior of The Faith within seconds. "What the strix happened? What do you think you are doing letting that idiot expose us all?" *And how did he evade my mind probe?* He watched the image in his hologram as other ministers tried to grab the young fanatic's arms and take him away from the cameras. Pareth, the Prior, disheveled and his eyes bleary, came into focus on the video screen.

"I don't know, Karm. We certainly did not authorize this. Crebot has always been a lead figure among the more fundamentalist clerics, but we have been watching him carefully. I already sent some of the Brothers to bring him in."

"I will be there as soon as possible. Get the fool in seclusion and shut him up until we can determine the extent of the damages." Karm punched the off button. "Kak!" He growled out loud to himself, pounding a fist on his desk in frustration. "How did this happen?" He held out his palm, waited for the faint glow, and ordered a system check of all the brain wave monitor links. Within seconds, the change to a green hue indicated all connections were still in effect and at full strength.

The phone lit up on all lines. Karm hit the monarch's line and watched as Brach's image appeared on screen.

"What's happening, Karm? Have you seen what some insane extremist is doing on camera?" The monarch pointed at a view screen behind him showing the chaotic scene as he spoke. "I just spoke to Lerit, or Pareth, or whatever the damnation he calls himself, and he claims to have no knowledge of what happened."

"Calm down, Brach. I spoke to the Prior, too. I'm going over there right now. You probably will want to join us. We need to coordinate our efforts to squash this as quickly and permanently as possible." He hung up on the monarch and called Maripa's line.

He swore into the phone as soon as he heard her pick up. "Have you seen what this religious fanatic is doing on the news?"

"Yes, sir. Who let him get in front of a news camera?"

"I don't know, but we are going to find out. Be ready in five minutes." Karm hit the off button and disconnected all of his lines. At that moment, the door burst open and Dr. Rocker ran into the room, breathless and sweating, stopping in mid thought as he saw Karm's dark visage behind the desk.

"Not now, Jontar. I have an emergency to deal with."

"I was going to ask if you saw Crebot on the monitors, but I can see you did. I need to talk to you about him." He moved, still breathing heavily, to pour himself a glass of water, drank it in one gulp, refilled the glass and sat heavily into the chair opposite Karm.

"You know this down-headed fool?" Karm asked, his brows raised in surprise.

"He was a former graduate student of mine at the university. Brilliant, but unstable, always reaching beyond acceptable limits of his research when he believed he knew what was right."

Karm leaned forward, focused, concerned. "You say he is unstable?"

"He was always trying to discover what he considered to be 'Truth'. The chancellors eventually had to remove him from the program when his research went far beyond the parameters he was given. Years later, I saw him standing on a street corner addressing a small crowd. When he recognized me, he berated me for my 'misplaced faith in science' and how we all needed to 'seek the truth in The Eternal'. To me, at least, he seemed to have lost himself in some sort of religious conversion fervor."

"So he is nothing more than a fanatic?"

Rocker frowned, placing both hands on Karm's desk as he leaned in. "No, far from it. He had a brilliant mind, one of the best I had ever worked with, and knows many of the details of my theories on cloning. He could be very dangerous if he is under control of The Faith and has turned his genius against us."

Karm clenched some papers in his fist and snarled. "I'm going to have them all filleted and served up on a platter!" He stormed out of his office and down to a waiting levicoach.

The lower levels of the Church of The Faith were dark and damp. The foundation, being built from large blocks of basalt, gave the appearance and feel of an ancient dungeon out of the mythologies. An elder escorted Karm and Maripa down to the third level. At the end of a long chilly hallway stood a heavy wooden door with two palace guards blocking their path. They raised their energy rifles as the group approached.

The elder raised his hands. "We are expected."

The guards unlocked the door and admitted them. The glare of a single bare bulb hanging by its cord from the ceiling dimly lit the small room. A table stood in the center of the small cell. Karm barely recognized the skeletal young man seated at the table. Disrobed and wearing only his loose undergarments, Crebot was haggard, but still defiant. He sat alone on one side of the table with another guard standing behind him. He scowled and his unblinking eyes stared at the Prior and the monarch who sat across from him. An empty chair waited for Karm.

"Alright," Karm said as he took the chair. "What have you learned so far?" Maripa stood to one side of the table and watched the zealot closely.

The Prior spoke first. "It appears this young fool simply lost his temper at a reporter and let his religious fervor get the better of him. The reporter is a well-known agnostic and critic of our beliefs and he was attempting to goad him into a reaction he could use on the evening broadcast."

"So this was a spontaneous outburst? Not something planned or pre-determined?" Karm rubbed his left forearm absently. *Certainly explains how he evaded my mind monitors.*

"It would appear so," said the monarch. "He simply lost his temper and his ardent radicalism took over what few brains he initially possessed."

The extremist raised his head and glared at each of them. "You still think you can manipulate the truth? The Eternal cannot be controlled or hidden. His truth will always be known."

"Silence, Crebot," commanded the Prior. "You will speak only when told to speak. You are defrocked and no longer hold any authority here."

"My authority comes from The Eternal, not from anyone on this world. I speak His Truth." Crebot raised his hand and pointed in judgment at the others in the room. "I am not concerned with your secrets. The souls of the people are my province. The Eternal commands that we bring all souls to Him and in this I shall not fail. Your dealings in worldly matters corrupt you and condemned you to damnation. Your plan to deliver soulless abominations to a holy new world proclaims your departure from His glorious teachings."

The young man rose to his feet, every limb trembling with the effort. He reached inside his shirt and scratched himself nervously. Maripa was suddenly alert, watching the deranged youth for the slightest sign danger.

"The Eternal has spoken to me. He tells me of your treasons and your plots against Him. He instructs me in the ways of His new church, which I am destined to lead."

"This man has obviously lost his mind," said the monarch. "Guard, return him to his seat and keep him quiet."

The guard stepped forward and placed one hand on the trembling fanatic's shoulder. Crebot screamed and struck the guard in the chest with a long thin knife he had kept hidden under his clothing. Blood sprayed and covered both of the men in red splotches. He yanked the blade free and turned to face the three leaders across from him. In an instant, Maripa sprang into action.

"Now you all will pay the price for your—.''The rest of the sentence died in his throat as Maripa landed on him. She had leaped onto the table and bounded high above the others in the room. Her heel crushed heavily into Crebot's temple sending him flying backwards. Before he could recover, she grabbed the knife from his hand and thrust it into his neck severing the arteries. With another kick she sent the dying man flying into the wall. He collapsed gurgling into a pool of his own blood. She stood over the body for a moment to be sure he was dead, then turned to face the others. The two guards from the hallway burst into the room brandishing their weapons.

She glared at the men around the table. "Didn't any of you think to search him?"

"Weapons of any kind are forbidden," said the Prior. "He should not have had a knife. Ours is a faith of peace."

"Maybe you ought to investigate compliance with your doctrines a bit more closely, Prior," said the monarch. "We wouldn't want to take a chance Crebot had recruited others to his holy cause."

"We will certainly be more cautious in the future," said the Prior. He faced Maripa for the first time. "I want to thank you, young lady, for saving our lives. The Eternal certainly provided you with some useful gifts."

"You're welcome, but your Eternal had nothing to do with it. I was protecting Karm. Saving you and the monarch was an unfortunate byproduct."

"That's enough, Maripa," said Karm. "We don't need to make any more enemies than we already have. Why don't you go get yourself cleaned up?"

"Yes, sir," She followed the guards out of the room as they removed Crebot's body.

Karm, Brach, and the Prior sat quietly at the table.

After a brief moment to gather his thoughts, Karm stood and paced the room. "We need to assess the damage and take immediate measures to quell any thoughts that Crebot was rational or even remotely plausible. We cannot leave anyone to wonder if what he said bore any measure of truth to it. What are our best options?"

Brach sat upright as he regained his composure. "I can call in the media and state unequivocally there is no value in the claims he made to that reporter. Our best scientists will back me up and denounce everything supporting his statements. People must believe he was no more than a raving lunatic."

The Prior joined in. "I can tell our followers the poor man had been given too many responsibilities and he suffered a nervous breakdown. I'll use the fact that he was a well-known zealot against him. We can blame his rants on dementia intensifying his fears to the point where he became delusional. The press release can state he is recovering from his illness secluded in a remote monastery. His few followers will be dispersed to a monastic life where vows of silence and isolation in some very small locked cells will keep them from ever communicating with anyone in the foreseeable future."

Karm thought for a moment before speaking. "Agreed. And I think it would be best if I played no role at all in any of this. My position is too well known and might be construed as suspect. I don't want any rumors of collusion developing so I need to be out of the public eye on this one."

"One more thing," said the monarch. "I think we need to reevaluate our launch date. Given this new development I am not so sure we can keep everything under wraps for another three years. We need to launch by the end of next year."

Karm ran the talons of one hand through his crest, shaking his head. "Impossible. We are already on double shifts to meet the current deadlines. I don't have enough people to move the date up so far."

"Find them. I am not asking you, I'm ordering you. As an incentive I will allow you to provide a small number of your people with credentials as crewmembers, but only on the provision you can launch before the end of next year. I don't think we can keep the lid on this any longer."

Considering his options, Karm stopped his pacing and faced the monarch and his brother. "I'm going to need some sort of cover story to hide the reason for the sudden increase in manpower I'll be taking on. Thousands of new employees are certain to raise a few questions out there."

The monarch smiled and winked at Karm. "You're a very creative man. I'm sure you'll_come up with something. Are we in agreement?"

"I want those credentials on my desk tomorrow if I am going to go along with this."

"Absolutely. First thing in the morning. Do we all agree on our cover story for why we are all headed into space?"

"Yes, yes," Karm replied. "As far as my staff and the press are concerned, this is just a publicity stunt to promote a new alternative to regular flights around the planet. A rocket large enough to take passengers up into orbit and land safely on the other side of the world in only a matter of an hour or so will revolutionize the airline industry. You and the Prior are going on the inaugural flight to emphasize the safety and reliability of the rocket.

Pareth took over the narrative. "Then a computer malfunction will prevent us from shutting down the engines so we are hurtled out into space. A tragic accident, certain to cause an upheaval, but not the worldwide panic any knowledge of our true mission would cause."

Brach nodded in agreement as he turned to address Karm. "Excellent. You can tell the press how construction and testing exceeded your expectations and you are ready to proceed ahead of schedule. The 'accident' will explain why we don't return."

"Alright then, let's get going. We all have a very busy day ahead of us."

The three men stood to leave, but Pareth grabbed his brother's sleeve. "Pardon me, Your Majesty. Might I have a moment? We should probably coordinate the timing of our broadcasts."

"Certainly, Your Grace. Until next time, Karm."

Karm left the room. Before the doors closed he noticed the two leaders deep in conversation.

"You should have discussed your plan to offer him additional credentials, Your Majesty. A quarter of the passengers belong to me. Do you intend giving up some of your seats to them?"

"I have no intention of giving up anything, Your Grace. I had to offer him something to get him to agree to the new launch date. We will ensure he and his friends miss their boarding time when it comes."

The Prior lowered his voice and held up a single finger in warning. "It occurs to me I will need to be extra vigilant to ensure none of my flock misses their departure times. I don't mean to appear lacking in faith, but prudence demands I take steps to protect their interests."

"You are welcome to take whatever steps you deem necessary," said the monarch. "Karm is our common enemy here. He would love us to tear each other apart in mutual distrust. I assure you, neither you nor your flock have anything to fear from me."

"This is good to hear, Your Majesty. Just the same, I will be cautious." The Prior stood and gestured toward the closed door. "After you, Your Majesty."

The next day, Karm monitored the news broadcasts on the screens across from his desk. The monarch was speaking on the main network channels.

"… and I guarantee you, all the ravings of the poor deranged individual have not even a speck of truth in them. The man was suffering from delusions and hearing voices. The Prior informs me he is currently being treated at an undisclosed location by members of his order."

The reporter turned his attention to the scientists who sat alongside the monarch. "Can you gentlemen spread any light on some of the claims the cleric made about the sun?"

"Rest assured there is absolutely no truth to his claims," said the scientist seated next to the monarch. "Every astronomer on the planet has been monitoring the sun for the past decade. Not one single bit of data suggests anything other than what we are telling you. The sun will continue to degrade and it will eventually go nova, but not for another one hundred years, at least. There is more than enough time to work on solutions. Nobody alive today or in the near future needs to fear being swallowed up by an exploding star."

"What about the claims of Dr. Bladett confirming what was said yesterday?"

Brach leaned into his microphone as he responded. "Dr. Bladett is an old and respected member of the scientific community, but he is retired and no longer privy to the most accurate information. His connections to The Faith and its most radical factions contribute to his misinterpretation of the old data he still works with." He raised his hands to quiet the reporters. "All of the data will be released and you all will have free access to our best scientists. I hope our transparency in this matter will quiet any concerns that have unfortunately arisen as a result of the ravings of one individual. I guarantee all of you are safe for the duration of your lifetime. Dyan'ta will continue to remain safe for the lives of your children." He stood and left the table. The scientists remained to continue answering questions.

Karm turned off his monitors and took a long drink. He stared at the ceiling for a moment before reaching for the phone.

Activate secure line and his palm glowed. When he heard the line change tones he punched lines three, five, and nine together.

"Yes, sir?"

"We need to step up production. Can everything be ready a year from now?"

"No problem, sir. We are well ahead of schedule so there is no problem kicking it up a notch. I'll send you the adjusted schedule and supply requirements in a couple of days."

"Very good. Proceed as usual." *Deactivate secure line* and the glow in his palm faded.

***

Maripa awoke warm and content under the heavy blankets of the room she shared with Rocker whenever they could escape. She stretched and turned over, reaching for her lover only to discover his absence. A crash of metal resounded up from the lower floor. "Oh, no," she sighed. "He's trying to cook again. I've got to tell him the truth before he poisons us." Groaning, she grabbed her robe and headed down to the kitchen, the smell of burnt smat eggs and grek sausage rising to meet her on the stairs.

"There are reasons why we have cooks and other servants here," she reminded Rocker again. "As much as I appreciate the effort, you don't really have to do this." She walked barefoot over the tiled floor and embraced him tightly, standing on her toes to kiss him good morning.

"I know," he said once she released him and he could breathe again. "I wanted to surprise you with something new I came up with for breakfast. You might actually like this one." He smiled down at her and kissed her again before turning back to the cabinets.

"Oh, no, you don't," she said, grabbing him by the hand and pulling him out of the kitchen. "I hate to tell you this, but you can't cook. Let the chef do his job."

"Now you're starting to sound just like Betha. She didn't like my cooking either."

Maripa felt her stomach lurch a bit. "I'm sorry, Jontar... I didn't mean to..."

"Hush!" he said, pulling her into his arms. "I'm okay with that now. She will always hold a special place in my heart, but I know she approves of us...and I love you."

Maripa's heart soared and she sunk even deeper into his embrace. "I love you, too, Jontar."

The air was cold, but the sun shone bright orange in the sky as they strolled the grounds that afternoon. The snow crunched under their feet, their breath formed clouds before them as they walked.

Taking Maripa's hand, Rocker stared off into the woods, not really noticing any of the beauty. "Do you really believe Karm can pull this off?"

Maripa hesitated for only the briefest moment before responding. "Without a doubt. I've known him my entire life and he has never once failed to accomplish what he set out to do."

"Even with the secrets he still hides from us?"

"Listen to me." She stopped and took both of his gloved hands in hers. "I trust him with every fiber in my body. I may not like his secrets any more than you do, but I know he has his reasons."

"The timeline and all that?"

"I'm not saying I understand it all, but he has managed to stay two steps ahead of everyone else all this time. I believe him even if I don't understand him."

Rocker thought about this and then came to his decision. "The scientist in me has a hard time accepting his claims of time travel and aliens, but he does seem to genuinely care about saving all of us." He stepped closer to Maripa, searching for something in her eyes. "Okay, if you trust him, then I'm all in, too. For better or worse."

Chapter Twenty-Six

"Are you sure this is the wisest move?" asked the Archbishop. "There are only a few months left before we launch. Karm is not causing any difficulties now that we are in control. Siege tactics might be more prudent than an attack at this time."

"No. I mean to squash Karm, not just control him. He has been a thorn in my side for far too long and I cannot escape the feeling that he is taking his defeat too calmly." The monarch shoved the food on his plate around with his fork as he spoke. The reports he read sat open beside him. He was feeling petulant. With so much at stake now, he could no longer afford to escape on another falcon hunt. Staying on top of Karm's maneuverings and keeping Pareth at bay trapped him in the palace. He missed the fresh air and relief from the constant pressures of the office.

The Archbishop set down his utensil and folded his hands on the table. "You have already won, Sire. There is no need for this show of force. Karm will never board the ship, so he will perish here with everyone else. This attempt may only serve to renew his determination to regain some measure of control. Who knows what trouble he might cause if he is pushed too far?"

"No. I will show him what true power is. He will know he lost and it was I who destroyed him. I want to see the look of defeat in his eyes before we leave this world. Now, go set your men to their task at the mines. I want this operation underway before the day is over."

"Very well, Your Majesty. As you command." He pushed his chair back, bowed to the monarch, and left the room.

Back at The Citadel a few days later Karm, Rocker, and Maripa enjoyed a rare weekend together. Karm rose early and sorted through his fly boxes as he finished breakfast.

"Off to try and catch your finned adversary again, Karm?" Rocker shuffled into the study and grabbed a cup of narl tea from the buffet table.

"What else? Who knows how many opportunities I have left? Time is growing short and we don't have any more free weekends as the launch approaches. I mean to get that quetzal of a fish before we go."

"Good Luck. Don't forget our lunch date in town later."

"I won't. By the way, I want you to keep an eye on Brach and the Archbishop." Karm held up his left hand and scratched at his palm. "I've been getting some indications that they might be up to something, but I can't quite pinpoint anything specific, yet. Brach has been raging for a few days now, which usually means he is up to some sort of mischief."

"Alright. I'll tell Maripa you want her to look into it. We'll let you know what she finds at lunch. She should be getting up soon."

"Alright. See you then." Karm grabbed his vest and rod, and then clomped out the back door wearing his waders.

An hour later, Maripa joined Rocker in the study. She was dressed in jeans, t-shirt, and a light sweater, crest feathers not yet preened. Her bare feet silently crossed the polished stone floor. She grunted as she sat in one of the upholstered chairs near the fireplace.

"Good Morning," Rocker said as he poured her some narl tea. He handed her the mug and kissed her lightly on the top of her head.

"Not until at least my second cup," she mumbled, sipping at the steaming brew.

One of the servants entered the room and placed a pile of papers on the table next to Maripa. "The morning reports, ma'am."

Maripa muttered a barely audible, "Mm…Hmmm…thanks," and sorted through the stack as she drank.

"Anything important?" Rocker joined her by the fireplace with a plate of smat eggs, grek bacon and sausage, and fruit from the assortment left by the cooks.

"Nothing out of the ordinary. Wait, here is something from one of the mining facilities up north. Someone out there is stirring up the miners, causing some strikes and a few delays to their deliveries."

"You don't sound too worried about it," Rocker said as he gnawed absently on some bacon.

"Not really. Nothing more than a few days, a week or two at most in delays to our time table. I'll send some people down there to settle the matter and we should be fine. Maybe only a short delay to the launch date. Nothing really." She finished her mug in a quick gulp and hoisted herself up out of the chair to get another.

"Karm was worried that The monarch might be up to something. We should let him know about this."

"Maybe. But right now I need to go for a run. Want to come along?" She stood and stretched her arms toward the ceiling.

"Sure. I could go for chasing you around in the woods again. Who knows? Maybe I'll catch you today."

Maripa smiled, pecked him on the cheek, and gave him a sly wink. "You can always try. I suppose there's a first time for everything."

It was one o'clock by the time Karm showed up to their lunch meeting. He still wore the waders and vest, with his fishing rod in one hand. He pulled up an empty chair to join them at the table in the sidewalk café. A waiter took their order and left a pitcher of water on the table.

Noticing the empty fish bag, Rocker couldn't resist provoking the old angler. "No luck today?"

"Not a nibble," Karm said, frowning as he scratched at his left palm again. "This darn thing kept distracting me all morning, but all I keep getting is Brach's anger. He is so focused on me and because of his hatred, I can't get a clear handle on his ultimate plan." He poured himself a glass of water and turned to Maripa. "What did you find?"

Maripa took another bite of her fruit as she gave her report. "Nothing out of the ordinary. At least nothing of any significance. The only thing going on is some disturbance at one of the northern mining facilities."

Karm bolted upright and his jaw dropped open, his eyes lost focus as if his mind was in some far off world. An angry red glow lit his palm. "What sort of disturbance? What mines?"

Maripa's eyes narrowed and she handed Karm the notices. "Some clerics are stirring up the workers at one of the copper mines, causing some strikes and other slight delays, but nothing too serious. I already sent a group down there to handle the matter. There shouldn't be any more than a day or two delay to the launch."

"That down-head! What does that mutes-brained quetzal think he is doing?" Karm jumped up and ran to the waiting levicoach. Rocker and Maripa ran after him and barely seated themselves before it took off.

Maripa sat across from Karm in the coach. "What's the matter, Karm? What's so important about some remote copper mine? What are you keeping from us this time?"

"That mine is a critical focal point in our timeline. We cannot allow Brach to interfere there. The repercussions could be catastrophic. This could destroy everything we have worked for," Karm clenched the report in his fist.

"Rocker sat next to Maripa and shook his head. "It's only a day or two at the most, Karm. We still have plenty of time to launch and escape."

Karm turned his anger on the scientist. "No. We don't have any time to spare at all. You just don't understand. Everything is proceeding according to a pre-determined and precise time schedule." He punctuated each point with sharp gestures as if stacking the events in order. "It all has to happen exactly as it did before. Any alterations or delays, even for a few hours could cause irreparable damage to the timeline and set everything to total chaos. Brach thinks he is showing me once and for all who is in charge, the feather fluffed idiot. In reality, he's unwittingly setting in motion events I may not be able to salvage." For the remainder of their journey, Karm sat rigidly staring out the window, occasionally erupting with vile epithets directed at the monarchs intelligence and heritage.

As soon as the levicoach arrived back at The Citadel, Karm jumped out and ran to his office. He hit the button for The monarch's private line and tried to remove his waders and vest while he waited for Brach to pick up.

"What in The Eternal's name do you think you are doing?" shouted Karm as soon as he heard the monarch's voice. "What could you possibly hope to accomplish by such childish games as a miners' strike?"

The monarch paused before he responded. His image in the view screen showed him sitting at his desk, smiling. "Ah, Karm. I see you received my message."

"Your message? Is that what this is all about? You're still obsessed with who's in control here? Is this nothing more than a game of power to you?"

"Yes, Karm. That is all anything is ever about. Power and who controls it. I wanted you to know once and for all your smug self-assurance and money are useless when those with real power choose to utilize it. I want you to understand I am in charge of the situation here, not you. I control the populace and the resources you need for your so-called empire. I want you to realize I can cut you off any time I choose. This is power, Karm. For now, my point has been made with just a small demonstration at one mine. Tomorrow, it could be hundreds of mines or factories. I could bring this entire project to its knees with just a few simple commands."

Karm stared at The monarch's image and slumped back into his chair. "You have no idea what you are doing, Brach. This is no contest of power. A contest would require that both sides have a reasonable chance of winning. You are completely out of your league here. Stop now before you force my hand. I cannot allow this action to continue."

The monarch's eyes widened in surprise at Karm's continued defiance. "You cannot allow? You are defeated, Karm. None of your bullying or posturing will help you now. Surrender and I may see fit to allow the workers to return to their jobs in a few days. The launch will happen, but according to my schedule, not yours."

"A few days is unacceptable, Brach." He sat up and stared directly into the eyes of The monarch's image. "The launch must take place as planned. If you persist in this you force me to take measures I have no wish to take. Thousands of lives are at stake here, Brach. Stop now before you learn what true power is."

The monarch shifted his glance a bit, but then returned his gaze to his monitor. "Forget it, Karm. No empty threats will help you now. You have until tonight to submit."

Karm closed his eyes, and sunk back into his chair. "You give me no choice, then. Contact your bevy at those mines and see what they tell you. Call me tomorrow if you want to discuss power again." He hit the off switch and The monarch's image vanished.

Karm tapped another button on his phone and activated the security features of his biocomputer. His left hand glowed red. "I am sending you the coordinates now," he told the voice on the other end of the line. "Launch the missiles immediately." He hung up and his palm returned to normal. Karm went to his liquor cabinet and poured himself a tall drink from the first bottle he saw and downed it in one long gulp. He then collapsed into a nearby chair and called for Maripa and Rocker to join him. *They'll hate me for this, but I had no choice.* He poured another drink and downed it just as quickly as the first. *How much longer before I can just disappear and no longer be such a monster?*

Karm sat with Maripa and Rocker in his office as they watched the wall of monitors relaying news of the disaster. The evening news broadcasted the breaking story of the catastrophe at the mines.

"Five thousand dead," reported the man on one of the video screens in Karm's office.

"Apparently the result of a military accident. Some sort of missile test gone horribly wrong," said the journalist on another screen.

"All attempts to reach the palace for comment have gone unanswered so far," said another reporter on another display.

Even with all my foreknowledge, I was powerless to save them. Time is a brutal and cruel taskmaster. She will have her due no matter the cost. She will not allow events of this magnitude to be altered. "He left me with no choice," Karm said as he hit the remote control and turned off the monitors. "I cannot allow any delays. Not at this late date. New workers will arrive in the morning and production will be brought back on schedule by tomorrow evening."

"Thousands of innocents!" Maripa, wiping tears from her cheeks, could not bring herself to turn away from the grizzly scenes on the monitors. "Why? Just to show The monarch you were still in control? I've killed before, but only when there was no other recourse. I would never have believed you capable of such horrors."

"Do you honestly believe I wanted this? You still don't understand." Karm downed another in a long succession of drinks. "Our entire future hangs by a thread. By sacrificing those few, millions more will live. They all died in my past, so they must die in this time as well. It is a critical moment in time that cannot be altered without horrific consequences. If I had done nothing, all of our efforts would have come to nothing and everyone on the planet would die. The future timeline must be maintained no matter what the cost."

"The future? All I can see is more secrets. You still won't let us in. And yet you still demand our trust in you. It doesn't work this way. How can we help if you won't tell us your plans?" Tears streamed down her face as she turned to face him.

"There is no other way. This is my burden and mine alone. I accepted this task with all it implied. You can either accept the fact or not. I will continue to do what I must."

Rocker stood and approached Maripa, placing his arm around her shoulder. "You know we will not desert you, Karm, but you need to know you have severely damaged our faith in you. You have just committed an atrocity, even if it was for some greater good in your view. Until you are willing to include us in this view of yours, we cannot condone or even understand what you have done."

They turned and left Karm alone in his office. In the darkness, Karm picked up the remote again and turned on the monitors. He took another long drink as he watched the reports of his destruction.

Chapter Twenty-Seven

The orange sun rose bright in the clear morning sky. Karm stood looking out his window at The Citadel, already dressed in his waders and vest. *Go ahead and do your worst now, you big ball of gas. We beat you. We are going to survive your assassination plans*. He stuck out his tongue and flicked it with the second talon of his right hand in defiance at the dying star, then clomped downstairs to eat some breakfast. He grabbed the sack with his usual hard-boiled smat egg, slice of grek ham and carton of hodak milk from the kitchen table. The butler handed him his rod and hat as headed toward his favorite spot along the stream.

"Send the others down to pick me up when they arrive," he called back over his shoulder and bounded down the steps.

On the flight to The Citadel, Maripa snuggled next to Rocker as they looked out the window at the world passing below them. "Will the new planet be as beautiful?"

"We can't say exactly what it looks like, but it will be livable. Everything we have been able to gather tells us there must be plant life of some sort. An oxygen atmosphere would require that. The temperature ranges indicate a dynamic ecosystem with enough liquid water to moderate any real extremes—"

Maripa jabbed her elbow into his side. "You down-head. You may be one of the smartest people on the planet, but sometimes you can be so dense." She wormed her way closer to him, pulling his arm around her. "Just tell me everything will be alright."

"Our new home will be beautiful, just like you." He held her tight, delighting in her warmth and the scent of her crest.

The plane landed and taxied to the waiting levicoach. The staff removed their luggage and stored it in the vehicle's trunk before they set foot on the tarmac. The Citadel shone bright in the morning sun. The trees had shed their leaves long ago and the grass had turned to a dormant brown for the winter. There was a stark beauty to the sight.

"Is he down at the river?"

The driver laughed. "Where else, sir? He wants us to retrieve him there and head directly to the launch pad."

Maripa rolled her eyes skyward. "Well let's hope he caught a few this morning. He'd just fuss all the way into space if he had to leave without at least one."

They found Karm in his usual spot by the deep pool. His rod bent sharply and he frantically pulled in the line. They heard him laughing and reveling in his triumph as they exited the coach.

Rocker cupped one hand beside his mouth as he called out. "Looks like a big one!"

"The son of an old quetzal who always taunted me!" Karm shouted back as he played out some line. "I may never have caught him, but I got his offspring!"

Just as Karm reached out to land the silvery beast in his net, the creature gave one last burst of desperation and snapped the line. Karm lost his balance and fell waist deep into the stream.

"Kak!" Karm yelled as he slammed his rod into the water. He struggled to stand with his waders full of the icy water. "You may have won this round, but I got your DNA. This isn't over yet." He shook his fist and rod at the large wake cutting across the stream to the opposite bank.

Maripa reached out to help him onto the bank. "Are you okay?"

"I'm fine," Karm grumbled back as he climbed the bank of the stream. "Just soaked. Get the heaters going in the coach."

Karm changed into drier clothes and joined his companions in the mag-lev. "Mutes, almost had him that time. Would have loved to actually land him just once before taking off. You two all set?"

Rocker and Maripa nodded. "All packed and ready to go." The levicoach accelerated down the dirt road, spraying gravel in its wake.

"Good. I sent my belongings on ahead yesterday so looks like we are good to go." He pulled a small silver case out of his pocket and removed a violet capsule. Karm tossed the pill into his mouth and chased it down with a swallow of water.

An hour later they arrived at the launch pad facilities. Guards checked their IDs at the gate while security officers searched the vehicle inside and out.

The guard snapped a crisp salute. "Welcome to Pad One, sir. You may proceed to the main hangar." He waved the vehicle on and the gate slid closed behind them. They were accustomed to the high level of security measures during the past year. Their frequent trips to supervise the installation of the equipment and DNA samples required regular trips to the site.

The levicoach pulled up to the main entrance of the hangar and more security personnel surrounded them. After a final inspection of all luggage and passing through security detectors they entered the facility itself. Once inside, they saw members of the monarch's staff and clerics of various ranks of The Faith, which embodied the rest of the crew. Each group was outfitted in their flight suits, but kept to themselves. Karm located the launch control room and headed in.

"The countdown is proceeding normally, sir," reported the flight director. "Crew insertion in one hour."

"Thank you, Captain. We'll be in the prep room getting ready." He left the control room and walked back to Maripa and Rocker.

"Time to suit up."

They followed him into the suit-up area and sat on the contoured chairs as the technicians helped them into their bulky pressurized suits. In thirty minutes, they finished dressing and headed out. They carried their helmets and coolant cases back to the waiting area joining the rest of the crew.

A tall soldier with rows of ribbons and medals on his chest entered the room with two armed soldiers in attendance. "Time to get you folks to the launch pad," he said in a booming voice that echoed throughout the room. "Follow me to the transport." He turned on his heels and led the way down the starkly lit hallway. The two armed soldiers stood guard as the crew followed. Three additional guards trailed behind them, weapons at the ready.

Loading the transport proved to be tricky while they struggled to maneuver in their pressurized suits. With the help of several technicians, everyone soon found themselves safely deposited into their seats and buckled in for the short drive to the ship. Three towers surrounded the gleaming vessel, each with a large freight elevator leading to different levels. The crew divided into three groups, each assigned to separate towers. Karm, Maripa, and Rocker were collected with The monarch's group. Security guards, led the way and accompanied each elevator to the designated level. When the elevator stopped, a guard raised the gate and the group began to board the ship in single file crossing the gantry to the open hatch.

As Karm began to exit the elevator the guards blocked his way and lowered their weapons, the red light of the firing contact indicating the weapons were fully charged and armed.

"What is the meaning of this?" Karm demanded of the soldiers.

Maripa found herself unable to act. She was blocked by both Karm and Rocker. Her pressurized suit proved too stiff and bulky for her to move effectively on the narrow gantry. She was definitely not in any position to attack trained soldiers with plasma beam rifles aimed at the group. The guards lowered the gate between them, trapping the three in the elevator.

"So now we say goodbye at last, Karm." The monarch walked back out across the gantry and stood behind the guards.

"This is outrageous, Brach. Let us through. The ship will launch in just a few minutes. We don't have time for any games."

Brach smiled at Karm's frustration. "I quite agree. I am done playing your games. You are no longer in charge here, and you certainly will not be boarding this vessel."

Rocker finally found his voice. "What if something goes wrong with the regeneration equipment? How will you fix it without us on board? I'm the one who designed the systems and I know them better than anyone."

"We have plenty of very smart people with us, Dr. Rocker and they are all well briefed in your designs and specs. My people assure me they learned your systems well enough to do just fine without you to hold their hands... but thank you for all your hard work. None of this would have been possible without you."

He turned to walk back into the ship. "Take them to the bunker and don't let them out until after launch. After that you can release them unharmed. They cannot do anything once we reach space. I think I'm going to enjoy the thought of your prolonged suffering over the next few years." He stopped and faced the small group of prisoners. "I want you to remember who finally outwitted you and condemned you and your friends to die here on this world while we survive to colonize a new world."

"Don't do this, Brach. You'll never make it without us."

"Still defiant? You still think you have the upper hand?" the monarch reached into a pocket in his spacesuit and pulled out a small beam pistol. "Come to think of it, I would rather see the look in your eyes as you die at my own hand." He pressed the firing contact.

At the first sight of the monarch's weapon, Maripa shoved her way forward and slammed the full weight of her body into Karm, knocking him to one side. As he fell to the ground, the orange beam grazed Karm's shoulder instead of burning into his heart. Rocker landed a sidekick to one of the guards who fell screaming over the railing of the gangway one hundred feet above the concrete below. He grabbed the second guard before the man could raise his weapon.

"Get down!" yelled Maripa as she ripped the metallic emblem from her portable oxygen tank and hurled it toward the monarch. The object embedded itself in his arm causing him to drop his gun.

"Now you die," she said to the monarch as he gripped his wound, her body coiled in the manner of a predator preparing to launch into its prey, her eyes firmly fixed on Brach as she sprang.

Maripa swore as she got caught in the struggle between Rocker and the remaining guard. She broke free just as Brach escaped into the ship and closed the hatch. She approached the porthole in the door and the two eyed each other. She punched the window with such force, The monarch jumped back in fear. She turned to see Rocker finishing off the remaining guard with a powerful twist, breaking his neck.

"Two minutes to launch," called out the loudspeaker from the elevator.

Karm sat up holding his shoulder. "Maripa, get back here now! We need to get down to the emergency bunker before this thing launches!"

She ran back to the tower as Rocker shoved the guard's body out of the way. He closed the gate and hit the emergency escape button. The elevator dropped at an alarming rate, braking only at the last possible moment, crashing them all to the floor.

Rocker helped Karm to his feet. "Maripa, Hurry! Get the bunker door open. I'll help him."

"One minute to launch," called the loudspeaker.

Maripa sprinted the twenty yards to the emergency shelter and keyed in the access code. The lock clicked and she pulled the door open just as Rocker and Karm arrived. She slammed the hatch shut behind them as they stumbled inside.

Karm sat silently on a chair in a corner. Maripa located the first aid kit and began to dress his shoulder. Rocker stood stunned in the center of the room.

"I should have killed him," Maripa said as she applied the bandages. "Is there a phone in here? Maybe there's still time to stop the launch."

Suddenly the ground shook and a deep rumble sounded through the bunker. The sound grew to a roar as the entire room quaked and then faded to silence.

"No! No! No!" Maripa ran to the door, but Rocker caught her before she could open it. "They can't launch! It can't end like this!"

Rocker took her by the shoulders and held her tight. "We're together and that's all that matters, my love," he whispered in her ear as she trembled.

The rumbling gradually subsided. Karm stood and walked over to Rocker and Maripa, still holding each other. "Alright, what's done is done. Let's get out of here and back to the control room."

"What's the point?" Rocker asked, cradling Maripa in his arms. "We lost. Shouldn't we go home and make the best of the time left to us?"

"Don't give up yet. You never know what the fickle future holds for us." He walked over to his friends, placing his free hand on Rocker's shoulder.

After a few moments they walked over to the transport and drove back to mission control.

"Karm! What are you doing here? Why didn't you board the ship?" The startled Captain sprang from his chair as the bedraggled trio entered the room.

"Apparently, the monarch had other plans and we weren't invited. He infiltrated some of our security forces with his own men and they prevented us from boarding the ship."

"I'll round up those men and court martial them!"

"No need. They're dead. Brach tried to kill us and these two," he said pointing to Maripa and Rocker, "were more than a match for them. You might find a few charred pieces of bone at the launch pad, but I doubt it."

A man at one of the computer banks suddenly interrupted. "Captain, I think we have a problem here. You need to take a look at these trajectory numbers."

The Captain looked over the engineer's shoulder at the screen. "This can't be right. These coordinates show them heading off into space. They were supposed to do a couple of orbits and reenter. What happened?"

"I'm not sure, sir, but it looks as though their computer changed the coordinates and ignited the engines. The new trajectory is taking them into deep space. We can't override it. They cut us out." The engineer frantically typed instructions to his console and reset switches. "Nothing is working. They're leaving orbit now."

The Captain turned to Karm and shook his head. "Looks like you were the lucky ones after all, sir. If we can't re-establish communications and telemetry control,

the ship is lost and everyone on board will die out there."
He stared helplessly at the monitors and the engineers.
"This was supposed to be a simple demonstration. The
monarch is aboard that ship."

Karm place a reassuring hand on the officer's
shoulder. "I know, Captain. There will of course be a full
investigation and every system will be torn apart and
analyzed until we find out what went wrong. If you can't
restore_communications or control in the next hour they
will be lost for good . Keep at it until then. I will start
preparing for the worst, though. I'll check back with you
soon." He signaled for Maripa and Rocker to follow him as
he left toward one of the nearby offices.

Karm quietly closed the door behind them and
turned to face Rocker and Maripa. "We need to maintain
the cover story and protect our people at all costs,
especially now. We don't want to live on a world in total
panic if the true condition of that ship ever leaks out." He
walked over to one of the chairs and sat down. "We need to
let everyone believe the ship became lost in a freak
accident in space. There will be some turmoil until the
government stabilizes again, but we can't risk the public
finding out the truth."

Rocker nodded in agreement. "We agree with you,
Karm. As long as we are stuck here, we will want to live in
peace until the end. How would you like some company
back at The Citadel?"

He smiled and took Maripa's face in his hands. "We
could find worse places to celebrate the end of the world."

Without warning, the door opened and in walked
The General dressed in his finest military uniform.

Karm stood and eyed the intruder. "You seem to
have had a relapse in your devotion to The Faith, General.
Why are you here and not on board with your friends?"

"I am sure you knew my role as a spy, Karm. You
are too good a strategist to have been fooled for long. An

unfortunate heart condition prevents me from joining His Majesty on this journey, but I still serve as required. His Majesty's final instructions were for me to deliver this message to you." The General pulled an envelope out of his jacket and handed it to Karm. He saluted and left as quickly as he arrived.

Maripa scowled at the closing door, every fiber of her being screamed to give chase and kill the monster. "What does that traitor have to say?"

Karm opened the envelope and read the message aloud.

My Dear Karm,

By now you are coming to grips with the fact that you have finally been outwitted. My companions and I are leaving orbit and on our way to Raince'to. I want you to know I have always considered you a most worthy adversary. I had almost given up hope of defeating you.

You should also know I will ensure your name and Dr. Rocker's live on in the colonies we build. You and your people will be given full credit for your genius and for saving our people. I give you my royal and solemn oath.

I also wanted to assure you that neither of us want The Faith to have any authority whatsoever in our new society. I have taken steps to eliminate the threat once and for all. If, somehow, you find a way to follow us to the new world you will probably find the path marked by the bodies of a few dozen clergy.

Farewell my old friend.

Brach

"He must have written this in one of his saner moments before he became obsessed with killing me." Karm folded the letter and stuck it in his pocket. "Let's go home. I need a drink."

Chapter Twenty-Eight

"Set course for Latonia base," said Karm to the pilot as they boarded the jet.

"Yes, sir. Estimated arrival time - four hours."

Maripa snapped to attention at the mention of the desert base. "What the strix are you doing, Karm? Why in the world would we want to go into the middle of that wasteland during a crisis like this?"

Karm looked at Maripa with wide innocent eyes while sporting a mischievous grin. "Now, you wouldn't want me to spoil the surprise, would you?"

"Don't play games with us, Karm. You don't want me getting angry right now."

Karm somehow maintained his virtuous expression.

"Me? I would never play games with you. Not in a million years."

Rocker straightened himself in his seat and scowled at Karm. "We don't have a million years."

Karm gave them a mischievous wink. "Oh, I wouldn't be too sure about that. Just sit back and enjoy the scenery for the next few hours. I promise, all your questions will be answered when we arrive." He waved a dismissive hand and buckled himself into his seat.

Rocker turned to Maripa, seeking guidance in her equally confused face. "Do we trust him once more?"

She shrugged her shoulders and took his hand in hers. "He's almost never let us down, so I guess one more time won't kill us. Not that it matters anymore." They buckled in and leaned on each other as the plane accelerated down the runway.

"Good. I'm glad that's settled. Wake me when we arrive. I need a nap." Karm pulled a blanket over himself and closed his eyes.

Four hours later the pilot's voice broke the silence in the cabin. "Beginning our descent to Latonia Base. Wheels down in fifteen minutes."

Maripa startled awake. "Have a nice rest?" Rocker asked as he brushed one stray crest feather from her face.

"Must have been more tired than I thought." She stretched, sat up and tousled her crest. "Did you sleep?"

"Not really. I've been trying to calculate how long it would take to build another rescue ship and replace all of our equipment. I don't think it's possible. Not with how little time we have."

Maripa held his hand and leaned over to kiss him. Her eye caught the view outside the plane. "What the strix? Why are we landing? Take a look."

Rocker turned to look out his window. "There's nothing down there. No town, no roads, only a broken down old runway." He turned back into the cabin, unbuckled his seatbelt, and stepped across the aisle. "Karm, wake up. You need to tell us what's going on. Why are we landing in the middle of nowhere?"

Karm looked out of his window. "Ah, Latonia Base. We're here."

"What do you mean 'we're here'? We aren't anywhere except the most desolate part of the most isolated desert on the planet. There's nothing out there." Rocker jabbed a finger toward the window.

"Sit down and buckle in before we land. I'll explain everything once we are on the ground."

Rocker and Maripa watched through their window as the plane lost altitude. They saw nothing except rock and dirt from one horizon to the next. The jet shook with the rumble of machinery as the landing gear lowered and locked into place. Then a single bounce and the plane taxied to the lone building next to the runway. It was a small adobe shack with a uniformed guard standing outside awaiting their arrival. The plane rolled to a stop in front of the weather-beaten shed. The pilot opened the doorway and lowered the steps. A wall of oppressive heat slammed into the three passengers as they departed. An intense sunlight forced them to shield their eyes until they reached the small bit of shade provided by the rickety structure. The sentry snapped to attention.

"Welcome to Latonia Base, sir. May I see your identifications, please?" He held out his left hand to receive the documents while his right hand rested on his sidearm. The soldier gave the papers a quick examination and returned them. "You may enter now, sir. They are waiting for you on level four."

"Thank you, Lieutenant." He waved to the others to follow him inside.

The interior of the shack proved no more revealing than the outside. Some broken wooden crates in one corner and an antique refrigerator hummed and rattled in another. The open window allowed a thin tattered curtain to flutter in the slight breeze. A single table occupied the center of the room, surrounded by four chairs looking as though they might collapse should a flieg land on them.

Rocker pulled out one chair for Maripa, and sat himself in the one next to her. "Having fun, Karm? Care to let us in on your little secret now? And what did he mean by 'level four'? This place barely has one level. One good kick would bring the whole building down around us."

"Yes, I'm ready to explain everything. You two sit down. This will take a while."

They sat cautiously in the suspect chairs and waited.

"Ready for descent to level four." Karm said in a voice too loud for such close quarters. The floor shook and started to drop into the ground. They were surrounded by metallic walls on all sides. The square of light receded into the distance far above them. Maripa and Rocker both grabbed the table to steady themselves as the elevator took them deep underground. A few moments later, their descent slowed and they came to a gentle stop. A doorway to their left slid open with a hiss.

Karm spread his arms as he stood and walked out into an enormous underground facility. "Welcome to my little secret,"

Rocker and Maripa followed and their jaws dropped as they looked around the space. A large silver spaceship shaped like a somewhat flattened sphere occupied the center of the hangar. Scaffolding surrounded the vessel and hundreds of men and robotic machines operated in a perpetual buzz of activity. Dozens of motorized carts delivered supplies to the men, then vanished down ramps along the walls. Cranes hoisted sheets of metal to men who welded them onto the ship's frame. Announcements of various schedules and orders were broadcast throughout the area.

Karm stood, hands on hips, gazing up at the vessel. "This is Hegira II; our real mission." He allowed his stunned companions a moment to realize what he had just said. "Follow me and I will explain everything." He led them through a doorway and into a control room where dozens of computer screens fed information to the men seated at the stations before them.

"Taket," he called out to the mission control officer, "have you been able to raise them yet?"

"Yes, sir. We have them located and we are ready for you to contact them whenever you give the order."

"No time like the present. Give me the microphone and hail them."

The man handed Karm the microphone and rotated a couple of dials, listening to the changing frequencies, nodding when he recognized correct signals. "Go ahead, sir."

"Hegira, this is Karm. Are you reading me? This is a secure channel."

"This is Brach, Karm. I see you survived despite all my efforts to the contrary. I'm glad, really. It might be even more satisfying thinking of you, stranded and helpless, watching the sun explode. Oh, did you receive my message?"

"I got your message. You do as you see fit. I was just checking our communication link. Nothing more to talk about at this time. Out." Karm handed the microphone back to the radioman and returned to Rocker and Maripa.

Karm opened the door and motioned for his companions to follow him. "Let's go into a more private room to talk."

"Will you please tell us what's going on, now?" Maripa asked as the door to the conference room shut behind them. "No more games or delays. Out with it."

"Absolutely, my dear. Where do I begin? I always knew neither the monarch nor any of The Faith could be trusted as allies. Each of us concocted an agenda that could not survive so long as the others existed. Therefore, I ordered the construction of this entire facility as an emergency back-up. Everything we need is here. All of the equipment built for the Hegira was duplicated in this facility for the Hegira II with a few special modifications, of course."

Rocker cocked his head, suspicion rising again in his thoughts. "What do you mean by special modifications?"

"None of the genetic equipment onboard the original Hegira will function for more than two minutes once it is turned on. Everything looks normal during the testing phase, but the circuits will blow under actual field conditions. The ship itself is also a fake."

"How can it be a fake?" asked Maripa. "We saw it launch, or at least its trail, and you just spoke to the monarch out in space."

"Oh, it's real enough for that. But the HyperIonic drive we constructed cannot achieve anywhere near the speeds required to reach Raince'to within three generations. All of the test data and specs were lies from the start. The monitoring equipment was falsely calibrated so all of the data looked exactly like it was supposed to. None of Brach's people could possibly have known any better."

Rocker's face scrunched as he considered the implications. "You sent them out there to die?"

"If you remember, they did everything they could to force their way onto the ship."

"And you let them prevent us from getting on board." He nodded his head. "Good. Let them rot out there in space."

"Yes. I had several contingency plans ensuring we would be left behind, but Brach was very accommodating." He looked at his companions and saw their confusion. "I am sorry I had to keep this a secret from you. The monarch's men are actually very good. Once again, events forced me to make sure that your reactions were genuine so he would be convinced he was in control."

Maripa's eyes lit up in anticipation. "Wait, you said the other ship's engines cannot get them to the new world, but this one can?"

"I assure you, this ship will bring us there faster than you ever imagined. We are still a few months away from our launch date, but everything is on schedule and nobody is the wiser. Even if they do become suspicious, you saw how well we disguised this base. We will need to stay here while the ship is completed so that our cover story is maintained. As far as the rest of the world is concerned, we are on that ship with the monarch. Those who saw us after the launch have been reassigned here to keep them in isolation. I took the liberty of having all of your belongings brought to your quarters here on the base. Let me show you to your new home."

The next two months passed uneventfully. Karm visited the communications center regularly to check on the Hegira, but nothing had been heard from them in weeks. Rocker objected strenuously upon discovering his credentials allowed only brief access to the genetic equipment he helped design, but he understood the deadline pressures and did not interfere. He and Maripa kept busy helping with supervision of loading supplies and equipment onto the ship. There appeared to be a few minor design changes, but nothing drastic enough to cause alarm. Then came judgment day.

The speaker on his desk suddenly crackled to life. "Karm, come to the communications room immediately."

Karm hit the talk button. "What's going on?"

"We have an emergency transmission from the Hegira. You need to come to the C-R right away."

"On my way. Call Dr. Rocker and Maripa and tell them to join us."

The speakers broadcast an unfamiliar voice as Karm entered the room.

"Over here, sir," said the lieutenant in charge. Karm noticed that Rocker and Maripa huddled with the lieutenant around the loudspeaker listening to the voice on the other end. He listened as he approached.

"Is any one there? Please answer. They're killing each other. Is anyone there?" The voice sounded weak and barely audible through the static.

Karm grabbed the microphone. "This is Karm. Who are you? What do you mean 'they're killing each other'?"

The voice was barely audible through the static. "Can you hear me? Is anyone there? This is Sergeant Vedak. Please, can anyone hear me? We need help."

The radio man adjusted the dials attempting to strengthen the signal. "That's the best I can do, sir. Try again."

Karm pressed the talk button again. "Sergeant Vedak, do you read me? What is going on up there?"

"Praise The Eternal! You can hear me. Please help. They're killing each other. Only a few of us are left. Most are badly wounded. Help us!"

"We can't help you unless you tell us what's going on, Sergeant. Talk to me."

"Yes, sir. The monarch ordered us to round up all of the clerics and confine them to their quarters, but they were armed and resisted. How did they get weapons, sir? Nobody but the soldiers were supposed to be issued weapons."

"Keep talking Sergeant."

"Yes, sir. As I said, sir, the clerics brought weapons onboard somehow and began firing as we approached. Our guys started firing back. A lot of us died in the first attack, sir. We set up barricades and tried to hold them off. We contained them in the lower decks around medical and some of the barracks, but they broke through our lines. They had knives too, sir. A lot of our guys got cut up pretty bad, sir. Once they gained access to the weapons lockers, they were able to fight their way up through the rest of the ship." The sergeant's voice broke off in a fit of violent coughing. "I'm hit bad, sir. You've got to send help."

"Sergeant, you know the situation. We can't send help, but finish your report...keep talking. Tell us what happened."

"Yes, sir. Some of our weapons fire penetrated the hull. We had to seal off most of the lower decks. A lot of people got trapped down there. They're probably all dead now from decompression. Some of us are left in the command deck. Our cartridges are almost empty. The enemy's going to break through soon, sir. Are you sure there's no way to send reinforcements?"

"No, soldier. There is no way to send help." Karm put his hand over the microphone and looked up at the others in the room.

"Yes, sir. I know, sir," said the sergeant. "It was a quetzal of a mission though. Wish I could say goodbye to my mother…before the end and all."

"I'll see what we can do, soldier. Hang in there, son." Karm looked up at the control room supervisor. "There must be some way we can contact this man's mother and get her on the line for him?"

"I'm not sure, sir. I'll find out right away."

After a few minutes of searching the databases, the supervisor pointed at his screen. "I found her, sir. Turns out she's also stationed here as a machinist. We can bring her here in ten minutes."

"Make it five minutes."

A few minutes later the control room door opened and in walked a woman dressed in grease covered overalls guided by a lieutenant.

Karm reached out to the woman as he stood to provide her with his chair by the microphone. "Over here, ma'am. Did they tell you what's going on?"

The woman looked fearfully around the room, then approached Karm to take the seat he offered her. "Yes, sir, they did," Her eyes were red and she wiped her nose on her dirty sleeve, but she remained calm. "Is he still up there? Can I talk to him?"

"Yes, ma'am. Right here. Just press this button when you want to talk." Karm stood back as she reached out for the mike and pressed the button.

"Kellend, are you there, honey?"

"Mom! Is that you?" came the sergeant's reply. "What are you doing there?"

Karm looked around the room and spread his arms, ushering everyone out of the room. "Let's give them some privacy."

Twenty minutes later the woman exited the room. Her cheeks were streaked with tears. "Thank you, sir...thank you."

The lieutenant took her by the shoulders, supporting her as he gently led her down the corridor. The others re-entered the control room.

"Just like it happened before," Karm said quietly. "Cut off all communication links. There's nothing we can do for them."

"Yes, sir." The radioman pressed a button and all lights on the panel went out.

Karm turned and walked slowly back to his office followed by Rocker and Maripa.

Maripa placed her hands gently on Karm's shoulders as he slumped in a chair. "What do you mean 'just like before'?"

Karm's head bowed and he kept his back to Maripa as he responded. "You remember I told you how my DNA was reconstructed by the aliens from a dead ship. Well, the Hegira is that ship. They trained me and sent me back to complete the failed mission from that crew. It has always been my responsibility...my destiny to ensure that everything happened in exactly the same way it had before so history would unfold in the manner it was supposed to."

"So you knew all this was going to happen?" She looked from Karm to Rocker and back to Karm. "I guess I never quite believed your story about coming from the future." She reached out and took Rocker's hand.

"Yes, it's all true. I am sorry about keeping you both in the dark so much. I could not risk anything happening to change the timeline. I had to make sure everything occurred not only the way it did before, but at the exact same time as before." He looked up at Maripa and

Rocker, then down at the floor. "This is why those miners had to die. The delays caused by a strike would have caused irreparable damage to the timeline. There was no other choice."

Rocker reached out to Karm with his free hand, and placed it on his shaking back. "I know, Karm. I understand, now, what a terrible burden you've been carrying for all of us. I'm not sure I would have had the strength to do the same."

Maripa released her grip on Rocker's hand, and gathered both of her men in a warm embrace.

"In my timeline, those people on the Hegira died many decades ago and our entire race died with them. It was my task to keep us from extinction. The Hegira II launches in one month just after the new year dawns. The miner's strike planned by Brach would have delayed Hegira II's launch significantly, setting in action a chain reaction whereby all of us, all of the Brin, would have perished. This mission will succeed."

Chapter Twenty-Nine

Everything was ready for launch. All of the supplies and equipment were securely stored away. The DNA samples were safely locked in dormant hibernation. Maripa, Karm, and Rocker were in the suit-up room getting stuffed into their pressurized suits.

"Hope this goes better than the last launch," laughed Rocker as he struggled with his left boot.

"Don't remind me," Maripa said connecting her coolant hoses.

With the final checks of their suits completed, one of the engineers led them to the main hangar. The roof had been opened over the past hour and they looked up into a starlit night. They continued on to the ramp leading up to the ship's main hatchway and on to the bridge. Karm took the Captain's chair on the left. Maripa sat in the center chair and Rocker on the right. Each of them had practiced with the controls in front of them and were familiar with their duties for the flight.

Karm flipped the communications switch at his side. "Command crew buckled in and secure for launch."

Maripa and Rocker turned dials and set their controls just as they rehearsed during training drills.

"Drive motors at max. Coolant flow nominal," called out Maripa.

"Stabilizers balanced. Internal environmental controls show five by five," said Rocker.

Karm examined the control panel and nodded. "Ready to close and seal hatches."

Maripa and Rocker jumped at his command. "Wait Karm, not yet. What about the rest of the crew? They haven't boarded yet. We still have another hour before we need to close the hatches."

Karm stared at the main view screen. "Sorry guys. another one of those vital secrets I had to hide from you. There is no crew for this voyage, only the DNA and equipment we are transporting. Launch is in one minute. No time to explain now. I can fill you in once we are in space. Oh, and don't worry about hitting any wrong switches. I'm in full control of the ship." He held out his left arm. The glow of his palm could be seen even through the heavy glove. In fact, his entire body seemed to shine.

The electronic crackle of mission control sounded in their headphones. "T minus 10...9...8...7...6... ignition sequence start...5...4...3...2...1... all systems go. You are go for lift off."

There was no vibration, nor any sound. But through the view screen Rocker and Maripa could see the shrinking shadow of the ship as they shot high above the desert floor. In no time, they saw the curve of the planet's horizon in the distance backlit by the dying sun. They could feel gravity diminishing as they reached orbit.

"Standard orbit achieved." Karm reached up and removed his helmet, then took off his gloves and placed them inside the helmet as it floated in free fall in front of him. Rocker and Maripa removed their helmets and gloves as well. Rocker took all of their unneeded equipment and stowed them in the bay next to his seat.

Karm unbuckled himself and floated free of his chair. "Don't start with the inquisition, you two. I can finally tell you the entire story, so follow me to the command crew quarters and listen."

Maripa and Rocker looked at each other, unfastened their restraints and drifted down the passageway after Karm.

Maripa gasped at the sensation of weightlessness. "This is fun!" She performed effortless somersaults and various combat maneuvers as she propelled herself toward the meeting room.

Rocker, in contrast, turned a ghastly green. "I don't feel so good." He barely managed opening the bag attached to his belt before retching violently into it.

They struggled a bit at first trying to match the fastening strips on their suits to those in the chairs, but did manage to secure themselves.

Maripa glared at Karm. "This better be good."

"Trust me. Once you hear the entire tale you will understand why I kept you and everyone else in the dark. You remember I told you about the alien ship that discovered the original Hegira and my DNA among the thousands of destroyed samples? Yours too, Maripa. Ours were the only survivors."

They both nodded in agreement.

"Those aliens, as I have told you, were from a civilization who call themselves the Skae. Technologically far beyond anything you can imagine. They only let me see a small part of their ship so I would be as free from contamination and knowledge of the future as possible. Their principal edict forbids them from interfering with the development of other races. Ours turned out to be a special case, but they never did tell me why. I always assumed they decided in our favor since an entire species, ours, was on the brink of extinction. After recovering the ship's logs and data bases they formulated a plan to save us. The key was finding the two surviving DNA samples. Once the DNA was grown, they could train one of our own species to carry out the plan. They could not directly take steps to interfere on their own, but apparently two members of the destroyed species, when specially trained and equipped, was permissible."

"You still haven't explained why we don't have a crew."

"I'm getting there. The Skae provided me with this biocomputer implant you both have seen me put to good use. However, it only provides me certain information and only allows me to tap into a fraction of what it is capable of doing. It always tells me just enough to succeed, but never so much that I might endanger the future. They also provided me with enough information to build this ship. As you have already seen, none of the bridge stations are functional. My biocomputer is the true control mechanism. Our engines are only powerful enough to lift us into orbit. My friends out there will help us with the rest."

"You mean the Skae are out here waiting for us?" Maripa searched outside her window for some sign of a ship.

As she scanned the sky, she noticed a tiny light moving across the star field in their view screen. The light grew and took the shape of a small spaceship. The speakers crackled as communication channels opened.

A gentle voice sounded over the speaker. "Hello, Karm. Congratulations on the success of your mission."

"Bolt, my old friend. It has been too long. Thank you for all you have done to help us."

"We could not allow your species to die. We did what we had to do. Are you ready for the jump?"

"Yes, we are. Is Zem with you, now?"

A second, somewhat more nasal voice sounded over the speaker. "I am here. I am pleased to hear you again. I will send the tow beam now."

"Thank you, Zem. I read a steady connection. Please take us to the string."

"The Skae are here? They really exist?" Maripa and Rocker said in unison as they watched the view screen.

"Yes, and now I should continue with my story. Our current technology does not have the ability to power a ship to even the nearest stars, unless we are prepared to build a ship of immense size capable of carrying generations of people. We are incapable of such an undertaking, so my friends out there devised this entire deception to hide themselves from us. They are about to connect us to a cosmic string and tow us to our new home. That's how they brought the two of us here," he said as he looked at Maripa. "cosmic strings can be influenced by their advanced technology to not only allow travel across space at incredible speeds, but also through time. Manipulating the time stream is how I arrived here decades before Maripa. Since I am from the future I knew most of what was supposed to happen and how to control it to my advantage."

Rocker ruffled his crest as he tried to assimilate what he was hearing. "But, didn't your manipulation of events on Dyan'ta disrupt the time continuum?"

"Those events stayed isolated to Dyan'ta, and when it is destroyed, there's no potential for those events to radiate out to the universe and interfere with the existing time continuum."

"This is unbelievable."

"Just wait until you hear the rest of the story. Despite all of their advances, the Skae were not able to reanimate me without some difficulty. My DNA started to spontaneously decay at an alarming rate. To keep me alive long enough to complete the mission, their scientists developed the pills I take to stabilize the decay and, hopefully, will allow me to live a long and productive life." He held up one of the violet capsules and swallowed it. "Fortunately, they improved their techniques enough to solve the problem before animating Maripa's DNA. That is why you don't need the pills. I just wish they had figured it out sooner. These things taste terrible.

Karm turned to face Rocker, pointing a talon at his companion. "Your discovery did something even they could not do. You learned how to reanimate the DNA without the degradation problems. Only now, having seen your designs and calculations, the Skae invented ways to greatly improve them. Our new equipment can grow a new clone to maturity in only one week!"

"Oh, great! So we have a batch of fully grown week-old babies on our hands." Rocker threw his hands up in exasperation. "Won't that be fun!"

"Not at all. You remember those CAT scans you questioned me about? We added a few alien enhancements. The scans were much more than an examination for genetic defects. Those probes collected the entire body of knowledge from each individual. We can implant their knowledge and grow fully developed and educated adults in one week. We don't need to bring along a large crew, only the thousands of DNA samples."

Maripa rubbed her temple. "So you kept us in the dark to preserve the alien's prime directive and the future timeline. They could help us, but nobody could know about it."

Karm applauded her and smiled. "Absolutely correct. Even now they cannot reveal the technology connecting us to the cosmic string or the location of our new home. We will need to learn these things on our own. Our isolation on the new planet will ensure secrecy for generations to come."

Rocker shook his head. "That still doesn't explain why we didn't bring anyone else with us. We aren't leaving all those workers behind to die are we?"

"Not at all. As I said, the cosmic strings can also manipulate time, so, after we left, the Skae sent another ship down to Latonia Base and gathered up enough of them to help us start a settlement on the new world. They should actually already be there working to build the new community. Unfortunately, we cannot save all of them, but we devised a lottery for those with the skills we will require, and remember, with the CAT scan pathways implanted, the clones will wake up with all the memories and thought patterns of their originals. They may actually believe they are the original and not a clone."

"Alright, Karm. I guess you're forgiven. You sure that's everything? No more secrets?"

"Well, maybe just one more, but that can wait until we arrive on the new planet and settle in. It's more of a present for you than a secret."

"Wonderful. You can't help yourself, can you? There always has to be one more trick up your sleeve." Rocker chuckled as he turned back to Maripa.

Maripa interrupted and pointed at the view screen. "Is that what I think it is?"

A bright ribbon appeared on their sensors and resolved on the main screen. It moved sinuously across the sky, reminiscent of a living thing.

"Looks like it extends on forever," she said, glued to the image on the screen. "It's incredible."

"That is our ride. It's a cosmic string. We better hurry back up to the bridge. This is going to be bumpy."

The journey along the string took only a few minutes. Their ship shuddered violently as it tossed about, but it was well built and everything survived, mostly in one piece. As the shaking subsided the ship slowly rotated to reveal a brightly lit blue planet ahead of them. Approaching closer to the shining orb revealed clouds in the atmosphere. Several large land masses grew in size with their descent.

"Adjust to coordinates 2268.910 by 427.336," Zem's voice directed them over the speaker.

"Heading in now. See you there in five minutes."

Karm's body glowed again as it took over control of the ship. Maripa and Rocker watched the view screen as the continent below them expanded. Forests and grasslands came into view. Large rivers and lakes crossed the landscape.

Maripa stared in amazement at the scene below. "Everything is so green. Not quite like home, but very pretty."

Rocker watched at her side, equally astonished. "And did you get a look at that sun? It's yellow, not orange. It must be a few billion years younger than our old star. That is a comforting thought."

The Hegira II set down on a grassy meadow not far from a meandering river. Karm stopped glowing as he shut down the ship's controls and opened the hatchway.

"Looks as though our friends have been busy," Karm said as he left the ship.

They stepped off the ship onto their new home and saw a small village waiting for them. Several homes sat along a winding dirt road. As the three travelers approached, they saw several large buildings, their construction almost complete, near the center of town. To one side of the village fenced pastures sat peaceful and green, waiting for the animals to fill them. The hum of electricity could be heard in the distance. A number of Brin could be seen busy with the new construction.

Karm pointed toward a rise in the distance. "They must have built the power plant on the other side of those hills. The much smaller spaceship that towed them along the cosmic string landed almost silently nearby. The hatch opened and two figures, dressed in flowing colorful attire, walked toward them. They stood about eight feet tall on long thin legs. Their arms were equally long and spindly with five fingers on each hand. Their wavy brown hair accentuated the deep blue of their smooth skin.

Karm ran to greet them. "Bolt! Zem! I am so glad to see you again." He caught himself suddenly and stopped in front of them. He raised his fist to his chest and bowed remembering the customary greeting he had learned many years ago.

The two smiled as they returned his greeting. Bolt extended his arms to embrace his old friend. "It is good to see you again as well. We can stay for a brief time to help you adjust and confirm everything is operating properly, but then we must leave you again."

"I understand. Let me introduce you to my friends."

Bolt grinned down at Karm. "Ahhh, friends…so, you did learn after all. I am glad."

***

Five months later, the three administrators sat at the kitchen table eating breakfast before starting their day.

"Looks as if the neighbors are getting an early start," Maripa said as she looked out the window. "How many more are scheduled for release today?"

Rocker looked up at the ceiling as he did a few calculations. "Twelve this morning and another ten this afternoon." He took a bite from his muffin. "We should be able to expand and speed up production once the new facilities are finished in another week. The new seeds are ready for planting just as soon as the additional fields are plowed."

Maripa grimaced as she shifted in her seat uncomfortably. "How long before we need a new town? This one is getting a bit crowded now. What is our current population? It must be over a thousand."

"One thousand and ninety eight healthy productive adults."

Karm strolled down the stairs dressed in his waders and vest, his new rod and reel in hand. "Gotta run now. I want to see how those fish we spawned last month are doing." He waved at the two of them as he opened the door, then paused and looked back. "I almost forgot. Here, Jontar. I want you to take a look at this." He reached in his pocket and handed Rocker a small glass vial with a yellow liquid inside.

"What is this?"

"Just a sample of my DNA, and the present I promised you when we left Dyan'ta. I'm off now. Have fun you two!" Karm whistled as he walked down the road to the river. He waved at some of the people he passed along the way.

Maripa took the sample from her husband, examining it closely in the morning light. "Why did he give you his DNA sample now? He never let us have it before. Do you think he's experiencing symptoms again?"

"No, the new treatments we developed cured his degeneration problem. He hasn't had to take any of those pills in a month now." He took the sample back, held up the vial to the light and swirled the liquid as he peered into it. "Maybe I better take a look at this." He went back into his private office and set the small bottle into the reader. A few moments later the monitor displayed row after row of base pair sequences.

Maripa was cleaning up in the kitchen when she heard his shouts.

"Maripa! Get in here! You're not going to believe this!"

She draped the towel over the back of a chair, stretched her back, and went down the hall to Rocker's office.

"What now?" she asked as she entered the room.

"That old conniving Quetzal. He did it again. One last present he called it. Look at these results." Rocker laughed as he pulled Maripa into his arms.

She looked at the screen and saw the flashing message above the images of Karm and Rocker.

DNA MATCH 98% certainty Karm / Dr. Jontar Rocker.

"That old coot is my clone! It was my DNA the Skae recovered from the dead ship." He shook his head and placed his hand on his wife's swollen belly. "This is going to be some story to tell you when you are born." He felt the tiny movement inside his wife and looked up into her eyes.

She looked lovingly into her husband's eyes, a wistful smile on her face. "Do you really need to go in to work today?"

"I'm the boss and father, at least according to the new clones we are raising. I can stay home any time I want." He stood and gathered her to him in a gentle embrace.

"Good," she said, pulling him closer.

About The Author

Jim Cronin is a retired middle school science teacher, currently working part-time as an educator/performer at the Denver Museum of Nature and Science. Born in Kansas City, Missouri, raised in Arlington, Virginia and Denver, Colorado, He became an avid science nerd at the height of the space race of the 1960's. Married for thirty seven years to the love of his life, Diane, together they have raised two incredible sons. After thirty-five years in the classroom, he decided to explore new worlds of opportunities, including volunteering, bicycling, and writing. After three years of learning how to write something others might enjoy, Hegira is the result.

Social Media

Website:
http://www.authorjimcroninhegira.com/

Facebook Page:
www.facebook.com/pages/Author-Jim-Cronin

Twitter:
https://twitter.com/authorjimcronin

Acknowledgements:

I want to thank all those who helped make this journey a reality. First, my loving wife, Diane, who, with eternal patience and many exasperated eye rolls and head shakes, put up with my endless ramblings and requests for proof readings, as well as the many hours I spent staring longingly into the computer screen instead of her eyes. Love ya sweetie! To my brother Mike, who spent countless hours over many weeks and months brainstorming almost every aspect of this story to help make it something worth reading. He really should be listed as a co-author, but I'm the one who did all the typing. I also want to thank my editors for teaching me how to write. Meredith, Arsen, Cat, Fred, the English language has always been a mystery to me, so your guidance and instruction has been invaluable. Finally, to all of you who read the early drafts and gave me so many wonderful ideas and suggestions, thank you for your time and efforts on my behalf. I hope this book makes it all worthwhile.

Hegira Reviews:

" I highly recommend that you pickup a copy of this opening tale in this series you won't be disappointed." - Joe Pranatis

"Of obvious appeal to sci-fi fans but the strong story-line gives this book universal appeal. So I would recommend to anyone who enjoys a good, well-written story." - Maria

"Science fiction at its best. A well written and well imagined alien world without being difficult to understand and follow. "   - Trypsin

"A thoroughly good read that reminded me very much of one of my old favourite SF authors Robert E Heinlen."   - Rea

"The author gives primacy to the plot, and the plot doesn't disappoint. The story of 'going back in time to save the world' might have a familiar ring to it, but the plot-line and well-timed twists sketch an unseen picture... the author comes up not only with a fresh plot, but more importantly with a distinct method of execution of the plot... I have to admit the author creates quite an impressive central character in Karm. I rate the book 4 out of 4 stars." Reviewed by: ananya92 for OnlineBookClub.

Awards:

www.ingramcontent.com/pod-product-compliance
Lightning Source LLC
Chambersburg PA
CBHW070444030726
47503CB00004B/883